CLAIRE HIGHTON-STEVENSON

ISBN: 9798346272250

Dedication

To every one of my American readers.

I see you, I hear you, I love you.

In difficult times, we pull together.

Authors Note

We are often forced to take drastic steps, to maintain our safety and our sanity. As many of you know, I have been taking those steps for a while now and slowly removing my presence from social media and the platforms that encourage hatred and division.

And it feels even more appropriate now to invite you all to join my free Patreon site. A space where we can gather without the algorithm and trolls.

I find it a much more peaceful and creative way to engage with you all. So, when you feel up to it, come and join us!

In the meantime, I hope you enjoy this new book, and the romance between Sammy-Jo and Daisy, as well as the appearance of many familiar face.

Merry Christmas

Chapter One

Saturday 21st December

Daisy Rose Foster was freezing and about as angry with herself as one could get, which was happening a lot lately, she realised, after she'd kicked the tyre and sworn several times, but it hadn't helped ease the annoyance.

The engine management light had been on for weeks, and she'd ignored it.

Because last time it had come on, it was for nothing more than a loose cap on some part of the engine she'd never even looked at. That was why you paid mechanics to do a service once a year, so you didn't have to worry. She'd just assumed it was that again.

How wrong she was, when the world around her was now enveloped in steam billowing out from under the bonnet.

She sagged a little more.

Snow fell in clumps, and she was already shivering without the engine running and being able to blow hot air at her. She felt a little aggrieved because she had managed to check the weather forecast before she'd set off, and it hadn't mentioned anything about it snowing.

She glanced up at the night sky and the flakes falling heavily in the wide-lit circle radiating from the streetlamp, and groaned.

"Why can I not just have a simple life? You know, a girlfriend that doesn't cheat, a job I like, a car that doesn't break down."

Within minutes of starting, the great big flakes had covered the ground and most of the parked cars along the street. The bright light from the streetlamp gave everything a moonlit shine, and it looked almost like daylight.

"Just a nice girlfriend would be fine, I'd take that." She continued to berate the universe. "One that doesn't cheat on me."

The only positive she had was that her parents' house was no more than a couple of miles away. The negatives were multiple: her phone was dead, so she couldn't call for a lift or find a local taxi. She'd have to walk, and that meant lugging her cases in the snow, and she wasn't dressed for this weather.

Looking down at her feet and the pair of old, worn-out trainers on them, she grimaced. The tread was never going to hold if it got icy.

"Fuck's sake." She swore again as she trudged around the back of the car and as if to prove the point, she almost went arse over tit.

If she hadn't been completely pissed off by then, the boot of her SUV raising up and dumping half a tonne of snow on her head would have made it so.

"Seriously, just fuck off!" she screamed at the car and frantically tried to stop any of the snow from heading down the neck of her jumper and down her back.

The sigh left her body like a prayer as she closed her eyes and tried to stave off the growing need to just cry and give up.

Life shouldn't be this difficult, should it?

She had a small case on wheels and a rucksack squeezed in beside a box of gifts she'd bought and lovingly wrapped. Okay, that's a lie. She'd paid for the store to do that, but whatever, she had picked them out and paid for them, so that had to count for something, didn't it?

Yanking the rucksack out, she flung it over a shoulder and then lifted the case out onto its wheels on the road. She slammed the boot closed and more snow slid off and landed on her feet. Her toes were already numb; she'd have frostbite at this rate.

"This is what happens when you don't say no," she muttered to herself, dragging the case up the kerb impatiently. When one of the wheels got caught, she breathed deeply and bit down on her lip to stop the tirade of absolute filth that was threatening to spill out.

The invitation to spend Christmas at home with the family had come months ago. Daisy had planned to decline. She'd just met Nadia and things were going well. She was hopeful of waking up Christmas morning all snuggled up with her girlfriend and spending a romantic day together, until she realised that Nadia's idea of commitment meant agreeing to come over, but not to stay out of anyone else's bed.

"I don't understand the problem. We never said we were..." Nadia laughed. "Right, it was always just..." She waved a hand, finger extended to point at herself and then Daisy.

"Are you serious?" Daisy asked, incredulously.

Nadia pinched her forehead. "So, you're upset about it?"

"I'm not upset. I'm livid. We had a thing Nadia, and you're doing it with half the fucking city."

"I mean, it's three, sometimes four. I think you're exaggerating a little..."

"Oh, just fuck off, Nadia. Seriously, get your things and get out."

Nadia puffed her cheeks out. "Right, so...it's nearly Christmas?"

"And?"

"You got me a gift, right?" Nadia grinned, and Daisy screamed in frustration.

Daisy had done the only thing that she could after dumping Nadia's cheating backside, deciding that Christmas at home with her family wouldn't be such a terrible thing after all.

Of course, her mum had been delighted, her dad too, and even the twins were looking forward to it. It was just Daisy who felt deflated.

"I swear to all that is bloody – if one person wishes me merry fecking Christmas before I get a hot shower, I won't be held res—"

"You alright there?"

A voice out of nowhere made Daisy jump and she twisted around, letting go of the suitcase, feet planted and fists raised, ready to ward off any unwanted attack.

"Woah, hold your horses." Someone approached with hands up, empty palms out. "I just thought you looked like you could use a hand. What with all the swearing and talking to yourself..."

Daisy relaxed, a little at least.

'Relaxed' probably wasn't a word anyone would usually use to describe her lately, she supposed. Life was kicking her arse far too often.

Looking at the stranger, she realised that despite the gruffness of the voice, the big brown eyes looking at her held just a touch of mirth. Her head was bound in blue and red wool, a ton of reddish-brown curls poking out from under it. At least she was a woman, Daisy thought.

Which was 50% less scary in an instant.

"Right, yes, I'm sorry about that. Broke down," Daisy said dramatically, opening her hands and arms to indicate the car on the side of the road.

"Ah, that's a bugger. Did you call the AA?"

Daisy smiled ruefully and sighed, her shoulders sagging and the rucksack strap slipping down her arm. She caught sight of herself in the bottom half of the car door window. Blonde hair was frozen to her head like rat tails, like she'd been dragged through a hedge backwards.

"Yes, why didn't I think of that? Instead of standing here like an idiot battling with my bags."

The woman stared at her.

Great first impression, she thought, sighing internally. This day was going from bad to worse without even trying.

"I'm sorry, that was totally out of order. No, it ran out last month and I forgot all about it." *Because I was too busy dumping my girlfriend, hating my job, and looking for somewhere else to live, and crying about it all*, she didn't add.

"That's a bummer." The woman reached up and pulled the scarf down and away from her chin to reveal a wide mouth and white teeth grinning at her. "Not sure you'll find anyone around here open till the morning. And even then, it's only a few days till Christmas. A lot of the businesses have shut down till January." She glanced around her as if to make sure. "Probably find a garage over in Bath Street in the morning though, I guess. Do you have far to go?"

"Just to my parents. They live over on Datchet Avenue, down by the river."

"That's a trek. Can't you call them and get them to pick you up?"

Daisy sighed again, a plume of white drifted away.

"Yeah, I thought of that, but…dead battery. And I don't know the number off the top of my head to use…" She smiled regretfully when the woman pulled her own phone free from her pocket and then thrust it back in again.

Daisy yanked the suitcase again and this time it came free and wheeled up the kerb.

"As you can tell, I'm completely organised," Daisy joked, and the stranger thankfully chuckled along with her because so far, she'd done nothing to help herself with the only person who'd stopped to see if she was alright.

"It's fine. Happens to us all."

"I'm really sorry. I'm not usually this neurotic."

The woman smiled. "Listen I don't live far from your parents' place. I could walk with you if you like, help carry something."

Daisy thought about the box of presents in the boot. She was pretty sure Amberfield was a safe place to break down and leave a car unattended, but so far, she hadn't had much luck with this trip, and she didn't have the finances to replace a heap of gifts should the worst happen.

"That would be a great help." Daisy beamed. She reached out a hand. "I'm Daisy."

The stranger pulled off a glove and took Daisy's hand. "My friends call me SJ."

Chapter Two

It was bitterly cold and Sammy-Jo's arms were aching already from carrying the box. It wasn't heavy really, just awkward, and her fingers were numb despite the gloves.

They hadn't got that far, and Daisy had twice fallen over – once landing on her backside, the next half-landing against SJ. Luckily, she'd been able to shift the weight of the box onto her left hand and grab hold of Daisy before she dropped to the floor.

Now, as they rounded the corner, she was a couple of steps behind and she couldn't help but notice the huge wet mark that had spread, and frozen, across Daisy's jeans-clad backside. A pretty nice backside if she were to really consider it, which she didn't, because that would just be rude. But still, it was hard not to notice.

"Are you sure you don't want to borrow my scarf?" Sammy-Jo asked again. "Or we could stop for a moment, and you could dig out something from your bag. You must be frozen."

"I'll live," Daisy called back, continuing to trudge forward. The streets were practically deserted, and Daisy stopped, swinging around to wait. "Do you need a rest?"

"No," SJ said quickly - too quickly. Her pride was getting the better of her. And then she remembered her therapist's words.

"*Your pride is often your downfall, Sammy-Jo. It's okay to ask for help or tell someone that something is bothering you.*"

"Yeah, I guess it wouldn't hurt to put this down for a couple of minutes," SJ admitted.

There was a wall to her left, a small front garden with dead plants and stick trees, all looking rather unkempt and sorry for themselves under a layer of snow.

Placing the box down, SJ shook out her arms and bashed her hands together to try and get some feeling back into the end of her fingers.

"What's in it anyway?"

"Presents. It's Christmas, remember?" Daisy laughed. "I'm visiting my parents. I've got two younger siblings, a surprise package my parents didn't expect."

"Oh, how old are they?"

"Seven, twin girls."

"Cool." Sammy-Jo moved from foot to foot. "What are they called?"

Daisy puffed out her cheeks and looked away down the road before she turned back to SJ.

"You're not allowed to laugh."

Sammy-Jo's eyebrows rose. "That bad?"

Daisy nodded. "I think it's bloody embarrassing, but my mum loves it, and well, Dad thought it was cute. Nobody listened to me. I'd have picked excellent names like Carrie after the actress who played—"

"Princess Leia?"

Daisy grinned. "Yes, or maybe Stevie, after—" She waited for SJ to jump in.

"No, you've stumped me on that one."

"Nicks, Stevie Nicks, the greatest female singer of all time?"

SJ shrugged. "Can't say I've heard of her."

"Really?" Daisy looked astounded, then broke into song. "*Now, here you go again, you say, you want your freedom... well, who am I to keep you down?*"

"Ah, yeah, I've heard that…dunno what it's called though."

"It's called 'Dreams.' Anyway, they didn't listen to me and so now the girls have to grow up with—" She shook her head.

"Go on then. What are they called?"

“Dolly and Polly.” Daisy rolled her eyes and blew out her cheeks again. “Can you imagine if they’d had triplets?”

“Molly?”

Daisy laughed and nodded.

“Good job it wasn’t quads, might have sneaked a Holly in there too.” Sammy-Jo smiled. She grabbed the box. “Ready?”

“Yes, my toes must have frostbite by now,” Daisy complained before giving an awkward grin. “It’s my own fault for not dressing for the weather, but to be fair, I didn’t expect to break down, nor did they forecast this.”

“True, British weather will always catch us out.”

“A white Christmas though, maybe that’s good.”

“You got a nice voice, by the way,” Sammy-Jo said, grateful that her scarf hid the blush.

“Aw, thanks. I do like a bit of a sing now and then,” Daisy admitted. “We have a karaoke bar in town, and I go there sometimes.”

They walked on, the silent streets echoing every crunching step, but it was comfortable, not that awkward silence that SJ usually found difficult around people she barely knew.

Daisy broke the silence, however, when she asked, “So, did you grow up around here?”

“I grew up in Woodington and then moved to Bath Street and then more recently I bought a little house in Amberfield. Figured I’d best get on the ladder.”

Daisy nodded, seemingly content with the answer.

“Did you have to drive far?” Sammy-Jo asked.

“East Kent. Stayed there after Uni, but…” She trailed off and concentrated on crossing the road. When they were safely on the other side, she added, “I’m being evicted, and my job is – well, let’s just say that I disagree with everything the manager wants to implement so…”

"Looks like you'll be on the move then?"

"Yeah, maybe."

"Amberfield is nice," Sammy-Jo said without really thinking. It was just one of those throwaway comments, wasn't it? Or was it the baby blues staring at her and the smile that was encouraging something that really wasn't there?

"Is it? I mean, I've only ever visited. Mum and Dad moved here about four years ago, because the school was supposed to be good, and the twins were their main concern."

"Well, I can understand that. Not that I know anything about schools, or kids, but…there's some nice pubs. And the riverside complex is really taking shape now. There are cafés and boutiques, and even a gay bar," she said rather enthusiastically and then thought better of it, despite having seen what looked like a rainbow sticker in Daisy's car window. People had those to support the NHS now too, didn't they? "Not that you might want…you know, a—"

"Gay bar?" Daisy said for her, her lips upturning just a little. "Do you…like gay bars?"

"Uh, I – uh, yeah, I mean…hm-hm, I go in there from time to time…or mostly I go to Art Too, in town, I mean Bath Street. Technically, both bars are in Bath Street, it's just that Blanca's is only just across the river, and I can walk it—"

She stopped speaking, aware she was rambling and even more aware that Daisy was smiling at her. Which wasn't such an awful experience, even if she was a little nervous. Pretty girls always made her nervous now. She could scream and shout with the best of them, but the minute a pretty face flirted with her, she'd start to feel anxious. Her last relationship had really done a number on her confidence, that was for sure.

"Sorry, I get chatty when I'm trying not to focus on something I don't like."

Now the smile disappeared, and Daisy's brow rose curiously. "You don't like me, wow that's—"

"Oh, no, that's not what—" Shoulders sagged, and SJ almost dropped the box. "No, I just meant, the cold. I'm trying not to focus on the cold and the snow." *And how pretty you are, and probably how straight you are, and totally not interested in me you are.*

They walked on a little further in silence and stopped to watch as a car slid along the street and only missed a parked car by a matter of inches.

"That was close," Sammy-Jo said as they turned the corner.

"Yeah, hope my car will be alright, though at this rate getting written off might be a blessing."

"I'm sure it's gonna be fixable."

"Yeah, I hope so. I do love the heap of crap." Daisy chuckled. She halted. "Well, this is me." Stopping outside and pointing at a small, terraced house with a big bay window with a twinkling Christmas tree in pride of place. "Thank you for walking with me."

"You're welcome, couldn't leave a damsel in distress," Sammy-Jo said. The blank look on Daisy's face meant she continued. "Not that you needed saving or anything like that. Nope, not at all."

Daisy smiled and took the box from her.

"It was lovely to meet you, SJ." She leaned in and kissed her frozen cheek. "Maybe I'll see you around."

The front door opened, and a man in his 50s stepped out. "Daisy? What on earth? We expected you hours ago."

"Car broke down." She shrugged. "SJ here was kind enough to walk with me."

He turned his attention to the tall woman all bundled up.

"Thank you. Do you want to come in and warm up? We've got some mince pies and mulled wine on the go."

Sammy-Jo thought about it. It would be nice to get warm. Maybe they'd offer a hot chocolate instead; she'd like to talk to Daisy some more. But common sense got the better of her.

"Thanks, but I'd best get going. I'm meeting some friends." She waved, and watched as Daisy walked inside, her dad now carrying the box. Before the door closed, Daisy locked eyes with her, and gave a little wave, and Sammy-Jo felt her heart melt.

Chapter Three

"Alright, let's get some Christmas cheer in," Ladonya drawled. Another year at Bath Street Harriers Women's Football Club had passed and she still hadn't lost her Texan accent.

"Sounds like a plan to me." Nora Brady grinned. "SJ? What are you having?"

The teammates looked at one another as Sammy-Jo continued to stare off into space.

"SJ?" Nora said more loudly.

"Huh, what?" Sammy-Jo blinked and stared at Nora, and then Ladonya. "Sorry, I missed that?"

Nora laughed at her. "Okay, you alright?"

"Yeah, I'm good." SJ nodded. "So, what was you saying?"

"I said…" Ladonya waved a finger at her. "We need some Christmas cheer, and she said…" She pointed at Nora, and in her best English mockney. "What are you having?"

"Oh…uh…" Sammy-Jo looked along the bar at all the options. "So used to not drinking, I can't make up—"

"Bloody hell, just get her a pint for god's sake, we'll be here all night," Handsy shouted before smiling at the bar staff. "I'll have a gin and tonic, ta."

"Right, pint for SJ, same for me," Nora said. "I'll grab us that table." She grabbed SJ by the elbow. "Come on, daydreamer."

When they were sitting down, they both watched the others messing around, joking and dancing about. SJ was still trying to warm her hands.

"You'd think they hadn't been allowed out for years." Nora laughed before turning serious. "You alright?"

"I guess," SJ answered. "It's been a good season so far; they all deserve it." Being professional footballers had its perks, she guessed.

"True. Who'd have thought we'd be sixth in the WSL at Christmas?" Nora said, tilting her head to look at her friend and teammate. Nora was captain, but everyone respected Sammy-Jo Costa, just as much as Nora did. "You got something on your mind?"

"Not really, nothing serious anyway," SJ answered. She spun around to face Nora. "I just…I kind of wish I could meet someone, you know? I haven't dated anyone since…well, you know…"

Nora nodded; they both knew who Sammy-Jo was talking about. Krista Rave. Another footballer who'd had it in for Nora and used SJ to get at her. It was something that had almost broken the team and seen Sammy-Jo transfer listed until things calmed down and they'd all worked through it.

"I guess that's understandable, but…life goes on. You should put yourself out there," Nora encouraged. "It's been a year almost."

"I know. And I will." SJ sighed.

"You've got three entire weeks with no game taking up your time. That's three weekends free. Get in here, get down to Blanca's…you know there are a lot of girls in there who'd wanna be a wag."

Sammy-Jo barged her shoulder against Nora. "Fuck, I don't want a wife. The girlfriend part sounds nice though."

"Don't knock the wife part. It's pretty good when you find the right one."

"I'm glad you and Gabby are so right for each other. You and she are just sickening." Sammy-Jo laughed, and Nora joined in. "But is it too much to ask, that all I want for Christmas is…" She shrugged. "I dunno."

"You'll find the one, when the time's right, and then nothing will stop it from happening."

When they both became quiet again, Sammy-Jo said, "It's good to put all that Krista stuff behind us, you know."

Nora nodded. “Yeah, I don’t hold grudges…well, I might with Krista.”

They laughed again.

“What’s so funny?” Ladonya asked as she put the tray down onto the table and they both reached for their pints.

Chapter Four

The knock on her door the following morning wasn't something Daisy needed. She was exhausted after traipsing two miles the previous night, in the snow, in all the wrong clothing. Her leg muscles and core ached from being all tensed up, trying not to fall over and break something.

She'd literally said hello to her parents, grabbed a hot shower and climbed into bed in the poky room they called a spare.

If she reached out her left hand, she could touch the wall on the other side of the room, but she wouldn't complain. It beat sleeping in one of the twins' bunkbeds.

As if by magic, just thinking about them could conjure them, the door swung open and two very excitable kids flew through the opening, gabbling about something incoherent until they landed on their knees on the small bed, one either side of Daisy's legs.

Literally pinned down, Daisy was then unable to escape the torrent of questions.

"When did you get here?" Dolly asked.

Before she could answer, Polly piped up, "Are you staying for Christmas?"

"Did you bring presents?"

"Have you seen Santa yet? We saw him at the shops. He's real you know!"

"Matty said he wasn't, but we don't believe him!"

"Matty tells lies. Doesn't he, Dolly?"

"Yep, always fibbing," Dolly said and was about to launch into further explanation when a knock on the open door had all three of them look up.

“Morning,” their mum said, smiling at her brood. “Did you two want to let Daisy get up?”

The twins groaned but quickly jumped off the bed and scampered off to do God only knew what.

“Thanks.” Daisy smiled. “They’re getting big.”

“I know. You’d know too if you visited more often.” She ignored the eye roll from her eldest. “Your dad has taken Bill from next door to get your car. In the meantime, breakfast?”

Daisy sat up, hands clasped together. “Is it eggy bread?”

“It’s eggs, and bread, so I guess that’s doable.” Her mum grinned and almost lost her footing when Daisy jumped up just as excitedly as the girls had and wrapped her arms around her mum’s neck.

“I’ve missed this,” she said with a squeeze.

“Me too.” Her mum kissed her forehead. “Now, get dressed and I’ll have eggy bread on the table waiting. You know where the towels are, and the good shampoo is in the cupboard, make sure you put it away. Otherwise Dolly will use the lot.” She winked.

When Daisy made it downstairs, the only voices she could hear were her dad’s and Bill’s from next door, discussing possible solutions for her car.

“Morning,” Daisy said brightly as she turned into the room and was met with three faces around the kitchen table, and a fourth space set out for her. A plate with two slices of eggy bread cut into four triangles steamed in front of a cup of equally hot tea. “Aw, this smells good.” Daisy slid into the chair and grabbed a piece, yanking the corner off and chewing as she said, “Hey, Bill.”

“Hello, Daisy. Got ya car back, but the weather’s too bad to get a real look at it.”

She glanced up and out through the kitchen window at her two little sisters, all bundled up, playing in the snow.

"Still snowing then?"

"Yep, though it's forecast to rain later, so…" Bill shrugged. "Maybe this afternoon, or tomorrow we can get a look under the bonnet and see what the problem is."

"Thank you. I hope it's nothing too serious," her mum said, elbows on the table and a hot mug of tea in both hands.

"Me too. Not the way I planned to spend the last of my savings," Daisy said.

"You alright for money, love?" her mum questioned, putting the mug down. "We don't have much, but if you need—"

"No, I'm fine, Mum, honestly. I just…" She sighed at the thought of it all again. "What with having to move and deposits and my job isn't really working out, a duff car is the last thing I need."

"Always welcome back here, if all else fails." Her dad grinned, looking up from his phone.

That idea wasn't something Daisy had plans for, but she guessed it was a credible option if all else failed.

"Christmas decs look good," she said, changing the subject. She'd seen them briefly when she'd arrived the previous night. The tree was especially beautiful with all its lights and baubles. They'd been buying a new one every year from the day she was born; there would be twenty-seven Daisy baubles and fourteen more for the twins. When the years were added, the tree got bigger and bigger each year just to fit them all on.

"The girls were beyond excited when your dad took them to buy it. And they're just as excited to go and buy this year's baubles."

"Maybe if the snow eases off, we can all go into town and find them?"

"I like that idea."

Chapter Five

Sunday 22nd December

Waking up alone had never really bothered Sammy-Jo over the years. Whenever she had been single, it had always been by choice, like now, but this was different. This was healing Sammy-Jo and not the toxic version that just did whatever she wanted.

Finding dates, or women to have some fun with, had never been an issue for her. Confident, tall, attractive enough, she could charm her way into many beds if she put her mind to it.

But since the whole Krista Rave debacle, where she didn't just end up with egg over her face romantically, but also almost lost her career and every decent friendship she had, she'd been less inclined to let anyone get within ten feet of her heart, let alone inside it.

"Are you up?" The voice through the door sounded muffled.

"Yep," she called back and watched as the door crept open and her flatmate, Allegra, came into view, a scarf wrapped around her face, coat zipped up.

"I'm going to the shops. We need milk, and I've got shopping to do. Do you need anything?"

Sammy-Jo flicked her wrist over and checked the time on her watch.

"I mean, yeah, but…can you give me ten and I'll come with you?"

"I suppose so, if it's ten and not twenty, SJ." Allegra narrowed her eyes at her. "I know what your ten minutes means."

Grinning, Sammy-Jo jumped out of bed and grabbed a towel. "I'll be ten minutes, promise."

Allegra was still grumbling when they wandered into Aston's.

"I said I'd buy breakfast, didn't I?" SJ said, rolling her eyes at the complaining. "I wasn't even that long."

"You were fifteen minutes and that's me being lenient," Allegra argued. "See, this is why people get annoyed with you. You agree to something and then just ignore it."

"I didn't ignore it. I didn't even wash my hair."

"But you shaved your legs, didn't you?"

Sammy-Jo said nothing for a moment. She couldn't lie about it. Instead, she pushed the door open and headed towards a free table.

"You don't have to admit it. I know when you do. You whistle," Allegra said, dropping into the chair SJ pulled out for her.

"Whistle?" SJ exclaimed, as she sat down opposite. "I do not."

"Oh, yes you do, and it's out of tune." Allegra handed her a menu. "I'm starving."

"You're always starving," SJ countered, much to the amusement of Georgia, owner of Aston's, who stood listening to them bicker.

"You two are like a married couple, you know that, right?" Georgia chuckled at her two favourite footballing customers.

"If we were, I'd divorce her." Allegra grinned.

"You wouldn't," SJ said. "I'd be too good in bed, so you'd suck it up for the orgasms."

Georgia held up her pen. "Too much information for this early in the morning."

Allegra laughed. "Like I'd let you into my bed anyway."

"Who said I'd fancy you?"

"Okay, just give me your order so I can get going," Georgia said with a hint of mirth. "I'm guessing it's the usual for you, SJ?"

"Yeah, no point changing now."

"I can't believe you can eat the same food every day and not get bored," Allegra said, still perusing the menu.

"Because there is nothing wrong with eggs, bacon and sourdough with beans. All healthy options to keep this body trim and fit," SJ responded, patting her flat stomach for confirmation.

"Whatever." Allegra looked up at Georgia and pulled a face. "She's always this dull. I'll have eggs benedict, please." Turning to SJ, she said, "With extra sauce, seeing as we have time off and it's Christmas."

"Righto, and drinks?"

"Coffee," they both said in unison.

Chapter Six

Dolly grabbed a handful of snow and threw it at Polly, who giggled and ducked out of the way just in time. Then she scooped up her own handful and launched it back at Dolly, who wasn't quite so fast and took it full in the face.

"Oh, you have to be faster, Doll!" Daisy shouted. Walking arm in arm with her mum, Daisy enjoyed the sensation of having warm feet in borrowed boots. "You know in a minute, they're either going to kick off or turn on us, don't you?"

"Absolutely," her mum said, squeezing her arm. "And if it's the latter, we're going to batter them, right?"

"Completely," Daisy agreed and giggled.

The walk along the riverbank was slower than usual, due to the weather, and the fact that everyone else seemed to be out enjoying the snow too.

A couple of other kids joined in the snowball fight with Dolly and Polly as they all passed each other.

"Do you want to get a coffee?" Her mum pointed towards Aston's, already bustling with people looking for breakfast and hot drinks.

"No, it's packed. Let's get a hot chocolate in town once we've completed our mission."

"I do love having you here. I know Kent's only a couple of hours away, but it feels so far. I miss just going for a coffee and a catchup."

"Mum, I'm twenty-seven and have lived away from home for almost a decade."

Her mum chuckled. "I know, but when you do visit, I miss it when you go again."

"Well, if my car doesn't get fixed, I'm gonna be stuck here forever, or go back on the train and be stuck there forever."

"I'm sure Bill will fix it; he's a dab hand with mechanics."

"I hope so."

"What are you staring at?" Allegra asked, twisting in her seat to look out the window in the direction Sammy-Jo was looking.

"Nothing," Sammy-Jo answered, still staring and leaning to her left to keep looking. "I thought I recognised someone."

"Who?"

"Nobody you know. You're so nosey; you know that, right?"

"I prefer 'interested,' if you don't mind."

Sammy-Jo ran a hand through the long curls that now hung freely down her back.

"You need a visit to the hairdresser." Allegra reached out and flicked a rogue strand back behind SJ's ear. "It's literally a living, breathing entity all of its own."

"This is my mane. I will not chop it."

Sitting back in her seat, Allegra put her fork down. "You know you almost took Kayla's eye out in training the other day. That—" she waved at Sammy-Jo's hair, "mane is a dangerous weapon when you tie it up."

Sammy-Jo smirked. "I know."

"Anyway, who did you think you recognised?"

Without thinking, Sammy-Jo said, "Daisy." She then pressed her lips together in annoyance when Allegra grinned.

"Knew I'd get it out of you, and who is Daisy?"

"She's nobody, just…she was stranded last night, and I walked her home."

"You walked her home, before you came to the pub?"

Sammy-Jo nodded.

"Why was she stranded?" she asked with barely any interest in her voice, cutting into her egg yolk and letting it drizzle all over the muffin.

"Her car broke down, up on Sefton Street."

"And she lives around here?"

Again, Sammy-Jo nodded. "Well, she's visiting her parents and sisters. She lives in Kent."

Allegra pushed the mouthful on her fork into her mouth and chewed slowly, eyes narrowing as she watched Sammy-Jo cut off a corner of her toast.

When she swallowed, she took a sip of coffee and then said, "So, you rescued her on Sefton Street, walked her Virtually all the way back to where you live, and then walked all the way back to the pub…in the snow?"

"I did," SJ said proudly.

"I see."

Now it was Sammy-Jo who narrowed her eyes at her friend. "What do you see?"

"You like her."

Sammy-Jo huffed. "Don't be ridiculous. I don't even know her. I wasn't going to leave a woman all by herself, stranded on the roadside, was I?"

"Is she blonde, and pretty?"

"What does that have to do with the price of fish?"

Allegra laughed. "Because you have a type, my friend. You have a type."

Chapter Seven

Arriving back home, bag-laden and soaked through by the downpour that had washed away almost all the remnants of snow, Daisy pushed the kitchen door open with her hip and backed into the room to find her dad at the table with Bill next to him and an oily lump of metal on an old rag in front of them.

"Water pump," Bill said, as though that in itself should be explanation enough.

"Okay…" Daisy said slowly, dropping the bags onto the floor as the twins came rushing through the door gabbling about their new baubles.

"Those are nice, girls," her dad said as Polly and Dolly both held their hands out, dangling a reindeer and a penguin from cold fingers. "Shall we go and hang them?"

"No, can't. Not till Daisy finds one," Polly insisted.

"Oh, right." He looked towards his eldest daughter, who shrugged.

"I didn't find any I liked."

"We're going to pop down to the garden centre tomorrow. Their grotto is amazing; Daisy is bound to find one there," her mum said as she bustled in behind them. "In the meantime, I'll get started on tea. Bill, you staying?"

"Oh, thanks Eileen, but no, I'm going to see if I can get this part ordered for Daisy." His chair pushed back, legs scraping on the lino.

"Thank you, Bill, you're a life saver," Daisy said, pushing up on tiptoes to kiss his cheek once he was standing.

"No trouble, lass." He patted her arm and moved past her enough that she could sit down in the chair he'd vacated.

With Bill gone, Eileen edged her way towards the fridge. "I was thinking a quick egg and chips for tea. Any objections?"

Polly groaned. "I don't like egg and chips."

"Yes you do," Eileen said. "You had it last week."

"But I'm vegan now," Polly insisted.

"Since when?" her dad asked, equally as baffled as everyone else.

Polly shrugged. "Since this morning."

"Oh, give over," he answered and picked up his paper. "I blame that TikkyTokky rubbish for this."

Daisy chuckled. "So, Pol, you serious about it?"

The youngster nodded furiously. "Yep, nothing with a face or a soul," she said, words far beyond her own understanding.

"I'm not," Dolly said, eager to get some attention too.

"Right, well I'm not arguing, Polly, you can have chips and beans. Everyone else gets eggs." She turned away and started to open drawers and cupboards.

"I was thinking I might go out later," Daisy announced. "SJ mentioned a couple of pubs that sound fun. I might check them out."

"SJ?" her mum asked over her shoulder.

"Yes, the woman who walked me home last night."

"Oh, yes, well, that sounds nice, doesn't it, Chris?"

"Oh aye, just make sure you have a plan to get home and charge your phone," he reminded her over the top of the paper. "I'd rather you call at one in the morning than get stranded again. There won't always be an SJ, you know."

"I will, Dad." She pulled her phone from her pocket and waved it. "See, all charged."

"Can I come?" Dolly asked, moving to sit on Daisy's lap.

"Ah, when you're older. You're a bit small to be going to the pub," Daisy said, wrapping her arms around the tiny waist and hugging her sibling close. "When you get to sixteen, I'll sneak you in," she whispered, and Dolly giggled.

"And me." Polly jumped on the spot beside them, close enough that she heard the whisper. From the look on her dad's face, Daisy was pretty sure he'd heard too, and she grinned at him.

Chapter Eight

Daisy rocked up to Art Too with only a tiny hope of bumping into SJ again. She wasn't sure why she was this interested, because she barely knew anything about her. In reality, she didn't even know what she properly looked like either.

But the deep brown eyes and the wide smile had definitely left an impression, and it would be nice to thank her properly for walking her home.

In hindsight, she should have exchanged numbers with her white knight. She giggled at that idea. Daisy Foster didn't need rescuing, but it was nice that someone wanted to.

Loud music blasted out every time someone opened the door and entered or exited. She watched as two women laughed together, one blonde and gorgeous, the other dark and handsome.

Neither were Daisy's type, but they looked happy, and she smiled at them both as they passed and then followed them in.

It wasn't like any place she'd been in before. There was a small bar area with cubbyhole seating and then stairs that led, she assumed, down to another space. That was where all the music was coming from and where the blonde had disappeared to. And something had exploded Christmas all over the place.

"I like it," she said to herself, nodding along to the upbeat music.

Daisy headed to the bar and waited. The handsome dark-haired woman stepped in beside her.

"Alright," she said when the dark-haired one smiled and nodded at her.

"Hey."

"First time here," Daisy said. She'd always found that striking up conversations with people was the quickest way to make friends or be avoided like the plague.

"Ah right, it's cool. Just takes a while to get served." She laughed and Daisy nodded.

"Yeah, I'm finding that out. I'm Daisy." She held her hand out just as the music switched into a fast beat version of "Rocking Around the Christmas Tree."

"Right, uh Shannon." They shook hands. "Merry Christmas."

"You too. Was that your girlfriend you were with?"

Daisy pointed towards the stairs.

"Oh, yes, that is absolutely my girlfriend," Shannon gushed. "Still can't believe it and it's been a year."

"Ah, that's so sweet."

"What about you, with anyone?" Shannon asked and looked around, expecting to see someone looking over.

"No, just split with someone, so…" She shrugged and left it unsaid; there was an obvious conclusion. "Actually, I was kind of looking for someone. Sounds stupid, but she walked me home last night when my car broke down and…"

"What ya want?"

Daisy heard the words and swivelled to face an overworked woman behind the bar with pink hair and something metal piercing most of her face.

"Oh, pint of lager, thanks," she said quickly.

"So, what's her name?" Shannon asked once the drink was ordered.

"Uh, she just said SJ."

Shannon shook her head. "No, I don't think I know her."

Before Daisy could answer, she felt a tap on her shoulder.

"She's taken," the blonde said against her ear before sidling around to lay claim to Shannon. She grinned at them both, Shannon smiling like a lovesick idiot and Daisy poised to run. "God, I'm only joking." She held out her hand. "Diana, and you are?"

Finally getting her wits about her, Daisy laughed.

"Daisy. Nice to meet you."

"She was just asking if we knew anyone called SJ, but I said I didn't recognise the name."

Daisy's pint was placed in front of her along with the card machine. She reached into her pocket and pulled out a fiver.

"No, I don't know anyone called SJ. Maybe Scarlett would know her," Diana mused. "I'll text her." She went to grab her phone from the bag and then paused and narrowed her eyes at Daisy. "Why are you looking for her? You're not a weird stalker ex, are you?"

"I am not," Daisy said indignantly. "I just wanted to thank her, properly. She walked me home last night when my car broke down and…it was late, and cold and snowing and it wasn't till after she'd gone, I realised I should have taken her number."

Shannon ordered their drinks.

Diana continued to study her. "I believe you. Let me ask Scarlett, or Bea. Bea knows everyone, I think she's slept with most of them."

Daisy's eyes widened at that. Why did it bother her if SJ had slept with some woman called Bea?

"Oh, I'm just kidding," Diana said, typing into her phone. When she was finished, she put it back into her bag. "Might take a while for a reply, they're on a date."

"Scarlett and Bea?" Daisy asked. Gossip was gossip, regardless of whether you knew the people involved.

"Good god, no." Diana laughed, and Shannon joined her. "Imagine that."

Shannon leaned forward. "Scarlett is her sister…and her stepmother."

"Woah, now that's a story."

"Yes, it is, but we won't be telling it tonight, thank you Shannon. We're trying to make new friends, not scare them off with my family secrets." Diana laughed.

"Oh no, I love a family secret. I have twin sisters, 20 years younger than me, and my parents called them Polly and Dolly."

"Maybe we are kindred spirits, Daisy, lost in a world of sadistic parents." Diana chuckled. "Come on, let's find a seat downstairs and then…we dance."

Chapter Nine

Sunday night had never been this dull, Sammy-Jo thought as she flicked the channels and searched for something to entertain her.

She blew out her cheeks and switched the TV off, dropping the remote onto the sofa.

"Should have gone out," Allegra said, glancing up from her book at the other end of the couch. She had her legs up, her feet almost resting on Sammy-Jo's thigh.

"Maybe," she answered, checking her watch. It was nearly ten. The night was either coming to an end, or just beginning for some people. "When did Christmas get so boring?"

Allegra closed her book and placed it on her lap. "Christmas isn't boring, you're just stagnant."

"Nice. Thanks for that." Sammy-Jo sniffed her armpit.

"I don't mean – this time last year was a shitty time for you. All that Krista business and turning up at the club's Christmas party off your face, getting in Gabby's face, suspended, thrown off the team and transfer listed…it's no wonder this year feels—"

Sammy-Jo rubbed her face. "I know I was an idiot. You don't have to remind me."

"I'm not reminding you to be negative, I'm saying it was a lot. And it took a lot to get over and you've worked hard to regroup and get your work life back on track…and maybe that's been at the detriment of yourself and your life away from football." She twisted her legs off the sofa and stood up. Looking down at Sammy-Jo, she said, "The Sammy-Jo of old would have been out every night, being the life and soul of the party, kissing girls and enjoying every minute of it, and while I am glad that you've calmed down a bit and might actually be somebody who is now dateable… You actually have to go out and be dateable and not sit in here moaning there's nothing on the TV."

Sammy-Jo watched as she walked towards the door where she paused, clearly not finished.

"Otherwise, you'll be needing one of those iVibe2000 things I keep seeing advertised." She grinned. "Get to bed, and tomorrow, try again."

"I don't need an iVibe," Sammy-Jo called after her. "I've already got one."

"Eww, grim," Allegra shouted back.

Sammy-Jo flopped back against the cushion. Pressing her lips together, she considered what Allegra had said. Most of it was true.

She checked her watch again. Art Too would be open till two. If she left now she could be there by eleven, and then at least she wouldn't be sitting at home like Billy bloody No Mates.

Jumping up, she felt energised as she checked herself. She was just wearing jeans and a Fletcher t-shirt. She could throw on her plaid button-up and if she just tied her hair up, she was good to go.

She opened the front door and froze. It was absolutely chucking it down. Stepping back inside, she closed the door.

"We'll go out tomorrow night," she said to herself.

Chapter Ten

Monday 23rd December

Everything ached the following morning when Daisy was woken by the shouting seven-year-olds having a barney on the landing. She lay there quietly and tried to ignore it but eventually, it exploded in through her door and onto the bed.

"Dolly said that I'm a baby because I still like Peppa Pig. Tell her she's an idiot." Polly pouted and folded her arms as she bounced on Daisy's knees, causing a tidal wave of nausea to flow through her.

"Stop bouncing," she pleaded just before Dolly launched into it. "Mum?" Daisy managed to shout over the cacophony. "MUM!"

"Will you two pack it in?" Eileen said, appearing at the door as if by magic.

"Well, she started it," Dolly continued. "I just said she should grow up."

"Go on, downstairs and tell ya dad. Let him sort it out." Eileen shooed them out and then turned to Daisy, crossing her arms over her chest and grinning. "Did we overdo it?"

"No. Yes." Daisy groaned. "To be fair, I'm not hung over as such, maybe a little bit, but everything aches… I haven't danced that much in years. Diana is a demon once the music kicks in."

"Diana? New interest?"

"Uh, oh, no, not at all," Daisy answered, pushing herself up the bed to sit against the pillows. "No, I met her and her girlfriend, fiancée? Can't remember. They were nice though. It was fun to have some people to hang out with."

"And they didn't mind you being a gooseberry?"

Daisy laughed. "No, their other friends arrived and so there was a gang of us in the end."

"Well, I am glad you had a nice time. Maybe making some new friends will mean you visit more often." Eileen turned to leave and muttered, "Or just move here."

"I heard that," Daisy called after her.

"Good, you were supposed to." Her mum laughed. "Breakfast is ready, if you're joining us."

"I'll be down in a minute."

Picking up her phone, she groaned again, this time at the time. It was only just after eight. She hadn't gotten in until well after two, creeping up the stairs like she used to when she was a teenager.

Didn't matter then and didn't matter now; her mother was always awake. She probably should feel guilty about that.

Other than the time, it was the day that stood out. Monday. Usually, a workday, but today it was the day before Christmas Eve, and that meant she didn't have to think about work, and marketing, or Stella, her annoying boss.

She had a message.

Diana: Hey, hope the hangover isn't too bad LOL. We're going into town later, wondered if you fancied it. Should be a few of us for lunch at Aston's, down by the river. Let me know, I'll save you a seat. About 1ish?

Daisy: Hey, was just rudely awoken by the double trouble. I'd love to meet for lunch, if you don't mind me crashing your party again.

She threw the covers back and stretched her back out, wincing as the muscles reminded her of the limbo dancing they'd done at some point, after far too many pints of lager. If she went out again tonight, she was going on to vodka. That was much better for her waistline.

Diana: Absolutely, not a problem, otherwise I'd have not invited. □See you there.

Chapter Eleven

Nora Brady and Ladonya Sinclair paused to look in every shop along the Riverbank Boulevard and if she were honest, Sammy-Jo was jealous. Another emotion she'd been working on this past year.

The problem was, other than her team, she had nobody to buy presents for. Her parents had moved to Spain years ago, too engrossed in their life in the sun to come home for Christmas, which was okay with her because her mother would drive her up the wall within 48 hours.

She'd been invited to go there, but had no intention of doing so because, see previous point. 48 hours was her limit and she'd be stuck there for two weeks, and Christmas in the sun - it didn't feel right. It was a no.

So, she'd sent them gifts in the post weeks ago.

There were no siblings, no cousins. She did have an aunt up north somewhere, but they'd not seen each other since Sammy-Jo was twelve, so that was a no too. And usually it was all fine, because like Allegra had said, she'd be out partying up like a storm. And last year, despite it all, she had at least had Krista to entertain her.

This year was different, and as she watched her pals mooching into store after store, looking for anything they could add to the ever-growing pile of stuff they'd bought their significant others, Sammy-Jo felt left out.

She glanced around.

The riverbank had been turned into a Christmas market. Loads of wooden cabins lined one side, and the shops and cafés lined the other. No wonder it was so busy.

A whiff of something sweet and chocolatey mixed with alcohol and woody spices wafted across and got her attention.

"Does anyone want a hot chocolate?" she asked, as Nora lifted up an item of sexy lingerie. SJ rolled her eyes and looked away. Her sight landed on the back of a blonde head, in a denim jacket.

"I'll be back in a minute," Sammy-Jo said, ignoring the pair considering the question, turning on her heel and walking as quickly as she could without falling over her own feet or bumping into someone.

The blonde head bobbed and weaved through the crowd, dropping out of sight here and there, but Sammy-Jo kept moving.

She contemplated shouting out to her, but then she thought what if it wasn't Daisy, and who really would hear her over the Christmas music and chatter? A bunch of overexcitable kids ran around in circles, blocking her from catching up.

"Blooming heck," she muttered, making her way around them. She navigated a woman with a pushchair and finally breathed a sigh of relief when she saw the blonde disappear into Aston's.

At least twenty people milled around outside, some smoking, some drinking warm drinks and talking. Sammy-Jo joined them, lurking outside as she built up the nerve to go and say hello.

It was pretty ridiculous when she thought about it, but still, here she was. Craning her neck, she stared in through the window, which wasn't easy as most of it was steamed up from all the heat inside, but her luck was in as a kid in a highchair rubbed their chubby little hands across it, clearing a space.

SJ crept closer and dipped down so she could look in and see Daisy. She was frustrated when she couldn't find her, but then, someone moved, and Sammy-Jo had a direct line of sight to see Daisy hugging a blonde woman.

A hot blonde woman.

"You bloody idiot," she said to herself. As if she wouldn't have someone gorgeous all over her. Daisy was smiling and laughing at something the blonde said, and then the pair moved further towards the back and out of sight.

Sammy-Jo straightened up and sighed, her shoulders sagging. Like it was going to be a Christmas miracle, she thought and kicked a lump of mud.

“Merry Christmas, merry Christmas,” a bloke dressed as Santa said to her, holding out a small, wrapped package.

“Thanks,” she said and took it.

“Christmas is a time for great things. Merry Christmas, merry Christmas,” he said, walking away and handing out small gifts to people as they passed.

“Great things huh? I’d take a little thing right now.” She stuffed the present into her pocket and headed back to search for Nora and Ladonya.

Chapter Twelve

"Daisy!" Diana called out, and quickly rose from her seat to come and greet her new friend. "You should know, I'm a hugger," she said before launching into a bear hug.

"Oh, well, I like hugs." Daisy laughed.

"Right, let me introduce you to everyone and then we can get some delicious food because I am starving."

She led Daisy across the café to the large table at the back that had several people crowded around it, none of whom were out last night, other than Shannon, who waved at her.

"Don't look so frightened. They're all quite nice when they behave." Shannon laughed and got a dig in the side from the woman who looked the youngest.

"So, this is my mother, Claudia." Diana pointed at the elegant older blonde on the end of the table. "Her partner, and my sister, Scarlett." She was the darker, and quite frankly hot, and much younger woman sitting beside her. When Daisy looked perplexed at that, she added, "I'll fill you in later."

"Okay." Daisy chuckled at the unconventional family dynamics.

"That armpit is my younger sister, Zara, and my gorgeous nephew is asleep."

For the first time, Daisy noticed the stroller.

"Ignore her," Zara said. "She just hates it that I'm the pretty one." She winked.

Daisy laughed, because this family hadn't been hit by any branch falling out of the ugly tree, that was for sure.

"Wow, okay, well I will do my best to remember everyone's names…but after last night, there might still be some fogginess."

"Diana tells us you're visiting your parents," Claudia said.

"Yes, here till new year and then back to Kent to decide what my life will look like next year."

"And what do you do?" Scarlett asked.

"Bloody hell you lot, let the woman sit down before you begin the interrogation." Diana smiled and indicated a chair beside her. "I vote for a round of adult hot chocolates, a little hair of the dog."

"Not for me, thanks," Zara said. "James is picking us up and taking us to the ice rink in the park."

"Isn't Jacob a bit small for that?" Diana asked, and Daisy sat back and enjoyed the family dynamics.

"No, you can skate with the stroller."

"Sounds horrific. And an accident waiting to happen," Diana concluded.

"So, Daisy, what are your plans for Christmas?" Claudia asked, interrupting any possibility of a sibling fight erupting.

"Well, it will be Mum and Dad, and the twins, and me. Probably Bill from next door as he's on his own now, since his wife died a couple of years go."

"That's sad, for him, but at least you all have each other." Claudia smiled as her attention was drawn towards a teenager in an Aston's t-shirt holding a pen and order pad. "Oh, I think we're all having hot chocolate."

"Adult ones!" Diana shouted.

"Not mine," Zara called out.

When the order was taken, Scarlett leaned towards Daisy and said, "I had a think about an SJ, but nobody comes to mind."

Daisy had forgotten all about the text message Diana had sent the previous night.

"Thanks for thinking about it. It's silly really, I don't even know what she looks like, not properly."

"How so?" Claudia inquired. "It sounds intriguing."

"Well, my car broke down, and I was having a bit of a meltdown, when out of nowhere SJ appeared. It was snowing, and she'd had the sense to dress for the weather, so she was all bundled up, hat on her head pulled right down her forehead, scarf wrapped around her face. She walked me home."

"Ah, that's so sweet," Zara said.

"Yes, and I wanted to thank her properly, but I didn't think to get her number, and I only know she's called SJ to her friends." The conversation filtered back into her mind. "I think she said her name was Sammy something, Jo, Sammy-Jo."

"Hm, still not ringing any bells, but to be honest, I'm not really chatting to anyone else now when I go out." Scarlett grinned and nudged Claudia's shoulder.

"I guess that I'm looking for a needle in a haystack." Daisy smiled sadly.

"It is Christmas though." Zara's enthusiasm was apparent as she added, "And magic happens at Christmas, Daisy."

"Well, I mean, it's cool, not like I want a romance or anything." Daisy blushed. Why had she blushed when Diana smiled knowingly at her? "Honestly, I have so much going on with work and finding somewhere else to live, I really don't have time for a long-distance relationship."

Shannon scoffed. "Hardly a long distance, it's only Kent." She glanced at Diana. "I think when you find someone you like, you should give it a go."

Daisy giggled. "I barely know her, we literally chatted for 30 minutes and then said good night." *So, why can't you forget about those eyes and that mouth, the smile, the way she got all awkward and wanted to impress you?*

"I'm just saying, if you find her again, maybe it's meant to be." Shannon grinned.

"I very much doubt that," Daisy said just as a tray of mugs filled with hot chocolate, adult or otherwise, was placed onto the table.

"Woo, here we go," Zara said loudly. "Merry Christmas everyone."

"Merry Christmas," they chorused back.

Chapter Thirteen

"Where did you go?" Nora asked when Sammy-Jo found them. "Thought you'd stalked off somewhere."

"No, just…went for a wander, fancied a hot chocolate, but the queue was huge." She shrugged. "Did you get everything you wanted?"

"Yep," Ladonya said. "Thought about a whirl around on the merry-go-round."

On this side of the river, there was a small funfair and what seemed like a million kids ran around screaming and eating. Harried-looking parents were wiping chocolate from faces, adjusting scarves and trying to watch three different children run in all different directions.

"Really?" Sammy-Jo scrunched her nose up at the idea.

Ladonya slapped her on the arm. "Hell no. We're going to the pub, come on."

They trudged past the queue for tickets to the merry-go-round, pushed through the doors of Blanca's, and marched inside to claim a booth.

It was relatively quiet for such a busy day outside. At one end of the bar, the owner, Sadie, was leaning towards Natalie, her partner – in life, not business, she'd told Sammy-Jo once when they'd been the only ones in here.

Sammy-Jo watched them for a moment, another perfectly happy and settled couple who'd found each other and were enjoying the fruits of that.

Nora noticed her looking and stepped in front of her. "Drink then?"

"Just a Coke. I'm going out later, so I don't want to get blotto day drinking with you two."

"Day drinking?" Ladonya laughed. "I like that."

"Might as well, Gabby's picking me up and that's going to be at least…" Nora checked her watch, "another thirty minutes."

"Okay, I'm gonna go get us something Christmassy, and Little Miss Sociable here, a cola." Ladonya winked and then took off towards the bar.

"So, off out tonight then?" Nora asked, by way of intro into a conversation.

Sammy-Jo nodded. "Yeah, I think so. Last night was boring, I can't do another night sat in front of the TV with Allegra reading."

"Things alright between you two?"

"Yeah, she drives me nuts but I kind of like the banter. It must be what it's like to have a younger sister to annoy." Sammy-Jo grinned. "Though I dunno how much longer she'll be around now she's seeing John."

"Oh yes, Bath Street Rovers' new winger. What's he like?"

"He's alright to be fair. Bit of a drip."

"You mean he's nice and romantic."

Sammy-Jo laughed. "I'm nice and romantic. He's…a golden retriever, all panting and slobbery and waiting on her every whim. Does what he's told."

"Oh, and you're such a black cat femme." Nora pushed her playfully.

"Not if my boxers are a sign, but I like to think I'm no pushover now."

"Don't do that," Nora said, shaking her head. "Don't let what happened with Krista change who you are. Stay soft, it's what makes you interesting."

"Give over. It's what got me in trouble."

"No, what got you in trouble was not talking about how you felt about me joining the team and your fears around losing your spot as top dog."

Sammy-Jo didn't speak, but she kept listening.

"Krista used your fears to turn you against yourself," Nora continued. "She's not who you should be using as a guide to determine how you live the rest of your life."

"I'm not…I just…I don't want to get hurt like that again, or to hurt others because I—"

"Because what?"

"Off the pitch… I dunno who I am anymore. I'm doubting everything, and I don't know how to change it."

Nora nodded. "Okay, well one thing I can tell you, you're alright as you are. Be vulnerable with someone; it's actually quite appealing to most people when someone can show up authentically even when they're not at their best. Stop trying to be someone you're not, don't put up walls before you've even started."

They both turned to see Ladonya shimmying her way, singing along to Mariah Carey's "All I want for Christmas Is You," carrying a tray with one pint of Coke and two glasses of God only knew what.

"What the hell is that, rocket fuel?" Nora asked, laughing at her.

"More like windscreen wash," Sammy-Jo joked.

The electric blue creamy drinks had a rim of what looked like coconut around the glass, and a bright red cherry floating.

"It's called a…hell I forgot. It's Christmas, who cares, get drinking." She passed the drinks out and then held hers up. "To a wonderful holiday. May we all be blessed with waking up Christmas morning to find everything we wanted under the tree."

"Amen to that," Nora said as they all chinked glasses in the toast.

They were all mid-sip when the door opened and in walked the vision that was Gabby Dean, who turned to look at them. She was all long legs, hourglass figure, and blonde hair swept back in her trademark style. She looked stunning in a red dress with white faux fur collar. She glared at them with a brow raised, along with the curl of her lip as she caught them all in the act.

"Hey Babe," Nora said, placing her drink down and standing quickly to rush forward and greet her wife. "Drink?"

"No, thank you, I have a meeting to get to once I've dropped you lot off."

"A meeting?" Nora stepped back and looked her up and down. "Dressed like…that." The word wasn't a negative, but it definitely came with an edge of 'holy fuck.'

"It's a works do."

"A works do? Is that what we're calling it these days?"

Gabby laughed, then turned to Natalie and Sadie and waved. "Yes, it's the WIB dinner dance."

"WIB?" Sammy-Jo asked.

"It's a local group for Women in Business, here in Bath Street. We meet once a month to discuss ways in which we can help each other."

"Oh, sounds good." Sammy-Jo nodded.

"Yes, in fact, if you're all good with it, I said I'd give Natalie a lift too."

"Yeah, all good. We can squeeze in the back, can't we?" Nora turned to the other two. Ladonya nodded.

"I can walk," Sammy-Jo offered. "I'm totally out of your way anyway, and its ten minutes over the bridge."

"If you're sure? I have no problem with dropping you home," Gabby insisted.

SJ waved her off. "I'll be fine, but you're staying to finish your drinks, though, right?"

"Of course." Gabby sat down. Turning to Nora, she said, "I'll have a spritzer."

And without a word, Nora headed to the bar and Sammy-Jo grinned to herself. Golden retrievers.

Chapter Fourteen

It had been a toss-up between getting the bus into Bath Street and a cab home, or just walking to Blanca's.

Blessed with the option of two gay bars within one small-sized UK town, Sammy-Jo didn't dwell too much on it and decided the walk was quicker, better for her health, and less hassle getting home again if she had a skinful. Which wasn't the intention; it was mid-season break but taking her eye completely off the ball – no pun intended – was not what she had planned.

But she also knew that she could be easily tempted if the right person were offering, and as she was intending to go out there and at least look at who was available, she had to consider that temptation might come her way.

The mass of curls still hung down her back. She liked them wild but in a styled way. Despite Allegra's insistence that she visit the hairdresser, SJ did actually take care of her luscious locks.

However, she did double check she had a hairband around her wrist, because at some point, she would get hot and have to tie it back, she was sure of that.

Wearing long black pants with a high waist, black bra under a well-fitted waistcoat and a black tie around her neck, with a solid pair of black boots on her feet, she felt good as she checked herself in the mirror one last time.

"Right, let's get back out there," she said to herself. "You have to let that shit with Krista go. You're not that person anymore."

"No, you're not."

Allegra's voice behind her made her jump.

"What the hell?" SJ said, feeling her cheeks burn. "Sneaking up on people isn't nice, Leggy."

"I wasn't sneaking. I was walking past an open door. Anyway, you look nice."

Sammy-Jo shrugged with just a hint of embarrassment still lingering. "Thanks."

"Actually, you look hot, and if I swung that way… Nah, I still wouldn't be interested." Allegra giggled.

"Fuck off. Like I'd want to date you anyway. John can keep you, now you've gone back to men."

"I didn't go back to men - they were always there. It's called 'bisexual.'"

"Whatever, slimebag."

They both tried to hold a serious face, but neither could manage it and they both broke into laughter.

"Seriously though, you're right. Put it all behind you. Everyone else has, and everyone is much happier with who you are now."

"Yeah, I know. It's just…sometimes I'm reminded that the old me had more fun," Sammy-Jo said, feeling a tad wistful. She'd been arrogant at times, but with that came confidence. She'd walk into a bar and never feel like she didn't belong, or that whoever she picked for the night wouldn't be clamouring to go home with her. But all that had changed after Krista, and therapy.

"Maybe, but old you got into trouble a lot too, so…" Allegra pushed off the wall she'd been leaning against. "Time for new SJ to start making a path for herself."

"True." Sammy-Jo nodded. "What are you doing tonight?"

"I'm probably going to go over to John's."

"Alright then, well, I'll see you tomorrow then." SJ grabbed her keys and wallet.

With it this close to Christmas Eve, Blanca's was already filling up when SJ got there. She slipped her coat off at the door for maximum impact when she opened the door and stepped in. There was no way someone wouldn't take a second glance. She knew that much at least.

She pushed her way through the crowd of women dressed as elves at the bar and wondered just what she had walked into.

"What can I get ya?" Sadie shouted above the noise from across the bar. They both turned to look at the elves once more before Sammy-Jo spoke.

"Whatever they're having?" she grinned.

"Pint of Amstel, right?" Sadie asked, predicting her actual drink. Clearly, she was memorable, or too much of a regular, she considered.

Sammy-Jo nodded. "Yes, please," she shouted back when a roar of laughter went up behind her. "Busy, eh?"

Sadie smiled. "Christmas work do. They've been here since four. It's going to be carnage, but I am not going to complain. Work dos are going to pay for my summer holiday."

Sammy-Jo laughed and took her drink, waiting patiently to press her bank card against the payment machine.

Just as she was about to reach forward and pay, her other elbow was knocked and her drink spilled out of the glass and all over her hand.

"Hey, watch it will ya? Don't blooming waste it at these prices," she said, spinning around to give the inconsiderate person a Sammy-Jo special glare.

But that didn't happen. Instead, she felt her tummy flip and a smile appear on her face.

"I'm so sorry," Daisy replied, oblivious to who Sammy-Jo was, now she wasn't all bundled up in her hat and scarf.

"Daisy?"

"Have we met – oh, hang on." She leaned in and studied Sammy-Jo's face, lingering on her eyes, and then her mouth. "SJ?"

"Yeah." Sammy-Jo laughed before sipping her drink.

"Blimey, you scrub up alright." Daisy grinned. "I've been looking for you."

"Have ya?"

"Oi, are you going to pay for that, or what?" Sadie said, one hand still holding the pay machine, the other gripping the pump.

"Oh, sorry, yes…oh." She turned back to Daisy. "Do you want a drink?"

"I should be buying you one."

"That's alright, next time." Sammy-Jo smiled awkwardly. Dressed up, Daisy was even more attractive than her initial assessment on Saturday night.

"You know, I do have other people waiting," Sadie said a little more firmly.

"Sorry, can I get a white wine?" Daisy shouted. Sadie turned to get the extra drink. "Seriously, let me get these. Why don't you go grab us some seats, if you can find any. It's packed."

Without thinking too hard about it, Sammy-Jo agreed, and shuffled her way through the crowd of elves again. Spotting a group about to leave, she beelined for the table and nabbed it just before a couple of fairies and a reindeer could sit down.

"I only need two seats," she said, but they waved off the offer to share. "Fair enough." She shrugged to herself.

Flipping her coat around the back of the chair, she waved at Daisy, so she knew where she was, and took a seat.

"Don't blow it. At least find out if she's remotely interesting or interested," she told herself, and then smiled when she saw Daisy coming towards her. *God, she's gorgeous. And yes, Allegra, I clearly have a type.*

Chapter Fifteen

Daisy flung her head back and laughed as Sammy-Jo did an impression of someone from the TV. In fact, she'd done nothing else but laugh as Sammy-Jo recounted stories and kept her entertained, along with the wine and now cocktails they'd been drinking.

"You're really funny," she said, and Sammy-Jo shrugged and pulled a face.

"Apparently, it's my go-to source when I'm feeling awkward, nervous or overwhelmed." SJ raised her almost empty glass and downed what was left.

"Do I make you nervous?" Daisy asked with just the right hint of flirtation. She twirled her hair around her finger for better effect and almost giggled when Sammy-Jo became very serious.

"No, well, maybe a bit, I'm…all this…" She looked around the bar. "I kind of haven't been out much lately, unless it's to meet friends."

"And what was you hoping for tonight then?"

"I dunno," Sammy-Jo answered honestly. "Just putting myself out there and seeing what's what, you know?"

"Yeah, I get it. I was dating someone recently, right blooming nightmare."

"What happened? What did she do?"

"It was more of a who didn't she do kind of situation."

Sammy-Jo's eyes bulged. "She cheated on you. What's wrong with her?"

Daisy smiled at the compliment.

"I know, can you imagine?" Daisy held her gaze. "You've got beautiful eyes, you know that?"

Sammy-Jo's cheeks reddened. "Thanks for noticing." She laughed awkwardly.

"So, what about you? Who was your last…I assume girlfriend?"

"Yeah, I only date girls…I mean women, I date women, mature and sophisticated women." There was a slight slur developing to her speech. "My last girlfriend tried to kill one of my work colleagues…friends, she's a friend, I mean, she wasn't at the time, but now, she's a friend… I think. No, I'm sure, she's definitely a friend."

Unsure whether to be shocked at the revelation, or amused at Sammy-Jo's oversharing, Daisy went with, "Another drink?"

"No," Sammy-Jo replied firmly. "I talk too much. Sorry, I guess that was a lot, I should keep my mouth—" She mimicked closing her mouth with her fingers.

"I like you talking. That's why I was offering another drink, so you could tell me more about this woman you dated."

"Oh, well…I don't really want to announce it to the world, you know." She glanced at her watch; it was almost eleven. "My flatmate is at her boyfriend's. We could go and chill out at mine, unless you have to be home or something."

Daisy thought about it. Wasn't like she had a curfew, and she was a grown woman after all, and could make decisions for herself. There was nothing about SJ that concerned her or gave a weird vibe. In fact, she liked her. Liked her a lot.

"Okay, why not?"

"Cool," SJ said, almost toppling back on her stool as she went to stand up. "Whoops." She laughed as Daisy reached out to grab her.

"You okay? Should I call a cab?" Daisy asked, looking up at her. There was maybe a three-inch difference in their heights, but that didn't mean she couldn't stare right into Sammy-Jo's eyes. Gentle eyes, something soft about them when they looked at her.

"Just for the record…you're very pretty," Sammy-Jo slurred. "I can walk."

"Alright. Get ya coat." Daisy laughed and helped her on with it. "Can you remember where you live?"

"Course I can, I'm not that drunk. I'm just not used to drinking this much."

"Uh-huh." She slid her arm through the crook of Sammy-Jo's elbow and led them towards the nearest exit. "Over the bridge?"

"Yep, then all the way along the riverbank until your road, and then to the top, turn right and then left. See, I know where I live."

Chapter Sixteen

It had started to snow again as they'd walked the streets. The Christmas market was already closed up and dark as they passed each cabin and talked about whether they liked mulled wine, or hot dogs and candy floss.

It wasn't long before they passed Daisy's parents' home and onwards to the little house Sammy-Jo shared with Leggy.

"See, told you I could walk," Sammy-Jo said before stumbling into her door. Daisy stifled a laugh, and then reached forward and took Sammy-Jo's hand, steadying it as she attempted to insert the key into the lock. "Thank you," Sammy-Jo said as the key turned and the door opened a crack, which was a blessing because it was freezing outside now, with a bitterly cold wind starting to blow.

Pushing the door open, she gave an exaggerated "shhh" before they stepped inside and closed the door behind them.

"Next door gets cranky if we make too much noise after ten," she said by way of explanation to the sudden drop into hushed tones.

Kicking her boots off, she hung her coat before turning to help Daisy out of hers.

"Thanks," Daisy said.

"I'll whack the heating up a bit," Sammy-Jo said quietly, rubbing her hands together. "Come on in. Hot chocolate? I think I've had enough alcohol tonight."

"Go on then, let's live dangerously." Daisy grinned and followed her down the short hallway to the kitchen. "This is nice, you lived here long?" she asked, looking at a framed photo collage of a football team, club crest and signatures.

"About six months," Sammy-Jo answered, opening cupboards and collecting mugs. "Decided I wanted something a little quieter and out of the way. And I didn't want to live by myself, so Allegra agreed to move in with me." She flicked the kettle on. "Which works out well. We get on."

"Sounds fun, and good that you get on. Imagine it would be a nightmare living with someone you didn't like."

"True," she said, pointing a finger at Daisy. "Most of my stuff is still in boxes. I keep saying I'm going to decorate and then put pictures up and stuff, but…never got round to it."

"You like football?" Daisy asked, nudging her head towards the picture frame.

"Oh, yeah, that's my team," Sammy-Jo said, without adding anything further. "Are you into sports?"

"No, not really, more of a nerd really. I like books and going to plays and concerts, but stuff that's not really popular?"

"Okay."

The kettle boiled and Sammy-Jo concentrated on pouring the hot water into two mugs and not burning her fingers, swirling it all around with a spoon before she filled them both with milk and shoved them into the microwave.

"It's quicker. And I don't have to wash up in the morning," she said at Daisy's face, grimacing at the microwave.

"I've had too much to drink to really care, to be honest."

The microwave pinged, and Sammy-Jo took out the mugs of now steaming hot chocolate, gave them one more stir, and then led the way into the lounge.

One large sofa took up the space along the back wall, with a long coffee table in front and a huge 65" TV opposite. So, she sat down on one end of it. SJ sat at the other end, and it felt like a giant chasm had opened up between them. Maybe it was the alcohol wearing off that would put a stop to the touchy feely flirting that had started.

A large bookcase filled the third wall, and a sideboard hid behind the door. It was cosy but distinctly lacking in one thing.

"No Christmas tree?" Daisy asked. There was literally nothing that indicated it was almost Christmas, other than a couple of cards on the bookcase.

"No. We decided not to bother. Allegra is going to be at her boyfriend's, and I'm…well, I'm not bothered, and I'll be out most of the time…anyway, it's nearly over now, bit pointless." Sammy-Jo laughed. "I bet your parents' place is like Santa's grotto, isn't it?"

"Something like that. I do love it though, all the lights and mince pies, and mulled wine around the fire…okay, we don't have a fire, but a radiator doesn't sound as fun. But you get the idea."

"I do…family." Sammy-Jo smiled but went quiet. "Christmas just has a few bad memories for me I guess."

"I'm sorry."

It was silent for a moment as they both reached for their drinks, smiling over the top of them as they sipped gingerly.

"So…" Daisy put her mug back down. "Tell me about this murderous ex of yours."

"Damn, I thought you'd forgotten about that." SJ half-smiled and placed her mug down too.

"Not a chance. I want to know all your secrets."

The raised brow was comical. "All of them?"

Daisy chuckled. "How many have you got?"

"Enough to make you run for the hills," Sammy-Jo said, her smile slowly falling away. "But I did say I'd tell you about my ex so…I don't want to go into details though, I'm just getting over it and the last thing I want is to be thinking about what she did."

Daisy wriggled forward and reached out, her fingertips gently touching Sammy-Jo's knee.

"You don't have to tell me anything, if you really don't want to. I just…well, I like what I see so far and—" She sat back and let her fingers trail away to land on the cushion beside her as Sammy-Jo watched them leave. When Sammy-Jo looked up again, she added, "I know I'm only visiting for Christmas, and I'm not looking to meet anyone, but isn't that Sod's Law?"

Sammy-Jo felt the disappointment hit. It *was* Sod's Law. She changed the subject.

"Kris used me to get to a friend of mine. Someone she disliked and wanted to harm, and almost did. She attacked Nora in her own home, and I – I didn't see it. I thought we had something, you know."

"That's awful, SJ, and I'm so sorry you had to deal with someone like that. You didn't deserve that."

"Maybe not, but I had my own shit going on with Nora at the time that made me easy prey for Kris, and meant in some ways, maybe I didn't want to see it."

"What does Nora think?"

Sammy-Jo tilted her head, a little surprised by the question.

"She thinks I've redeemed myself and we should put it behind us. She's a good person."

"And you're not?" Daisy probed gently.

"I'm trying to be," Sammy-Jo answered with a rueful smile. "But the thing is…my ego allowed someone like Krista to manipulate me, and if I'm completely honest, I don't think I was a particularly nice person."

"In what way?"

Sammy-Jo shrugged. "I struggled to be emotionally available with anyone, my friends, my teammates…my therapist has her work cut out for her." She smiled.

Daisy picked up her mug again, and over the lip of the cup she said, "I think you're doing alright."

Chapter Seventeen

Daisy crept in at just after two A.M. Closing the door as quietly as she could, she leaned against it and thought back to just ten minutes earlier.

"You could just stay here? I can sleep on the couch," Sammy-Jo had offered when Daisy had yawned for the fifth time and decided she should get going.

As Daisy pulled her coat on, she said, "You're very sweet, but it's only round the corner, and Mum will worry if I don't get home. I can guarantee she's still got one ear on the door, listening for me."

"Okay, then I'll walk with you," Sammy-Jo said, reaching for her own coat off the hook.

Daisy reached up for her hand and enclosed it with her own, pulling it away from the coat but not letting go of it.

"I'll be fine. It's cold and raining; even the perverts won't be out in that. I'll be okay...but thank you, for caring." She raised up on her toes and placed a deft kiss against SJ's cheek. As she pulled away, their eyes held each other for a long moment. Long enough that either of them could have created space if they'd wanted to, but neither did.

Instead, Daisy felt fingers hook into her belt loops and pull her hips closer. The hand she'd been holding was now free and cupping her cheek as Sammy-Jo leaned closer.

"Tell me no and I won't," SJ whispered.

Daisy glanced down at her mouth, her plump, kissable lips. Her answer wasn't spoken aloud. She just closed the gap between them and met Sammy-Jo's advance.

The kiss was sweet, gentle pressure and movement without the need for anything urgent and intense and sloppy. Just lips brushing against one another reverently.

"Okay?" Daisy heard Sammy-Jo speak but couldn't quite get the gist of it. Was she okay? Of course she was. That was...

"Yeah, that was...I liked it."

"Good." Sammy-Jo straightened, taller in actual height but also in something else: confidence. "So, wanna hang out tomorrow or something?"

"Yes, I do," Daisy answered, spotting SJ's phone on the side with her keys. She picked it up, but it was locked. "Open it." She grinned and waited while Sammy-Jo pressed her thumb to the security spot.

Handing it back, she grinned at Daisy. "So, I just had to kiss you to get your number?"

"Hm, I kissed you," Daisy said with just the hint of a smile, typing her digits into the contacts list.

"No, I kissed you, it was definitely me."

Daisy saved the information and held the phone out to her. "I'm not arguing. I closed the gap and kissed you, so, I win."

"Nah-uh, that's not..." This time when Sammy-Jo pulled on her belt hoops, Daisy didn't get a chance to argue about it before she was kissed again. This time it was more urgent and intense, her lips nudged apart by an intruding, but welcome, tongue.

"Okay, fine." Daisy sighed contentedly when this kiss finished. "You can win."

"I always do." Sammy-Jo grinned.

She took each step up the stairs as slowly and lightly as she could to avoid as many creaks as possible, but at the top of the stairs, she saw it: her parents' door ajar.

"Daisy, is that you?" her mum asked in a hushed voice.

"Yeah, it's me. You can go to sleep now."

"Alright, night night."

Daisy smiled to herself again. Maybe being home for Christmas wasn't going to be a bad thing after all.

Chapter Eighteen

Tuesday 24th December- Christmas Eve

Sammy-Jo almost jumped out of her skin when she looked up from her phone and found John standing in front of her, staring down.

"Alright?" he asked, looking concerned.

"No, what the bloody hell are you doing here?"

He looked perplexed, like the answer was obvious.

"Sorry, SJ, I meant to text but we uh…anyway, yeah, we decided to stay here last night," Leggy said, strolling into the living room in just her knickers and John's oversized football jersey hanging down her thighs.

She perched on the end of the sofa, and brought her legs up, mug of tea in her hands. "Did you bring someone back last night?"

Sammy-Jo turned to face her. "Might have."

"Ooo, do tell?" She looked at John. "Make SJ a brew while I get the filthy details out of her."

John rolled his eyes but wandered off to the kitchen, while Allegra grinned at his obedience.

"He's well-trained," Sammy-Jo snarked, but the grin couldn't stay away from her lips.

"Just how I like them. Willing, and perfectly able…so, filthy details…did you f—"

"Unlike you, I don't have filthy details."

Allegra stretched up and sighed, before she slid down onto the sofa cushions. "Hm, I do have so many filthy details, but John would die of embarrassment if I shared them." She bit her lip and groaned. "So filthy."

SJ pulled a face. "Grim."

Giggling, Allegra pressed her bare foot against Sammy-Jo's thigh. "So, come on, who is she?"

Unable to contain her excitement any longer, Sammy-Jo twisted around. "You remember the woman I walked home, the other night?"

"Yes, was it her?"

"Uh-huh." SJ nodded. "I went to Blanca's, and she came in. We spent the whole night talking and then she came back here and—"

"And?" Allegra urged.

"And we drank hot chocolate and talked some more and—"

"Yes, and?"

"And then we kissed and…and she went home."

"She went home?" Allegra said incredulously. "She's not hiding out in your bedroom wearing a pair of your skanky boxers and a—" She pulled the jersey she had on. "Football shirt?"

"No, she went home, and we're going to hang out today, so, that's good. No pressure. She's not looking for a relationship and she doesn't live around here, so, it's all just a bit of fun."

"I thought you weren't doing a bit of fun anymore?"

John returned with a mug of tea and held it out for Sammy-Jo to take.

"Uh, thanks," she said to him.

He turned to Allegra, and then looked at the sofa and the space between her and SJ that was taken up by legs.

"Thank you, Darling," Allegra said sweetly. "Why don't you go grab a shower and I'll be in in a minute." She smiled all demurely and Sammy-Jo almost stuck her fingers down her throat.

When he was gone, Sammy-Jo said, "God, it must be awful being straight and having to pander to a grown man like a defenceless damsel."

"Shut up, I do not."

"'Thank you, Darling, why don't you go grab a shower…'" Sammy-Jo repeated the conversation using an overtly girly voice. "I'll be in in a minute.' …to let you have your way with me again."

"Fuck off." Allegra laughed. "Just for that I might let him, and I'm going to be so loud that old misery guts next door comes knocking."

"And I'll let him in to knock on your door." Sammy-Jo smirked.

"You're a shit, Costa." Allegra smiled. "So, where are you going to take your own damsel in distress?"

"I was thinking the ice rink, in the park."

"Is that allowed? If you hurt yourself—"

"I'm not going to hurt myself, but fair point, freak accidents do happen." She sighed. "I guess the Christmas market is nice. It's Christmassy and lots to look at, and talk about, and we could get something to eat, or end up in the pub."

"There you go. Perfect."

"I mean, she's not…it's just a Christmas visit. It's not like I'm impressing her to be my wife or anything."

"Wife? Blimey, imagine any poor woman stuck with you for life." Allegra laughed and jumped up off the sofa before SJ could launch a cushion at her. "Just have fun, idiot," she said, running out of the door up the stairs.

"I will," Sammy-Jo said to herself. Picking up the phone, she opened the text she'd been writing and finished it off. Hitting send, she sat back, sipped her tea and waited.

Chapter Nineteen

With her hands in the washing up bowl, covered in suds and holding a plate that she was currently scrubbing clean with a sponge, Daisy couldn't check the text message that had just beeped, but she had a good idea who it might be.

At least, she had a good idea of who she hoped it might be. Smiling to herself, she started humming.

"You sound happy," her mum said, coming over with a tea towel to start drying the dishes.

"Yeah." Daisy grinned. She handed the plate over. "I forgot how fun it is to meet new people and make new friends."

"Oh, how many people have you met? You've only been here two days."

"I know, impressive, huh?"

"Very. I'm glad to see you enjoying things." She waited for Daisy to finish up the next bowl. "So, what are they like?"

"Well, I mentioned Diana, she is lovely. I thought she was going to be a little stuck up, but she's a sweetheart, and Shannon, her fiancée adores her. It's very sweet."

"Sounds like they met their one."

"Yeah," Daisy said, staring into the suds. "And I found SJ."

"Oh, that's good."

"Yeah, we're going to hang out later." Daisy knew if her mum looked at her, she'd see the way her cheeks were heating up and know more than Daisy was ready to share.

But if her mother did notice, then Daisy was spared the interrogation by the doorbell ringing.

She rinsed her hands and dried them on another towel and reached for her phone, just as Bill wandered into the kitchen.

“Ah, young Daisy. I bring good news—”

“Thank goodness.”

“And bad news,” he finished. “I can fix your car, and it’s not going to be more than a couple of hundred quid for the parts.”

“Okay, that’s great,” Daisy said slowly.

“It is,” he said just as slowly. “The only problem is, I can’t get the parts until after New Year.”

“New Year?” Daisy slumped against the counter.

“Yeah, most of it’s generic, but one part is a Vauxhall part. They have to order it in and with it being Christmas—”

“It’s not going to be till the New Year,” Daisy repeated.

“But it’s ordered and as soon as it arrives, I can get the car back on the road for you.”

“Stella is going to kill me,” Daisy said, sliding into a chair at the table.

“I’m sure she will understand,” Eileen offered, flicking the kettle on to boil. “And if she doesn’t… Well, there isn’t much you can do about it.”

“I know, I just already have enough issues with her and her management style.”

“How’s that?”

“Well, she doesn’t have one for a start. She’s all over the place, takes on too many projects and then dumps them onto me, or someone else in the office. It’s a nightmare.”

“Maybe it’s time to move on.”

“It is, but I can’t, not until I’ve sorted somewhere else to live because they will want references and proof that I hold down a steady job.” She huffed. “So, I’m stuck with her for now.”

"You could just come home, love."

"And do what? I appreciate the offer Mum, I do, but I'm a grown woman, and I'm used to having my own space. I'm not sure moving into your spare room and having all my stuff in storage is where I see myself."

Eileen smiled. "It would only be temporary, until you got on your feet. Just think about it. Life is too short to be miserable."

"I guess so." She finally picked up the phone and read the text message.

SJ: So, want to meet up around 2?

Daisy grinned and started to type.

Chapter Twenty

Sammy-Jo hopped from one foot to the other in anticipation and from the cold. It had been snowing on and off but had ceased for now. Though there had been enough of it to put a layer of white across the ground and almost anything that had stood still.

In all honesty, it looked magical, just like every Christmas card depicted, though the reality was that it rarely snowed like this as far as Sammy-Jo's memory could recall.

A group of children shrieking loudly as they ran past her caught her off guard, but she smiled as their mothers, pushing strollers with babies bundled up underneath plastic coverings, passed her by.

She shoved her hands into her pockets and stamped her feet again, and this time when she looked up, she saw an arm raised and waving at her.

"Daisy," she said to nobody other than herself when she felt those fluttering butterflies in her tummy. Stepping forward, she closed the distance between them.

"Hi." Daisy grinned at her.

"Hey," Sammy-Jo replied. She opened her arms and moved closer. "Can I?"

"Oh, a hug…absolutely, I love hugs," Daisy answered, already moving into the space as Sammy-Jo enveloped her, squeezing gently until they parted.

"So…" Daisy said, twisting one way and then the other. "What did you want to do?"

A gust of wind blew the aroma of cinnamon and sugar at them, and Sammy-Jo breathed it in. "Donuts?"

"Maybe later." Daisy reached out and grabbed Sammy-Jo's coat pockets and pulled her closer again. "I already have something sweet."

"Me?" SJ laughed, but didn't step away.

Tilting her head up, Daisy asked, "Who made you doubt that?"

"I think there are a multitude of names my friends might call me, and none of them are sweet," Sammy-Jo said, her face solemn as she spoke honestly. "In fact, arrogant and brash would probably be more like it."

"Hm, I guess I must be getting a different version of Sammy-Jo then." Daisy chuckled. "So, I noticed there is a funfair. Wanna share a horse on the merry-go-round?"

Sammy-Jo considered that. "I'm not sure we'd both fit on one horse."

"We would…if I sat facing you…and then…" She leaned closer. "You could kiss me again."

Smirking, Sammy-Jo said, "Oh, so you admit now that it was me who kissed you."

"I didn't admit to anything. I'm simply saying…"

"That I can kiss you again. This sounds like something I would enjoy. But…" Now, it was SJ who pulled Daisy closer. "I was hoping we'd spend the afternoon, maybe even the evening together, and so, I'm not willing to risk injury at the first hurdle."

Daisy laughed. "Fair enough." She slid her gloved hand into Sammy-Jo's. "Let's go then."

By the time they had ridden the merry-go-round and attempted to try every indulgence a Christmas market had to offer, and with the snow starting once more, Daisy's suggestion of a drink in the pub made a great choice.

"Mulled wine again?" Sammy-Jo asked when Daisy ordered them at the bar.

"It's Christmas, and we already had one, so it makes sense to keep drinking it."

"If you say so," Sammy-Jo scoffed. "Wanna get something to eat in a minute?"

"And spend more time with you?" Daisy winked. "Yes, I do."

"Cool," Sammy-Jo said, sipping her drink.

"So, I want to know more about you. I've been doing all the talking all day."

"You're more interesting."

Daisy raised a brow at her. "Are you avoiding?"

"No, I just don't think I'm that…" She paused when the brow rose higher. "Okay, what do you want to know?"

"Tell me something that makes you happy."

"That's easy, football."

Daisy glanced at the woolly hat on the bar and the way that Sammy-Jo instinctively touched the emblem. "Your team?"

"Yep. Bath Street Harriers. You ever been to a game?"

Shaking her head, Daisy then sipped her own drink. "No, I'm more of a good hike kinda gal. Team sports have never been my thing, though to be honest, I haven't done much hiking recently, what with work—"

"Work, the work you don't enjoy?"

"That's the one." Daisy pointed a knowing finger at her. "I need to find another job, but marketing is…anyway, let's not worry about that now." She gazed at Sammy-Jo. "We're talking about you."

SJ laughed before she became quite serious and placed her palm down onto the bar. "I'm 29, I'm single, and if I'm honest, I think I might like you more than I'm supposed to."

"We barely know each other," Daisy said but couldn't stop her hand from reaching out and touching the back of Sammy-Jo's.

“I know, and that scares the shit out of me,” Sammy-Jo admitted. She was about to say something else when the bell behind the bar rang and the rendition of “Underneath the Tree” ended abruptly.

“Ladies and gentlemen,” Sadie called out and climbed up onto a chair. “We’ve been advised by the local police and council to close up and for you all to make your way home. The snowstorm is expected to gain momentum in the next two hours.”

Sammy-Jo turned to look out of the window. “Blimey, it’s blowing a hoolie. Come on, let’s get you home.”

“But dinner?”

“I know I’m taller than you, but you can see out of the window, right?”

Daisy turned and stared. The blizzard was almost a whiteout.

“Okay, I guess you’re right,” she said, pulling her hat onto her head. She grabbed Sammy-Jo’s hat and pulled it down onto SJ’s head, just as something caught her attention pinned to the shelf above the bar where the glasses were stored.

Sammy-Jo noticed and looked up, grinning when she realised what it was: mistletoe.

Leaning up, Daisy placed a quick kiss on her lips. “I like you more than I am supposed to, too.”

She hadn’t had a chance to step away when Sammy-Jo took hold of the lapels on her coat and pulled her forward into a searing kiss that left them both breathless.

“I’m ready for someone like you, Daisy,” she admitted. Taking either side of the zip and putting it together, SJ yanked it up until her hand was underneath Daisy’s chin. She let her fingers slide over Daisy’s cheek. “Can we talk about it?”

Daisy nodded slowly. “Yes.”

“Alright lovebirds, time to skedaddle before you end up stuck here all night.” Sadie shooed them towards the door.

Chapter Twenty-One

On the street outside, people scattered in every direction, out of sight within seconds as the snow and the wind that whipped it up and blew it hard into their faces created a barrier.

"Hold my hand," Sammy-Jo said. "And don't let go."

"I won't," Daisy answered back. Her fingers grabbed Sammy-Jo in a vicelike grip. This was not the kind of weather either of them had experienced before.

With their scarves wrapped tightly around their faces and hats pulled down as far as they could without completely covering their eyes, Sammy-Jo led them towards the bridge.

It was slippery underfoot, where hundreds of other feet had recently walked across it and trampled nearly a foot of snow down into icy mush.

"How is it so deep already?" Daisy asked, trudging carefully with every step.

"No idea. I never even thought to check the weather."

"Me either," Daisy shouted. "We get snow in Kent sometimes, but it hasn't been like this for years."

"Global warming I guess," Sammy-Jo said, stopping on the other side of the riverbank. Two very distinct paths had been trodden thoroughly in both directions. The problem was it had become compacted and icy. "We're going to follow the path, but in the deeper snow. We'll be safer."

Daisy nodded, still gripping SJ's hand. The snow was relentless, blowing almost sideways at them.

Every step was cold, and wet, snow dropping down inside their boots.

By the time they finally saw Daisy's parents' house come into view, the direction of the wind changed and was almost howling as the street acted like a wind tunnel.

"Come on, not far now," Sammy-Jo encouraged and before they knew it, she was pushing the gate against the snow just enough that they could slide around it.

The door opened before Daisy could get her glove off and find a key. She was grateful; her fingers were numb.

"Daisy, thank god, get inside," her mum said, opening the door wider and almost dragging her eldest through and into the warmth.

Sammy-Jo was about to turn and make her way home when she felt a hand grab her collar.

"Oh no you don't," said Daisy's mum. "I'm not letting you walk any further in that. Inside, come on."

Daisy grinned at her when she stepped across the threshold and the door closed behind them both.

"Right, the pair of you get those wet things off. I'll find some dry clothes."

"I see where you get the bossiness from," Sammy-Jo said, feeling just a little bit uncomfortable at being ordered to strip in a house she'd never set foot in before and by a woman she was yet to be introduced to.

"Oh, I'm a pussy cat, don't let her ask twice." Daisy laughed and unzipped her coat, yanking her arms out and dropping it, along with a huge pile of snow, onto the floor.

Sammy-Jo huffed but realised that A, there was no point in complaining, and B, she was freezing and soaked through. The coat came first, then the jumper that wasn't that damp. Her t-shirt was dry, so she left that. She bent down and undid her boots, pulling them and her socks off. Drenched through to the skin, her toes were frozen as she wriggled some life back into them.

Her jeans were soaked too, and the cold wind had frozen them. Skin-tight before, they were painted on now as she unzipped and tried to roll them down her numb legs.

When they were halfway down her thighs, the sound of footsteps racing down the stairs stilled her movement and she looked up to find two small faces popped over the banister. The girls looked exactly alike, with blonde hair like Daisy's and the same grin. Only they both had a tooth missing each, not the same one though.

"Daisy, you're home," one said.

The other piped up, "We were worried."

Both of them spoke as they continued to stare at SJ.

"Not embarrassing at all, Daisy," Sammy-Jo mumbled, much to Daisy's amusement.

"Yes, I am home. How about you two bugger off and give SJ and me some privacy, eh?"

"Alright," one said as they both walked the last few steps down the stairs. "Are you staying for tea?"

It took a moment for Sammy-Jo to realise she was being spoken to, but she needn't have worried, because Daisy's mum answered.

"Of course she is, now go and find your father and pester him for a bit." Eileen grinned and held out two piles of clothing. "You're a bit taller than me and Daisy, so I got you these."

Sammy-Jo took the pair of joggers and a matching top.

"Don't worry, they're brand new. I had them under the tree as an extra for Chris. But he won't know, and he wouldn't mind even if he did." She chuckled.

"Are you sure? I don't want to be a nuisance." Sammy-Jo offered them back to her.

"This is SJ, Mum," Daisy said.

"I gathered that," Eileen replied. "It's not a bother, and it's the least we can do. That's twice now you've made sure our Daisy got home safely. A proper Christmas hero you are." She turned to leave. "I'll get the kettle on. Nice brew will warm you both up."

The jeans finally gave in, and Sammy-Jo was able to step out of them. There was no way her boxers were coming off, so she pushed a foot into the leg of the joggers and quickly pulled them up.

Now dressed and feeling a little warmer, she noticed Daisy staring at her and smiling.

"What? Never seen legs before?"

Daisy laughed. "Not as firm as those thighs." She winked and picked up their wet clothes. "Come on."

Chapter Twenty-Two

"Bloody hell, it's you," a male voice said just as Sammy-Jo was pulling her hair up into a tidy ponytail.

There were two middle-aged men sitting together at the table, engine parts on top of newspaper in front of them. They both had oily fingers and faces and were staring up at her open-mouthed.

The table and two bench seats took up most of the space, although the kitchen would probably have felt cosily over-cramped under usual circumstances, but suffocated was how it felt right now to Sammy-Jo.

The man on the left had spoken and Sammy-Jo stood motionless, waiting to find out who he thought she was, because there were a lot of potential outcomes to that statement and some of them not as good as others.

"It is, isn't it? Sammy-Jo Costa?"

Daisy frowned. "How do you know SJ?"

He stood up and wiped his hands on a rag. "This is SJ? The woman who walked you home the other night?" He grinned at them both.

"And tonight, yes," Daisy answered. "Dad, what's going on?"

The fact he was grinning gave Sammy-Jo a little less anxiety.

"I'm Sammy-Jo Costa, yes," she answered, breathing in deeply as she prepared herself. Her involvement with Krista Rave hadn't escaped the local press or social media, and even though it had all died down and gone away, that didn't mean it couldn't get dredged back up again.

"Bath Street Harriers. Number eight," Daisy's dad said, just as the other man joined in to sing, "Flat White, Flat White, Flat White."

Sammy-Jo closed her eyes and grimaced as the rendition of the chant fans sung for her on the terraces rang out loudly in the small space.

"Blimey, can you believe it Bill, Sammy-Jo Costa in my kitchen!" He turned to Eileen. "Get that brew on, E."

"If you can boil the kettle any faster, Christopher, have at it," Eileen said to him. "Otherwise, pipe down and stop embarrassing Daisy's guest."

"That was a bloody bullet you scored against United though, wasn't it." Chris grinned.

Bill said, "Season ticket holders." Pointed to himself and Chris just to be clear. "Block D."

"Oh, right, that's cool." Sammy-Jo caught Daisy staring open-mouthed at her. "I said I liked football."

"*Liked* SJ, not played it, or was a professional," Daisy replied.

"Seriously, if I had, would it have meant anything to you?"

Daisy ran her tongue over her teeth and considered it. "No. of course not, but at least I could have bragged a bit." She smiled. "Look at these idiots, so many brownie points missed."

"Oi, she's one of our star players," Christopher said in all seriousness. "You and Nora Brady in that midfield has been a right tactical masterstroke."

Daisy's mum waded in carrying mugs that she placed down onto the table. "Will you leave the poor girl alone? She's Daisy's friend, so can we all act accordingly?" She glared at her husband. When the glare was finished, she turned to SJ and smiled. "Sit yourself down, love." She twisted back around and lifted the huge teapot complete with knitted cosy. "Now, did you get anything to eat while you were out?"

"No," Daisy answered. "We planned to, but then the pub chucked us out." She grinned. "They said they'd been advised to tell everyone to go home as the blizzard wasn't easing up."

"Good job, too. It's unlike anything I've seen for years," Bill added. "When I was a kid we had a Christmas like this once, sledging down the hill at the park, snowball fights with Bath Street kids. It was great." He laughed.

"Can we go sledging?" a small voice from behind piped up.

"We haven't got a sledge," the other small voice said.

"We'll make one, won't we, Bill?" Christopher said, clapping his hands together.

"Yes, let's do that. I've got some old scraps of wood in the shed."

Sammy-Jo watched as the conversations moved from one subject to another seamlessly. She could barely keep up and when she looked towards Daisy, she found herself lost even more, this time in the smiling eyes that had been watching her take it all in.

"What's for tea?" someone asked, but Sammy-Jo didn't care. Not while Daisy Foster was an option to enjoy.

Chapter Twenty-Three

The Fosters' living room was like the rest of the house: just big enough. They'd squeezed a two-seater sofa with matching armchairs in, along with a coffee table, bookcase and sideboard that doubled as the TV stand.

Every inch of space was filled with photos and books and trinkets of the life they'd built together.

How they managed to get a Christmas tree in with full décor, Sammy-Jo had no clue, but they had. It was shoved into the bay window with a multitude of wrapped gifts beneath it already, boxes of all shapes and sizes. Some were clearly for the younger ones with Barbie images and more childlike elves, Santas, and reindeers.

It shimmered and sparkled and twinkled and flashed, and Sammy-Jo was almost mesmerised by it.

Daisy had gotten herself comfortable, leaning up against Sammy-Jo's right side. At one point, she'd turned and frowned at SJ before lifting the footballer's arm and putting it around herself in order to snuggle in more easily.

The twins had gone to bed with barely any argument once they'd been reminded that Father Christmas wouldn't come if they were still awake. Now, Chris and Eileen frantically wrapped last-minute gifts and filled the two large stockings while Christmas music played in the background.

Sammy-Jo stared out of the window. The snow was still falling hard, illuminated in the streetlamp's brightness.

"I should think about getting home," she said, glancing at the clock. It was almost midnight, and she didn't want to outstay her welcome.

Eileen interrupted what she was doing, Sellotape mid-stretch. "You can't go home in that. You can sleep on the sofa. At least in the morning you'll be able to see where you're going."

"I don't want to put you out. You've all been very kind and—"

"She can sleep in my room," Daisy said without moving.

"In that tiny bed?" Eileen laughed.

"Have you seen how tall she is?" Now Daisy sat up. "There's no way she can sleep on here. I can't even sleep on here."

"Honestly, I can go—" Sammy-Jo attempted to speak but Daisy wasn't finished and placed a finger to SJ's lips.

"And at five in the morning when those two come thumping down the stairs to discover if Santa came or not?" Daisy finished her argument and moved her finger away.

Never the one to feel as though she were being told what to do, Sammy-Jo said, "Yeah, so I probably should go home and let you all—"

"No," Daisy and Eileen both said together. Chris raised his brows and pressed his lips together, a clear signal that neither women would be beaten on this.

"You can sleep in my room, with me," Daisy reiterated. "Okay?"

Sammy-Jo nodded. "Okay."

Daisy stretched. "We might as well go up now." She yawned.

At the top of the stairs, Daisy opened a door and Sammy-Jo wandered in expecting the bedroom and finding instead the bathroom.

"Do you want a shower or anything?" Daisy asked as she began to rifle through a cupboard.

"No," Sammy-Jo answered, sniffing her armpits.

Daisy produced a toothbrush with a flourish. "Mum always keeps spares. The kids are forever using theirs to clean things other than their teeth."

Sammy-Jo nodded. She'd been the same as a kid.

“Thanks.” She took it and felt their fingers touch. “Um, did you want a shower?”

“Nah, had one before we went out, and honestly, I am too cold to be getting wet again.” Daisy grinned. “Not that kind of wet anyway.” When Sammy-Jo’s cheeks had gone as red as she’d hoped, Daisy laughed and handed her the toothpaste. “I’ll go and get everything organised. We’re in the room opposite.”

“Okay.”

Sammy-Jo closed the door quietly behind Daisy and stood for a minute. Was this really happening?

“Merry fecking Christmas,” she said, grinning to herself.

Chapter Twenty-Four

Daisy opened the door to her bedroom and panicked. She'd forgotten about the three hours earlier where she had gone through all of her clothing options trying to find something to wear that would be sexy, yet casual. A complete waste of time as it had turned out; with the weather, she'd barely taken her coat off.

Though she did catch Sammy-Jo's attention at the pub, that much she was sure of. Why she wanted that attention so badly was another question that she didn't have time to dwell on right now.

The room was the smallest in the house. Most people would call it a box room, or an office, but somehow this did actually work as a spare room. Her dad's carpentry skills had seen to that.

He'd built shelving and space to hang clothes in the alcove, the single bed pushed against the wall, with a bedside table next to it that had a lamp, and the phone charger, make-up and hair products filled every inch of it.

Her case was open on the floor, and she literally swept everything except the lamp and charger off from the top and into the bag. Then she grabbed at her clothes, threw them down on top and somehow managed to close the lid and push it all under the bed.

Turning the small lamp on and the bigger room light off, it didn't look too bad. She sat on the bed just as she heard the light pull switch being tugged off in the bathroom.

A moment later and Sammy-Jo knocked lightly before pushing the door open and stepping inside.

Daisy hadn't prepared for that.

The sweat top and jogging bottoms her mum had given SJ to wear were now being carried over Sammy-Jo's arm. And the sight of any girl – but especially Sammy-Jo – in just her vest and boxers, with that mane of hair now hanging loose, was quite sexy.

"I thought I'd sleep in these. That okay?" Sammy-Jo asked.

Daisy had felt her mouth dry and all she could do was nod.

Placing the clothing onto the bed, Sammy-Jo set about folding it neatly. Every movement edged her t-shirt up and down just enough. Small muscles constricted and relaxed and Daisy felt the gentle urge of her libido waking up. Not just now, in the moment, but generally. Since Nadia, she'd barely shown any interest in anyone, but something about Sammy-Jo was doing it for her. Who was she kidding? Lots of things about Sammy-Jo were doing it for her. And that was the answer to the question she'd ignored earlier: why she wanted Sammy-Jo's attention.

Maybe she did need a shower after all, a cold one.

"I'm just going to—" She stood up abruptly and bared her teeth. "Won't be long."

Outside in the hallway, she gathered herself and wondered if this was a good idea. It had felt so an hour ago when she'd glanced at the snow out of the window and decided she wasn't letting SJ walk home.

Now though, the temptation was strong.

Sammy-Jo placed the folded clothes onto the floor at the foot of the bed, and then looked around, chewing on a nail as she took it all in.

In the dim light from the lamp, there wasn't much to see. Just a small box room with a bed in it.

A single bed.

A very small single bed.

She felt herself shiver and wasn't sure if it was due to the anticipation, or the weather. Touching the radiator, she found it was cool. So, the heating had gone off.

She rubbed at her arms to try and put some warmth back into her skin, but also because she felt the need to fidget nervously. She hadn't slept with anyone, for sleep or sex, since Krista, and she hadn't really planned to be doing it now with Daisy.

Should she just climb under the covers, or was that too presumptuous? Old Sammy-Jo would have been stripped off naked and been under the covers ready to pounce on the woman who had shown enough interest over these last few days to suggest her advances wouldn't have been declined.

But new Sammy-Jo – thoughtful, proactive not reactive, clearer thinking, and pause the moment Sammy-Jo – was a different prospect, and one she herself hadn't dealt with until now.

"Hm." She twisted her mouth left and right as she considered the conundrum. "Man up, Costa for fuck's sake." She gripped the corner of the duvet and slid in.

Her long legs slid against cold sheets until her feet hit something hot. She moved her toes until she found it.

"Aw that's so good."

A hot water bottle had been placed in the bed.

She was still focused on it when the door crept open, and Daisy peered around it before stepping into the room with just a towel wrapped around herself.

Sammy-Jo sat up.

"Are you naked?"

Daisy grinned at her. "Well, I have a towel." She fingered the edge of it. "Do you want me to take it off?" she asked coyly.

"No, yes, I mean…no. I'm not having sex in this bed with your parents next door."

"So, you would have sex if they weren't next door?" Daisy bit her lip and smirked.

"No. I mean, maybe." She grinned. "Probably."

"Their bedroom is next to the bathroom…" Daisy leaned down as though she were about to kiss Sammy-Jo and then swerved at the last minute to put her mouth next to her ear. "It's the girls who are next door."

Sammy-Jo gasped. "Ew."

Daisy stood up and laughed before turning and sitting down on the edge of the bed. She reached for a t-shirt and pulled it on over the towel. Pulling the towel out from underneath, she looked over her shoulder at Sammy-Jo, whose eyes were focused on her naked thighs.

"Like what you see?" Daisy asked. Sliding down onto her knees, she reached into her case under the bed and found clean underwear.

"You know I do," Sammy-Jo answered, dropping down onto her elbow, palm supporting her head as she continued to watch Daisy.

"Good."

Sammy-Jo kept her eyes fixed on Daisy's face as the smaller woman raised one leg and slid into the opening of her underwear. Only when both legs were in and Daisy bent to pull the material up her thighs did Sammy-Jo allow her line of sight to move lower, catching a glimpse of white buttocks.

Slowly, Daisy inched forward, until Sammy-Jo lifted the corner of the duvet for her.

"I can be very, very quiet, you know," Daisy said once she was under the duvet and Sammy-Jo's arm had fallen gently across her waist.

Face to face, she leaned in and kissed Sammy-Jo's lips. "Very quiet." Her hands moved towards Sammy-Jo and under her t-shirt.

"Maybe I don't want you to be quiet."

"Hm, that would be a problem in such a small house," Daisy said, letting her fingers trail up and along the side of Sammy-Jo's torso.

"So, maybe we wait until we can—" Daisy's palm cupped her breast, her nipple hardening at the touch. "Daisy, we can't—"

"We could…" Daisy answered, squeezing gently. "You could touch me…kiss me when I moan, and I will moan, Sammy-Jo. You make me want to moan." She edged closer and pressed her lips against the soft skin of Sammy-Jo's chin. "You want me to writhe for you, don't you?"

"I do, yes…I just..."

Daisy moved her hand away, lower and lower until it was pushed between them. "I can touch you, or I can touch me…pick one."

Sammy-Jo's breath hitched. "You. Touch you."

Daisy bit her lip and grinned. "Kiss me." Her eyes closed as the finger of her right hand slid inside her underwear, and she found her own wetness. "Kiss me till I come."

Chapter Twenty-Five

Wednesday 25th December- Christmas Day

Waking up to the sound of squealing was a new experience for Sammy-Jo, discounting Allegra's overexuberance whenever John did anything remotely interesting.

She had no idea what time it was. She couldn't move. Her torso and chest were pinned down by the heat of Daisy virtually lying on top of her, her head tucked into Sammy-Jo's neck.

One leg was hooked over her own and when she tried to move, she realised something else.

Daisy's hand was still cupping her between her legs.

"Morning," Daisy whispered against her skin. "Oh, what have we here?" she said, wriggling her fingers and causing Sammy-Jo's hips to buck. "Merry Christmas."

"Daisy," Sammy-Jo said sternly. "We can't—"

"You said that last night and we did." She pushed up onto her elbow and continued her movements under the cover.

"That was different—" SJ gasped. "Fuck." Her hips rolled with a mind of their own, in agreement with Daisy.

"Mm you like that, don't you." It wasn't a question and Sammy-Jo didn't need to answer. Daisy pulled her knee and opened the gap between Sammy-Jo's thighs, giving herself more room to move. "I know what else you like too."

"You think you're so – uh. So…smart."

"I do…" Daisy grinned and pressed her mouth against Sammy-Jo's neck. "Tell me to stop and I will."

"Don't."

"Don't?"

More sounds on the landing. People were moving around, not just any people but Daisy's parents and sisters. The kids were jabbering excitedly.

"Deny it," Daisy said.

"Deny what?" Sammy-Jo questioned before she stifled the need to groan and thrust her hips instead.

"That it makes you hot, turns you on that my family are practically on the other side of the door."

"Fuck off. No."

Daisy laughed. "Yes, it does. You tighten around me every time one of them feels near."

"That's cos I don't want to get…uh, uh, fuck."

"Caught?"

"Hm-hm." Sammy-Jo managed. Her hips lifted. She was so close. So close, and then the door handle began to lower. "Shit," she whispered, eyes wide.

"Dolly, leave them alone. Go on downstairs," Eileen said loudly enough to be heard, but in a whisper still. The handle reverted back to its usual place.

"Oh fuck," Sammy-Jo said, bringing her hand up to stuff into her mouth as she cried out around it.

"I think it turns you on." Daisy giggled, but didn't dare stop her movement. Not a chance; she was enjoying it too much. For all Sammy-Jo's bravado, it was very clear Daisy was the top.

"I want to watch you come," Daisy said. "Come for me, SJ."

"I can't… What if—"

"Yeah, baby, what if… That's the point…"

Chapter Twenty-Six

"'Snow is falling, all around me, children playing, having fun, tis the season, love and understanding, Merry Christmas, everyone.'" Eileen sung along to the music playing down in the kitchen.

"Prepare yourself." Daisy grinned as they reached the bottom of the stairs. "Christmas morning at the Fosters' can be a little over the top."

"Good morning," Eileen said when they both entered the room. Sammy-Jo was dressed in the jeans and jumper she'd worn the day before that had been left outside the bedroom door. "Found your clothes, I see."

"Yes, thank you." Sammy-Jo smiled a little nervously when Eileen continued to stare at her and then Daisy. "Merry Christmas," she added just as Chris rounded the corner with both girls hot on his tail.

"Are we building the sledge?" one said. Sammy-Jo still couldn't work out which one was which yet, but they both looked excited.

"You've got an entire sack of presents you've just unwrapped, don't you want to play with those for a bit?" Chris answered.

"Yeah, but we can do that any time. The snow will melt soon."

"Merry Christmas," Chris said to Daisy and Sammy-Jo. "Sleep well?"

Sammy-Jo felt her cheeks heat, and she looked away quickly when Daisy poked her in the side and said, "We did our best."

"Yes, slept great, thank you," Sammy-Jo said.

"Dunno how in such a cramped bed." Eileen laughed, "I guess you young'uns are used to such things."

"Dad," both twins whined.

"Yes, girls. Let me have some breakfast and then we will find Bill and build a sledge, alright? Go and play, I'll call you when I'm ready."

"Yes!" The girls grinned and danced around until one halted and looked at SJ.

"Are you Daisy's girlfriend?"

"No," Sammy-Jo answered quickly, catching Daisy giggling out of the corner of her eye. "We're friends."

"Kissy friends?" said the other one before they were shooed out of the room by Eileen.

"Has it stopped snowing?" Sammy-Jo asked, changing the subject back to something a little safer.

"Yes. It has. Thank goodness, thought we'd be snowed in," Eileen answered. "Tea? I'm doing breakfast in a minute."

"Oh, I'll get out of your hair, you must have loads to do."

"Nope. Turkey's in the oven. Bill's doing the spuds and stuffing, all I need to do is cook the veg. Chris prepared it all yesterday. So, tea?"

"Go on then." Sammy-Jo giggled when Daisy nudged her again and they sat down beside each other at the table. Within seconds they were pounced on by Dolly and Polly, with armfuls of toys they'd unwrapped.

"Look Daisy, I got a new Barbie. And a car for her to drive around in."

"Wow, that's awesome, Poll," Daisy said, "Don't you think so, SJ?"

"Oh, yeah, just like Gabby…I mean my boss's car," she said, looking at the plastic pink Land Rover.

"Is it pink too?" Polly asked.

"No, it's white, but it's nice," Sammy-Jo said, trying to sound convincing.

"Gabby drives a Land Rover, eh? Nice." Chris said.

"Yeah, it's a step up from the Mini she had when I first met her," SJ answered, taking the mug of tea Eileen now offered. She noticed Daisy staring at her. "What?"

"Nothing." She smiled, but it was obvious she had something on her mind.

"You dated her before she married Nora Brady, didn't you?" Chris asked, dropping the bombshell like it was a throwaway comment.

She almost spat out her tea. Did this man know everything about Bath Street Harriers and every person connected to it?

"Long time ago, yes," she answered, again, noticing Daisy smiling at her. "What?"

"Nothing," Daisy repeated.

"Wasn't she married to that tech guy? What's his name…" Chris clicked his fingers searching for the answer. "Rick, something."

"Yes, she was married to Rick—"

Daisy grinned at the blush that appeared when she stopped speaking.

"Go on."

"You know what, it's been a really fun adventure, but I think I should get going before we get any more snow," Sammy-Jo said, putting down her half-empty mug. "Thank you for looking out for me and getting my clothes dry, and I hope you have a wonderful day." She got up and smiled at everyone.

"Back at three for dinner," Eileen said. "I'll not see anyone on their own at Christmas."

"Oh, I'm fine—"

"I said, three," Eileen repeated and gave her a stern look that had clearly been perfected over the years with her children, and probably her husband.

"Three…okay then."

Daisy grinned. "See you later, Sammy-Jo."

Chapter Twenty-Seven

Sammy-Jo had barely gotten to the end of the street when she heard her phone beep. Pulling her glove off with her teeth, she reached into her pocket and checked the screen. Daisy.

She couldn't stop the smile that spread across her face underneath the scarf.

Daisy: So, that was fun.

Fun. Sammy-Jo couldn't deny it. Daisy was not who she'd first imagined she'd be. Which was a little confusing.

SJ: Yes, it was. You're different.

The response came back almost instantly.

Daisy: Different, how?

SJ: To people I've been with in the past.

She trudged on. The snow wasn't as deep at the top of the hill, and it was weird there not being any cars on the roads actually driving. But kids were making up for it. Every kid in Amberfield must have been out, dressed in enough winter gear that they wouldn't look out of place on the Swiss Alps.

Daisy: I bet if we dissected it, I'm exactly like people you've been with in the past.

Sammy-Jo frowned. She was pretty sure that wasn't the case. Daisy wasn't trouble for a start – well, not the bad kind, she thought.

SJ: Well, why don't we swap details later? I want to know all about your past people.

Daisy: All of them?

SJ: Yes.

She stopped at the corner shop, most likely the only one open on Christmas Day. Mr Singh was adamant about that. He opened 365 days, 7-11. The big sign on the window said as much.

"Morning, Mrs Singh," Sammy-Jo said, entering the shop along with the bee-boo electronic sounding bell.

Mrs Singh narrowed her eyes and only smiled when Sammy-Jo moved her scarf down and pulled off her hat.

"Oh, Sammy-Jo. Merry Christmas."

"Merry Christmas."

"Last-minute supplies, huh?" Mrs Singh said, coming out from behind the counter.

"Kind of. I've been invited to dinner sort of last minute and I need to…" She looked around at the shelves. If Mr Singh didn't sell it, it probably wasn't worth having. "Gifts, or something I can bring and not turn up empty-handed."

"Oh, well I'm sure there are lots of things." She handed Sammy-Jo a basket. "Take your time."

"Thanks." SJ smiled and took it from her. Wandering the first set of shelves, she picked up a gift set of olive oil and mixed olives. It wasn't exactly what she'd choose had she known she was buying gifts in advance. She put it back on the shelf.

Behind her was the huge section of magazines and newspapers, as well as colouring books and puzzle books.

"Perfect." Grabbing two Barbie colouring books. She popped them into the basket and carried on with her mooch. By the time she'd gone around the entire store, she had a large box of biscuits, a box of chocolates, and two bottles of wine added.

At the last minute, she decided to take the olive oil set too.

"Got everything?" Mrs Singh asked as she began to ring it all up.

"Oh, I need wrapping paper and Sellotape."

"Just there." Mrs Singh pointed to a large box that was almost empty. "Tape is on the shelf to the left."

"Great," Sammy-Jo said, grabbing the first one that came to hand.

With everything bagged and paid for, she bid Mrs Singh farewell and headed back out to the street. The sun had come out, but it was still brutally cold. As she was pulling her gloves on, her phone beeped again.

Daisy: Do you want to know what I'm doing, right now?

That was a question she very much wanted the answer to, and she felt a sudden surge of her old confidence come back.

SJ: Does it involve your hand inside your knickers?

When the phone beeped again, there was an image of Daisy holding her phone up to show a steamed mirror. She could just about make out the shape of her body, her naked body blurred by the condensation.

Daisy: No knickers.

"Fuck," Sammy-Jo muttered as she staggered towards her own home.

She sent back the mind-blown emoji and closed her phone before she lost focus and fell over.

Chapter Twenty-Eight

Daisy put the phone down and laughed at the situation. This was just typical, wasn't it? The one time she met someone who seemed half decent and on her wavelength, and she lived miles away.

"Enjoy it while it lasts, Daisy," she said to herself once she'd rubbed her hand over the mirror and cleared the steam that just moments earlier had hidden her from view…well, most of her.

That was the excitement of it though, wasn't it? It was daring. She liked daring, she liked risky and spontaneous. That was what turned her on.

She was pretty sure it was what turned Sammy-Jo on. She just wasn't sure if SJ was aware of it.

It's going to be fun finding out, she thought to herself as she rubbed moisturiser into her clean skin. *So much fun.*

"Daisy!!!" The banging on the door followed instantly. "Come on, we've got the sledge."

"Alright, I'll be out in a bit. I'm not dressed yet," she answered. "Polly?"

"Yeah?"

"Shall we have a snowball fight and gang up on Mum and Dad?"

"Yeah!! I'll tell Dolly, keep it secret Dais."

"Alright, see you out there."

Her phone beeped and she laughed again when she noticed the emoji SJ had sent. "Mind blown, huh? Oh, I'll blow your mind, Sammy-Jo Costa."

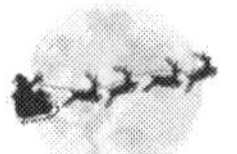

Every kid in the street was lined up in the middle of the road to get a go on the two sledges that her dad and Bill had knocked up for the twins.

Daisy had to admit, it looked like a lot of fun as races took off and the winner lined up again. Dolly was plotting her victory along with Polly, though Polly was out of the competition.

From the kerbside, Daisy stood beside her mum and watched the entertainment.

"Sammy-Jo is nice," Eileen said without moving.

"Yep, she is," Daisy answered, equally still. "Dad did a good job with those in such a short time."

Now Eileen turned. "They built those two years ago when the weather promised snow before. It didn't happen, so they left them in the shed and didn't tell the girls."

Daisy laughed. "Sneaky."

"So, you and Sammy-Jo, think it might be serious?"

"Mum, we literally met less than a week ago. I know I'm gay but even I don't move that fast."

"You look cute together, and she's clearly smitten." Eileen looked at Daisy. "As are you."

"Oh, behave." Daisy tried to brush it off.

"It's Christmas, magic happens." Eileen grinned. "And you've got two weeks to work it out. Most people would only see each other once or twice a week, so, you're getting almost two months' worth of dating into fourteen days. If you wanted it."

Daisy reached out and filled her hand with snow off the back of a parked car and compacted it into a ball. She caught Polly's eye and winked, watching as the twins followed suit.

"I do want to. But I'm very aware that I don't live here. And I'm not good with distance."

"So, move here then." Her mum was about to follow that up with something more when the first snowball came flying in and hit her on the shoulder. "You little sod." she laughed.

Daisy launched her own snowball at her dad. Dolly hit up Bill, and just like that, the great snowball fight of Datchet Avenue was born.

Chapter Twenty-Nine

Sammy-Jo heard the commotion before she'd turned the corner. What looked like a riot was taking place halfway down the hill, and in the middle of it was Daisy, orchestrating a mob of kids into the biggest snowball fight SJ had ever witnessed.

She stopped in her tracks and considered her next move. Because it was a guarantee that the moment Daisy, or anyone really, noticed her, she was going to be their next victim, and with her hands full carrying her bag of gifts and an overnight bag (just in case), she had no chance of defending herself.

Not unless she could get closer undetected, put her bags down safe, and then take them by surprise.

Ducking down, she squatted and inched forward like a crab in a sideways motion, keeping her head hidden by the snow-covered car windows.

When she got to a gap, she moved a bit quicker. Car by car, she made her way closer until she was only metres away from Bill's front garden. Her issue now though was that all the snow on these vehicles, including Daisy's car, had been swept off and used, meaning she was now almost visible to anyone who swung around and looked in her direction.

"Right. This will have to do," she said to herself. Standing quickly, she ran to Bill's and dropped her bags into the snow. She leaned over the wall and grabbed a handful of snow, ready to turn and launch at the first person she saw.

Unfortunately, she hadn't been fast enough and as she turned, she was pelted by as many as fifteen snowballs and greeted with cheers from Daisy's gang.

"Don't just stand there, SJ. You're on the grown-ups' side!" Chris shouted, before ducking just in time to avoid being hit. "You little monkey." He laughed and went after the grinning kid on the other side of the street.

Daisy stood in the middle of it all, smiling at her.

So, she launched her snowball at Daisy and leapt up cheering when it hit her bobble hat almost off her head.

"Oh, you wanna play?" Daisy laughed. "Come on then, Flat White. Let's play."

Sammy-Jo laughed and grabbed for more snow, rolling and throwing, rolling and throwing, hitting anything that moved. Her aim was pretty good.

Sammy-Jo dropped down behind a car and searched for more snow. It was running low now and some of the kids were drifting off, parents calling them in for Christmas lunch. And to be honest, she was a little bit grateful when Eileen did the same and a truce was called.

Glancing up, she saw a halo of blonde hair, now free from its hat, the smiling face looking down at her.

"You alright there, SJ?" Daisy smirked but held a hand out to help her to her feet.

"Yeah, just giving you a break from the onslaught," Sammy-Jo tossed back as she brushed herself down. "So much for making an effort and trying to stay dry this time."

Daisy reached over the wall into Bill's garden and lifted both of Sammy-Jo's bags.

"Looks like you came prepared."

Sammy-Jo closed the gap and took the bags from her, so close she could kiss her if she wanted to.

"I figured with you around, I need to be prepared for anything."

"Quick learner - like that." Daisy laughed. "Come on, let's get you undressed…and into dry clothes."

"We could just go back to my place—"

"And spoil the fun…tut tut." Daisy winked. "We've got dinner to eat, drinks to drink, and then…who knows what games we might play…"

Daisy went to walk away, but Sammy-Jo grabbed her wrist and spun her back around.

"Just so we're clear, we need to talk before we play any more games, okay?"

Daisy licked her lip and then bit it.

"Good idea. Now, are you going to kiss me like you want to or come inside?"

She didn't move, holding Sammy-Jo's gaze while she worked out what she wanted to do. And then Sammy-Jo moved, her hand releasing Daisy's wrist in order to reach around the back of her neck and pull her closer.

Grazing Daisy's lips with her own, she ignored the whoops of some kids passing by them. Her eyes were wide open and locked onto Daisy's.

"I want to do more than kiss you."

"Really? What's stopping you?"

Sammy-Jo pulled her eyes away and looked around them, and while Daisy focused on her face, Sammy-Jo reached between them and cupped her between her legs.

"Naughty." Daisy chuckled.

"You like it naughty, don't you?" Sammy-Jo responded, bringing her attention back to Daisy's face.

Daisy smiled slowly. "So do you," she said quietly and just in time before Sammy-Jo did indeed kiss her like she wanted to.

Chapter Thirty

"Table's not going to lay itself. Daisy, get off your backside and sort it please." Eileen was in her element, giving orders and having everyone run around, except for Bill who was still next door finishing off the spuds, and Sammy-Jo, who she insisted was a guest, and the twins who'd, "Just get under my feet."

"I really don't mind helping," Sammy-Jo said, only to be shooed out of the kitchen.

She wandered into the lounge and found the twins on the floor playing a game. They looked up at her in unison, as though they had some kind of telepathic thought process that worked as one.

"Alright?" she asked, and they nodded in synchrony.

The Christmas tree was twinkling, and Sammy-Jo sat down on the couch and watched it for a while. It was a little hypnotic the way the fairy lights blinked on and off slowly and then faded into a different colour. Blue to red to green to white and back round again.

Maybe next year she'd get a tree, nothing else. She didn't want all the other paraphernalia, but a tree would be nice, wouldn't it?

"Dolly said, you kissed Daisy," the one she now supposed was Polly said.

Sammy-Jo looked back and forth between them both. "Uh-huh."

"So, you are her girlfriend then?" Dolly now asked.

"Hm no, I don't think it really works like that," Sammy-Jo answered as honestly as she could.

The twins both frowned.

Then Polly said, "Daisy needs a girlfriend."

"Does she? Why?" Sammy-Jo felt her brow raise, intrigued.

Dolly piped up, "No, she needs a nice girlfriend. All her others have been horrible."

"All of them?" Sammy-Jo asked. She sat forward, inching closer to the edge of the sofa.

"Yep," Polly said. "Well, the ones we met were, and they always make her cry. Mum spends hours on the phone telling her she needs to find a good one."

"Not that we are listening," Dolly whispered.

"No, you wouldn't eavesdrop, would you?" Sammy-Jo said in a conspiratorial whisper. "What makes you think I'm nice?"

It was a sincere question. Over the years she'd gotten used to being the not-nice one. The bitch. The wife shagger. And more recently, the psycho-shagger.

"Mum said so. And Dad says you play football, so you must be good, or they wouldn't want you."

"Thanks…I think," Sammy-Jo said. That hadn't been the answer she'd hoped for, but then Dolly got up and came to stand in front of her.

"And Daisy is happy."

"Daisy is happy?"

Polly joined her sister, and they both nodded. "Yep. She's always smiling and singing. She's not hid in her room once and all she talked about was how she couldn't find you, and then she found you and brought you home, and she's happy."

Sammy-Jo smiled at them. Daisy was happy. Because of her.

"And you played snowballs with us, and didn't complain when Dolly hit you in the face."

"Twice," Dolly said proudly.

"So, you must be nice."

There were times in Sammy-Jo's life when she'd have mocked anyone who'd said she was nice. In fact, she'd have gone out of her way to prove them wrong.

But now, she had to admit…it felt kinda nice.

"Dinner!" Daisy shouted from the kitchen, and the pair of them scarpered.

"Bagsy sitting next to Bill," one of them said as they left the room.

Daisy appeared in the doorway.

"Did they bore the shit out of you?" she smiled.

Sammy-Jo stood up and grinned. "No, they're pretty cool, actually."

"Oh, you've been here too long." Daisy laughed and let herself be pulled against Sammy-Jo's chest. "Not that I'm complaining."

"Good." Sammy-Jo craned her neck lower and kissed her mouth. Slowly, but firm, a kiss of intent. "I'm starving," she said when they pulled apart.

"Me too."

Chapter Thirty-One

Everyone wore the paper crown. Everyone laughed at the silly joke inside the cracker, and everybody absolutely stuffed their faces with all of the delicious food on offer.

Rarely did Sammy-Jo eat anything like this, which only made it all the more wonderful. She poured extra gravy over her vegetables and tore into a Yorkshire pudding that was almost the size of her face.

They drank wine, and she ignored the pleas of Polly to, "just try some."

The popular Christmas tunes had made way for a more classical version. Jingling bells and things dashing through the snow all sounded a lot more magical as they laughed and told stories.

"When Daisy was your age," her dad started, to which Daisy groaned and Sammy-Jo poked her to let him finish, "we lived in a small cottage that had a real open fire and on Christmas morning I came down the stairs and found Daisy head to toe covered in black soot."

"Dad, really…" Daisy smiled as she continued to pretend to be bored by it.

"Do you know what she did?"

Polly and Dolly both shook their heads, rapt in the story and its outcome.

"What did she do?" Sammy-Jo asked, just as interested.

"Tried to climb up the chimney to see if she could catch Santa on the roof."

Bill and Eileen laughed, and the twins gasped.

"And did you?" Polly asked. It was getting a little bit easier to tell them apart now. Polly had a slightly wider nose, and Dolly had a small scar on her chin.

"I'm sworn to secrecy," Daisy said with a grin.

"Oh my God, you did, didn't you?" Dolly said excitedly. "But that means…did you not get any more presents?"

"I told ya, I can't say anything about it." Daisy shrugged and cut into a spud. "These are the best potatoes, Bill."

"Followed the recipe," he said. "It's all about shaking them and then coating in a light dusting of flour before chucking them into hot lard."

"You made a beaut job of it, Bill." Eileen smiled at him.

"Honestly, I haven't eaten this much in years," Sammy-Jo said, cutting up a crispy honey roasted parsnip.

"I imagine it's all macro controlled for you on a daily basis, isn't it?" Chris asked.

"Yes. I have a dietician who plans my meals for me." She put her fork down. "Oh, I forgot…" She went to get up and then stopped halfway, remembering her manners. It was something her teammates constantly reminded her of. "May I leave the table for a moment?"

"Of course, we don't stand on ceremony here, SJ," Eileen answered, turning to the twins who were about to speak. "Not you two. You stay put and finish your dinner. The toys will still be there when you have."

"But Mum…" Sammy-Jo heard as she left the room and grabbed the big bag of gifts.

When she returned, she placed the bag on her chair. "I just wanted to say thank you for allowing me to share this day with you all. If I'd been able to plan, I'd have come up with something a bit more…well, anyway, I got you all some things."

She delved into the bag and pulled out two equally sized presents and handed them to the twins. Eileen got the chocolates and the olive set, the biscuits and wine.

"Goodness, Sammy-Jo, you didn't need to—" Eileen said, accepting her gifts.

"I did," SJ answered. "I just wish it was something more exciting."

The twins ripped at the paper and pulled out matching copies of the Barbie mags, and then squealed when they saw £20 notes stuck to the front.

"Thanks, SJ!" they both shouted, holding it up to show everyone.

"You're welcome." She grinned, thankful that cash had been a good idea. Turning to Chris and Bill, she said, "To be fair, you were both a lot easier." She handed them each a wrapped gift and waited.

"What have we got here then?" Chris said, opening his gift, his eyes widened. "Oh, this is awesome." He lifted up a pair of signed football boots.

Bill grinned, opening his and pulling free the shirt. It said *Costa* on the back, the white number 8 showing her scrawled signature.

"It's going in a frame," he said, grinning. "Thank you so much."

She glanced down at Daisy, who stared up at her expectantly.

"So, this is just something to unwrap. I want to get something a lot nicer when the shops open," Sammy-Jo said, her cheeks flushed pink.

Daisy grinned. "Okay."

"Cos this is just something I thought was funny."

"Sammy-Jo, will you stop worrying and hand it over." Daisy laughed, and then grabbed the gift from her. She began pulling the paper free as Sammy-Jo moved the now-empty bag to the floor and slowly sat back down on her chair.

When Daisy pulled it free, it was obvious that it was a t-shirt. But nobody else could see what was on the front of it. They all stared at Daisy for her reaction.

Pressing her lips together, Daisy stared at it, and then she turned to Sammy-Jo. She turned back to the t-shirt, and then she laughed and pulled it towards her chest.

"Oh, that is priceless."

Finally, Sammy-Jo breathed and laughed nervously.

"I know, it's a bit nuts, right?"

"What is it?" Polly asked.

Holding it up, Daisy turned it around for everyone else to see. The image was Sammy-Jo's face, imposed onto the body of a Costa Coffee barista with a speech bubble that had her saying, "If you have to fucking explain it, it's not funny."

"My teammate Kayla made it for me cos she's forever explaining why they call me Flat White, and that's what I always say to her."

"I love it." Daisy smiled. "It's quirky."

Chapter Thirty-Two

Coming into the bedroom for the second night running, Sammy-Jo felt a little more comfortable in her surroundings. She closed the door and then leaned against it and stared at the woman already in bed.

Daisy was pressed up against the wall, her back to it as she lay on her side, duvet pulled up under her chin.

"Are you asleep?" Sammy-Jo asked, her voice sounding a little disappointed as well as surprised. She hadn't been that long in the bathroom, brushing her teeth and quickly showering. Her mane of curls was piled up on top of her head still.

"No, I'm just comfortable."

"Oh," Sammy-Jo said, not moving. "I'm glad about that."

"Are you?" Daisy smiled slowly and opened her eyes.

"Yes."

"So, why are you still standing over there?" Daisy raised her head just enough to take her all in. "Let your hair down."

"Why, it's going—"

"SJ, I'm not asking." Daisy grinned. "I need to work out how I'm going to deal with it."

"By leaving it up," Sammy-Jo quipped, taking it down. She shook it loose and let it all fall down her back, running a hand through it to push it off her face.

"Come here."

"You're very commanding tonight." Sammy-Jo laughed but did as she was asked and moved closer to the bed, wearing the same style of vest and shorts she'd worn the previous night.

"I've worked out that you're very good at taking orders, if there's something in it for you."

"Something in it?" Sammy-Jo mused. "You mean if I'm sexually interested in someone."

"Precisely," Daisy said. "Are you getting in?"

"Are you letting me in?" Sammy-Jo stared at her. "You seem to be bundled up quite—"

Daisy threw the duvet off.

SJ's mouth hung open as she took in Daisy's nakedness.

Her alabaster skin was only marked here and there by light-coloured moles and freckles. The cool air and the excitement had peppered her flesh with goosebumps, tight nipples puckered.

Without being told, Sammy-Jo gripped the bottom of her vest and lifted, pulling the material over her head and dropping it to the ground. Her eyes were transfixed by Daisy's face as her new lover focused on her bare breasts.

They were smaller than Daisy's, smaller than most women's she'd known over the years. Her body was lean and athletic, muscular and sinewy. Not like Daisy at all. Daisy had curves, and was a quarter of a foot shorter.

"Well, I suggest you don't stop there." Daisy sat up as she spoke, twisting around until she was sitting up against the wall with her feet hanging over the side of the bed.

Pulling the hair band free from around her wrist, Sammy-Jo began scooping her hair up, tying it in place, not taking her eyes off of Daisy's face.

"You know, I'm not sure if I'm going to allow this bossing me around to continue." She sank down to her knees, slid her palms around Daisy's calves and pulled her closer until she slid down the wall and her thighs parted.

"You do whatever you need to do—" Daisy gasped as she was taken a little by surprise at the speed with which Sammy-Jo's mouth covered her and her tongue slid around her clit with such ease that she needed to grab a pillow and smother her reaction.

If her mouth hadn't already been busy, Sammy-Jo would have smirked at the sight as she glanced up and over Daisy's stomach. It was rippling with every stroke, her breasts jiggling with the movement.

Pushing up on her knees, she changed up the angle of her assault and added her fingers to the mix, thrusting in rhythm with every lash of her tongue until she felt strong thighs begin to squeeze against her ears, Daisy's buttocks lifting from the bed and the muffled sounds music to Sammy-Jo's ears.

When finally, her lover stilled, Sammy-Jo gently lapped and nipped and forced the final echoes of Daisy's orgasm from her body.

Daisy didn't move other than her hips jolting every few seconds and her chest heaving in breaths.

"Are we going for round two?" Sammy-Jo asked, just a little smugly. And when Daisy's response was to raise her hips, Sammy-Jo chuckled and dove back in.

Chapter Thirty-Three

"Tell me about Gabby," Daisy said as they lay facing one another in the tiny bed. Both were still naked, wrapped around each other.

"What about her?"

"How long ago did you date her?"

Sammy-Jo blew her cheeks out. "A long time ago."

"I know that; how long?" Daisy poked her.

"I was nineteen. So, a decade ago," Sammy-Jo finally answered.

"And she was married?" Daisy asked, letting her fingertips drag down Sammy-Jo's arm. Sammy-Jo bristled, pulled away slightly, but Daisy held on. "I'm not judging."

"It's just not my finest hour, you know?"

"So, she was married?"

Nodding, Sammy-Jo said, "Yes, she was married."

"And this Krista, she was—"

Sammy-Jo sat up suddenly. "Look, what is this? Pick apart SJ?" Her face had flushed, and she spun around to sit on the edge of the bed.

In an instant, Daisy got to her knees and flung her arms around Sammy-Jo's neck. "No, not at all, I just…I have a theory and was…" She flopped sideways and looked up at her. "I like you. You interest me, and I just want to understand you better and—"

"What theory?" Sammy-Jo asked, turning to her.

Smiling, Daisy sat up again and rested her chin on Sammy-Jo's shoulder. "I just wonder if you're looking for something within a relationship that leads you to choose the wrong people…because you haven't quite understood what it is that's so attractive about them."

Squinting at her, Sammy-Jo frowned. "What does that mean?"

"Dating a married woman, it's…taboo, out of bounds, risky if you get caught. Same with Krista, a woman who clearly had an issue with a teammate. She's taboo, out of bounds—"

"Risky," Sammy-Jo said. "What's your point?"

"What are we doing?" Daisy asked and then answered it for her. "Okay, it's not taboo or out of bounds, but there's an element of risk, of being caught, but also reward… That's what turns you on but somehow you equated that to women who were out of bounds and taboo. When all you need to do is find someone who equally likes taking risks for reward."

"I guess that makes sense." Sammy-Jo scrunched up her mouth as she considered the women she'd dated in the past. "I have dated a lot of out-of-bounds women. So, it doesn't bother you that I did something horrible to a friend?"

"I mean not as much as it bothers you, and that kind of tells me that whatever was going on with you, you've made some of the right changes."

"So, you're not running for the hills?"

Daisy grinned. "Put some clothes on." She jumped up and grabbed her dressing gown, sliding her arms into it as Sammy-Jo stared at her, confused. "Clothes on," she repeated and threw Sammy-Jo's vest at her.

"Where are we going?"

"Downstairs," Daisy said, opening the door quietly. She turned back just in time to see SJ drag her shorts up her legs. "Come on," she whispered.

Rolling her eyes, but silently following, Sammy-Jo closed the door quietly behind her. Then she tiptoed along the landing to where Daisy was waiting at the top of the stairs.

One by one, they both descended. At the bottom, Daisy grasped her hand and pulled her into the kitchen. It was chilly. The heating had gone off hours ago, but when Daisy untied the belt on her robe and let it fall open, Sammy-Jo soon felt the heat rise in her.

"Put your mouth on me again," Daisy said as she leaned her weight against the edge of the table.

They both grinned at each other like naughty kids up to no good.

She didn't hesitate.

Daisy was right. The risk-reward was off the charts, and she dropped down onto her knees again without any other thought than how much she wanted to taste Daisy on her tongue.

The hand on the back of her head spurred her into action.

"Just like that," Daisy whispered. "Make me come."

Chapter Thirty-Four

Thursday 26th December-Boxing Day

Sammy-Jo had made her excuses and left the following morning after breakfast, because Eileen wouldn't hear of it any other way.

Daisy glanced towards the spot they'd been on earlier that morning, when everyone else had been asleep, and smirked at Sammy-Jo. It was impossible not to at least blush as she considered what they'd got up to.

And as much as she wanted to spend the rest of the day with Daisy doing more of those things, she also knew she needed to process it all because she did have a habit of diving all in and getting herself into trouble, and Daisy could easily lead her into danger.

Hot, sexy and exciting danger.

She'd promised to call later, and she would, but right now, she needed some time out.

Pathways and roads were, for the most part, now clear and gritted, quieter roads less so, but the route to the park was pretty clear and Sammy-Jo was walking through the gates within thirty minutes.

She kicked her feet through the snowier parts and smiled at a group of teenagers throwing snowballs. Her mind went back to the day before and the snow fight at Daisy's.

"SJ!" a voice called out and she spun around to find someone waving at her, all bundled up. She couldn't tell who it was from this distance.

Standing still, she waited for the person to catch up.

"Nora?" she said once her friend was closer and had pulled her scarf down from around her face.

"Hey."

"How did you know it was me?" SJ asked.

Nora laughed. "Have you ever seen yourself walk?" She chuckled at SJ's expression. "Like you're on a mission and nobody had better get in your way."

Sammy-Jo barged her with her shoulder playfully.

"Why you out here anyway?"

"Giving Gabby some space before she divorces me." Nora laughed.

Stopping, Sammy-Jo grabbed her arm. "You're joking, right?"

"Course I am, but she does have the hangover from hell…and I'm not suffering the grumpy stage till the painkillers kick in. So, I went for a walk and left her in bed complaining about every noise I make."

"Serves her right." SJ laughed.

"Self-inflicted," Nora agreed and looped her arm through Sammy-Jo's elbow. "So, why are you out here?"

"Clearing my head I suppose."

Now it was Nora who stopped them. "Are you alright?"

"Yeah." SJ nodded. "Yeah, I am, I just…I met someone and—"

"Whoop, see, I told you if you put yourself out there—"

"Yeah, and she's great, I just…I really like her."

Nora frowned. "So, what's the problem?"

"I'm not sure if I'm just…a game for her."

There was a bench up ahead. Someone had already cleared the snow from it, and Nora led Sammy-Jo towards it.

"What makes you think it's just a game?" she asked once they'd sat down.

Sammy-Jo pulled her gloves and hat off, unwound her scarf from her neck and plonked it all down beside her. Most of her hair was still tucked beneath her jacket.

"You know when someone just gets you?"

Nora nodded. "Yeah."

Sammy-Jo sighed and looked up at the sky. "You're going to say I'm an idiot and maybe I am," she said, turning her attention back to Nora. "I barely know her. We met days ago, but we've spent the last few days together. I was invited to Christmas dinner by her mum. Her family is lovely."

"Okay."

"I barely know her and yet, she knows me. Like she sees right through me and there's nowhere for me to hide."

"And that's a bad thing?"

"It is if she's not staying."

"Oh." Nora bit her bottom lip as she considered that. "Is she too far away to visit?"

"No, I guess I could drive over, and she could drive over, but she works Monday to Friday, and we have a game on Sundays and training through the week. When would we see each other, really?"

"So, what are you going to do?"

Sammy-Jo shrugged. "Enjoy it while it lasts, I guess."

"And try not to get too invested."

"Yeah."

Chapter Thirty-Five

Eileen sat in the armchair, feet curled up underneath herself as the girls coloured in quietly on the floor. The TV was playing in the background, the annual showing of a James Bond flickering away unwatched.

Chris had gone down the pub with Bill, and Daisy was reading a book, whose page she hadn't turned for several minutes. At least, not that Eileen had noticed.

She picked up her mug of tea and sipped, eyeing her eldest daughter over the top of it. Every so often, Daisy would sigh, but nothing more.

"Sammy-Jo coming over again later?" Eileen asked. Polly looked up and smiled but carried on with what she was doing. Daisy remained oblivious.

"Anyone fancy a bit of cake?" Eileen tried again. This time it was Dolly and Polly who looked up and nodded gleefully. Daisy remained staring at her book.

"Right." Eileen stood up, taking her now-empty cup with her. She paused beside Daisy and looked down. Daisy's finger was pressed against the page as she clearly was contemplating something.

Making her way into the kitchen, Eileen flicked the kettle on and then rinsed her cup quickly before tossing a fresh teabag into it. The Christmas cake was still on the table under the big plastic dome.

She'd made it in October, with a weekly feeding of the fancy brandy she'd bought especially for it, and proud of herself she was too, because it was bloody delicious.

Cutting two small slivers for the twins, she was just about to cut a larger wedge for herself when she heard feet shuffling slowly into the room.

Looking up, she saw Daisy frowning at her.

“Are you alright, love?” Eileen asked, putting the knife down. “Only you look a bit…away with the fairies.”

Daisy chuckled and pulled a chair out. “Do you think you can fall in love with someone you hardly know?”

The sound of the kettle boiling and flicking off diverted Eileen’s attention for a moment, which she was glad of as it gave a moment to digest the question.

Without asking, she pulled another cup from the cupboard and dropped a teabag into it.

“Is this about Sammy-Jo?”

“Yes,” Daisy answered without a pause.

Eileen poured the water and gave each cup a stir, handed one to Daisy and went to the fridge for the milk.

“The romantic in me wants to say yes, and I like Sammy-Jo. She seems like a good woman—”

“But?” Daisy said, taking the milk from her and pouring a little into the cup.

Eileen sat down at the end of the table. “I’m your mum, and I don’t want to see you rushing into something and regretting it.”

Daisy nodded. “I didn’t plan to meet her, that’s what has thrown me. And now I have, I want to keep seeing her.”

“Well, that’s good and there’s nothing stopping you from doing that.”

“Except her life is here and mine is in Kent. When would we see each other?”

“That, my darling, is what you both have to work out. But let me say this once more…” Eileen stood up and moved to stand next to Daisy, cupping her cheek when she looked up. “You are always welcome here, you know that. If you want to take a leap of faith and start over, you have a bed to sleep in.”

Daisy smiled and placed her hand over her mum’s. “Thank you.”

"Does Sammy-Jo know you're thinking like this?"

Shaking her head, Daisy said, "No, but I don't think she'd be against it."

"Maybe that's where you start then, a conversation about how you both feel."

"Mum!" screamed Polly. "Where's the cake?"

Eileen patted Daisy's shoulder. "I guess I should sort them out before they start." She paused. "Life is short, Daisy, for regrets, and for sticking with things that don't make you happy. Maybe this is your sign that something else is on offer."

"But it's weird, isn't it? Feeling this way about someone I've known for less than a week?"

Reaching for a tray from the top of the fridge, Eileen placed the plates and her mug on to it.

"You've spent over twenty-four hours with her. Split that into four hourly, weekly dates and you've known her for six weeks?"

Daisy laughed. "Thanks Mum, that actually makes sense."

"Course it does. I do know a thing or two, you know."

"Mum!!" the twins shouted.

"I'm coming," Eileen yelled back. "Why don't you take a couple of days not seeing her and see how you feel about that?"

Daisy nodded. "Yeah, that sounds sensible."

Chapter Thirty-Six

Allegra swanned in, still wearing her big furry coat that made her look like a bear, her arms filled with fancy, glossy cardboard bags that most likely contained overpriced gifts that John and his family had smothered her in.

"Merry Christmas," she said cheerily as she dumped it all down onto the floor and flopped into the space at the end of the couch, kicking off her heels in one swift movement.

"Alright," Sammy-Jo responded, taking in the chaos. "Have a good time?"

Allegra grinned and sighed. "Yes, it was wonderful. He's just so…" She trailed off dreamily. Sitting up abruptly, she said, "His mum loves me. Of course she does, why wouldn't she?"

Sammy-Jo stared, wondering if she was meant to have an answer to the already answered question. "Uh."

"How was your day? Did you watch James Bond?"

"No, actually, I wasn't here either."

Turning slowly, Allegra's pursed lips moved seamlessly into a grin. "Oh, and where were you?"

"So, I went on a date with Daisy on Christmas Eve, and we were having such a good time that we didn't notice the snowstorm, and so, by the time I'd walked her—"

"Home again?" Allegra's grin widened. "You really are taking this white knight business seriously, aren't you."

"Shut it. It was the right thing to do."

"You're right, sorry. Carry on."

"Basically, the snow was so bad, and we were frozen."

"Uh-huh." Allegra nodded, eager for more. She wriggled free of her coat.

"Well, Daisy's mum wouldn't let me leave and walk home alone, so I…" Now she grinned herself and shifted in her seat to face Allegra properly. "I stayed over."

"Holy fuck, is SJ back? The huge, inflated ego has returned?"

Sammy-Jo laughed and held her thumb and forefinger together to denote something small. "Maybe a little bit. The following morning, I was about to leave and then her mum insisted I return for lunch. So, I did, and then I stayed over again."

"And you and Daisy? Did you…" She made a circle with thumb and finger on one hand and pushed a finger through it with her other hand, laughing at Sammy-Jo's inability to hide the fact that they did. "You did, you dawg."

"Hey, I am only human, and she is gorgeous."

"Good for you. Get back on that horse, so to speak."

Sammy-Jo nodded. "Yeah, last Christmas was—" She sighed. "This Christmas has at least erased some of that."

"Krista Rave doesn't get to ruin your life any longer. Nora has forgiven you, the team has gotten over it, and now it's only you holding onto any residue left over from that twisted little bitch."

"I'm trying, and Daisy is definitely helping." She grinned again. "I just have to not let myself get too excited about it. It's just a Christmas fling."

"John was just a summer fling." Allegra shrugged. "Sometimes, we just meet the one."

"I've known her for five days. I need to keep my feet on the ground, but…" She wagged a finger. "If she decided to hang around, then…" She shrugged. "I would be interested in continuing."

"Hell yes, you would." Allegra high-fived her.

Sammy-Jo's phone beeped, and the screen lit up. She grinned when she picked it up and saw the name on the screen.

"Oh, you've got it bad." Allegra laughed at her. She jumped up. "I'll get out of your hair and put all this away."

"Okay, dinner later?"

"Yep."

Sammy-Jo watched her pick up all of her bags and saunter off. She flicked the screen and read the text.

Daisy: Hey, you okay?

SJ: Hey, yeah, all good. Allegra just got home, so we're going to get something to eat. You alright?

Daisy: Yes, the girls are running me ragged. Took them over the park and made a snowman. I was wondering if you wanted to do something Saturday night.

Saturday? Not tomorrow. Her ego felt it bite just for a second before she considered it again. Saturday would be good, wouldn't it? They could both have a little space, even if she really didn't want space. She liked being around Daisy.

SJ: Yep, Saturday would be great. Did you have anything in mind?

Daisy: No, I just thought that I'd like to see you again, but I realise that spending every day together probably isn't healthy.

Sammy-Jo smiled. At least they were on the same page.

SJ: Gives you a chance to miss me. □

Daisy: Maybe I will.

SJ: You don't already? LOL

Daisy: Like I'd tell you. Wanna play a game?

SJ: Depends on what it is, and do I get a prize?

Daisy: I mean…there might be a prize at some point. I was thinking, speed dating by text.

SJ: Rules?

Daisy: No rules, we both get to ask twenty questions and can decide to answer or not, it's no biggie. I just thought it would be a fun way to spend an hour, if you wanted to.

SJ: I do want to. Go on, ask your first question.

Chapter Thirty-Seven

Sitting back in the armchair, legs slung over the arm and her phone in hand, Daisy typed out her first message. She'd been intent on following her mum's advice, but something urged her to connect with Sammy-Jo still. The speed dating idea had been a bit of a spur of the moment idea, but maybe it was genius.

Daisy: Okay. What's the most spontaneous thing you've ever done?

SJ: That's easy, finished last game of the season couple of years ago. Got changed and on the way home decided I needed a break, so I went to the airport and flew to Santorini.

She sat up. That was an answer she wasn't expecting.

Daisy: No clothes, or passport?

SJ: I'd had to pick something up at the post office earlier and needed ID. Left my passport in the car. Bought clothes when I got there.

Sammy-Jo just went up another notch in her expectations.

Daisy: That's pretty spontaneous. I'm seriously impressed. Go on, your question.

SJ: Alright, what's your full name?

Chuckling, Daisy shook her head. She knew what was coming; she'd had it her whole life. If Sammy-Jo was on the same page and paying attention, at least.

Daisy: Starting easy, huh? Daisy Rose Foster. Are you actually Sammy-Jo, or Samantha something?

SJ: Just Sammy-Jo, my mum was a country music fan. Wait, D R Foster…you're DR Foster.

Daisy: Not from Gloucester! I told you my parents are evil with their children's names.

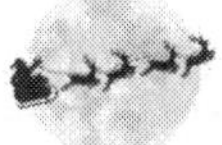

Sammy-Jo smiled at that. An image of Eileen and Chris came to mind. Nice people with a sense of humour, a little on the dark side.

SJ: Did you grow up in Kent?

Daisy: During my teenage years, yes. Then I went to Uni at Canterbury, got a job and stayed. Up until 10 though, we lived all over. Dad was in the military, so we moved around a bit. What's your favourite way to relax after a busy week?

Stretching out on the sofa, Sammy-Jo looked around the room at all of her stuff. She didn't really watch TV. If she were honest, she didn't do much anymore, but she didn't want to sound dull.

SJ: All sorts really. Xbox, pub, hanging with friends. Go for a walk. I like wandering along the riverbank in the summer. I'll throw that back at you.

Daisy: Hm, spa day. All over body massage and a facial, if I have the spare cash, which isn't often. So, maybe I'd take myself out on a date, dinner and cinema or something like that. Have you got any pets?

SJ: Only if you include Allegra. LOL Nope, no pets, I like animals, but life doesn't really fit for me to have one at the moment. How many girlfriends have you had?

She'd hesitated just a moment before adding that question. A tiny streak of jealousy shot through her that anyone else had been lucky enough to be that close to Daisy, but she breathed it out. Shook herself off. It wasn't important, or something she could control, but she held her breath, watching the screen as Daisy typed her reply.

Daisy: Girlfriends, as in relationships, or are we including hook-ups?

Daisy: And I am throwing this back at you.

Sammy-Jo relaxed. She liked the way Daisy was straightforward. Krista would have used a question like that to ramp things up, pushing all of Sammy-Jo's insecurities. It had taken a lot of therapy sessions to finally understand that Krista was a mastermind at that.

SJ: Let's clarify it as anything longer than six months.

Daisy: Okay. When I was 17. My first GF was Gwen. She was in my A-level class. We were together until she went to Uni in Liverpool. At Uni, I dated Becky for a year, then after that it was Jane. We were together for 3 years. I haven't been in a serious relationship since, though as I told you, I did attempt to with Nadia. So, what about you?

SJ: Well, you know about Gabby, that was just over six months, then on and off for a bit till it was finally done and then I met Sandy. We lasted two years. There was nobody serious for a while and my last relationship would be Jordan. Since then, I just had some fun until Krista, and well…less said about that, the better.

Daisy: Would you say you had commitment issues?

The question irked her into sitting up. Was she coming across like someone who had issues?

SJ: No, I'd say I have picked the wrong person issues. You?

Daisy: Maybe a little bit. It's not that I can't or won't commit. It's that I'm not prepared to waste my time on the wrong person.

SJ: I think that's fair enough.

Daisy: Yeah, so, the right person, obviously I'd want to commit to.

SJ: Me too. I think that's the point, isn't it?

Daisy: Yep.

SJ: Do you want to get married?

Daisy: Is that a proposal?

She really did laugh out loud at Daisy's reply.

SJ: No, LOL. It's my question.

Daisy: Just checking. □Yeah, maybe one day. I think it would be nice to have a relationship like my parents do. Do you want kids?

Blowing out her cheeks, she re-read it over and over. She knew the answer. And for a lot of people, it was a make-or-break question. How could you be with someone who wanted something so fundamentally different to you?

So, there was no point in being untruthful.

SJ: I don't think so.

Daisy: Me neither.

She released a breath. "Thank god for that." She grinned before typing out her next message.

SJ: Pool or beach?

Daisy: Private pool…use your imagination.

SJ: I was…on the beach too.

Daisy: Okay…I like that. Do you drive?

SJ: Of course. I just don't have a car at the moment.

Daisy: Why not?

SJ: It was just costing too much with repairs and stuff, and I can walk to most places. Allegra takes me to work.

Daisy: Are you going to buy a car?

SJ: Depends on if I have a need for one. Do I have a need for one?

Daisy read the question and then chewed on her bottom lip as she considered it.

"Daisy!" one of the twins yelled down the stairs.

"What?" she yelled back.

Her mum and dad both turned and looked at her.

“Maybe you could get up and see what they want without the need to holler?” Eileen said.

“Moi?” Daisy pointed to herself. “But they can scream from upstairs?”

“Daisy, you’re not seven,” her dad said, turning back to the film on the TV.

“No, and when I was, I wouldn’t have been allowed to scream down the stairs at you.” Daisy huffed and put her phone down. Launching herself up from the couch, she stomped out into the hall and looked up the stairs. “What?”

It was Polly whose head popped over the banister first, followed by Dolly.

“Can we go to the park?”

“The park? Really?”

They nodded simultaneously.

“I’ll take you tomorrow, it’s too late now. It’s pitch black out. The snow hasn’t melted completely. And you’ll be in bed in an hour.”

They turned to have a silent conversation with each other, nodding when they came to an agreement.

“Okay, tomorrow,” Dolly said, before she was pulled away by Polly.

Daisy huffed again, but then smiled to herself. It was kind of nice they wanted to do stuff with her.

“See, wasn’t difficult, was it?” Eileen said when Daisy reappeared and flopped back down onto the sofa. “Now you can continue talking to Sammy-Jo.”

“I—” She stopped talking when her mum’s brow rose. “Fine, I was.” She poked her tongue out, picked up her phone again, re-read the message, and noticed Sammy-Jo was still online. Probably waiting for her reply. Probably getting all anxious about waiting so long for the answer. Which was kind of cute; there was something hot about a confident woman showing up in her vulnerabilities.

Daisy: Maybe. x

Chapter Thirty-Eight

Friday 27th December

"Why are we doing this again?" Kayla asked. They were running in a line. She was second to the end on the right, between Jas and Nora, with Sammy-Jo and Ladonya further along. Everyone else had taken off and were racing each other to the boat house.

"Because it's good for us," Nora answered. "Don't you miss your mates?"

"Yeah, but I'd rather meet you all down the pub."

Nora side-eyed her and grinned. "We're going there later."

"I do this most days anyway," Sammy-Jo said, keeping her pace with the rest of them. "I like it."

"I like running around chasing a ball. Just running for no reason isn't as much fun," Kayla continued to complain.

"Honestly, last year we couldn't calm you down. Now you're all—"

"She's just pissed cos she missed out on the under-21s squad," Jas piped up and got a dig in her side for her troubles.

Sammy-Jo offered some words of wisdom. "I know it's disappointing. Just keep at it. You know how it is with the top four clubs; we're the last place they look at."

"I know," Kayla said with little enthusiasm. "Just makes me think…you know?"

"Think what?" Sammy-Jo asked. "You're not going to leave, are you?"

"No, well, maybe…one day," Kayla answered.

In synch, they all turned the corner and jogged on around the lake and up the slight incline until they reached another bend, and the park stretched out in front of them, a huge mass of green splotched here and there with white patches. Kids were running around chasing a ball.

"See, even the kids love chasing a ball," Kayla pointed out.

Halfway past and one of the boys booted the ball. It rolled towards them and Ladonya was first to it. She kicked it up and bounced it on her foot, passing it to Jas, who'd moved in front of her. Everyone else came to a halt, catching their breath a little.

Jas hooked the ball to Nora, who flicked it up and bounced it on her head. One by one the kids began to move closer, intrigued and interested in the small group of women who knew how to handle a football.

"Man, you lot are good!" one shouted just as the ball arrived at Sammy-Jo's foot. If there was one thing SJ was a star at, it was juggling a ball.

"We should give 'em a game," Sammy-Jo said.

"Seriously?" Nora answered.

She'd taken on the responsibility of team captain and was married to the team's owner. If any of these players got injured, she'd be in for it, on and off the pitch. She glanced around at Kayla and Jas, who were nodding eagerly. Even her sensible pal Ladonya had a mischievous glint in her eye.

"Fuck it. Come on then," Nora said, grabbing the ball out of the air when SJ kicked it up next. "Alright, who wants a game?"

Every pair of hands went up and a lot of excitable screaming started. "Do you play for Bath Street?" one of the girls, no more than ten years old, asked, looking up at Nora.

"Yep, we all do."

"You're Nora Brady," the same kid said, all wide-eyed now. Turning slowly, she looked at the others. "Oh, my days, Kayla Smith, Jas Khan, and Ladonya Sinclair!!" And then she turned to the last person in front of her.

Sammy-Jo fidgeted on her heels, trying not to get upset that everyone else had been recognised in awe except for herself.

"Sammy-Jo Costa?" the kid finally said, rushing towards SJ and slamming into her legs, arms wrapped around her. "You're my hero."

"Ya what?" Sammy-Jo said, not quite able to believe it. "I'm…"

"I have your shirt, and you're my favourite player."

Nora and the rest of them all stood together grinning. "Seems like you have a fan." Ladonya laughed and snatched the ball from Nora. She turned to Kayla. "You'd leave all this?"

"I said one day."

"I can't believe you'd even think it," SJ responded. "It's—"

"Are we playing or what?" Ladonya said, stopping this discussion from going too far. "I'm getting cold here. I ain't used to this arctic weather like you all."

"Yeah, come on. Let's lighten up, eh? It's still Christmas," Nora said.

"Alright, I'll referee," Ladonya said, doing a quick head count. "Nora, you're on one team with Kayla. Sammy-Jo and Jas, you take the other, got it?"

They all smiled and nodded as the kids began jumping up, shouting, "pick me, pick me."

Sammy-Jo looked at the kids. The obvious pick if she wanted to win was one of the bigger boys, and there were three of them.

"You," she said, picking the girl who'd already fangirled longer than anyone ever should. Her little face lit up as she walked towards her hero.

Nora followed suit, picking one of the smaller kids. One by one they took turns until they had a six-a-side game.

"Jumpers for goalposts," Jas said. "Well, hats and scarves." She laughed, pulling hers free and creating a goal when she dropped them to the ground six feet apart.

"You better be ready to lose, Brady!" Sammy-Jo shouted, getting her team excited and psyched up for the pitch battle ahead. "Okay, gather in," she said, pulling them all closer into a small huddle. One more glance at Nora and she caught the wink. They were on the same page.

Make this fun.

"Are we gonna annihilate them?" one of the boys asked, fist pumping the air.

"We are," SJ agreed. "But only if we act like a team. No showboating or holding onto the ball cos you don't want to pass. We win together, we lose together, got it?"

"Got it!" they all shouted back and covered the hand that she held out with their own.

"Okay. Names."

Each one of them shouted out a name. There was a Pete, Esme, Krishna, and Stella, all of which she was sure she wouldn't remember but she'd at least attempt to.

Pete stuck his hand up. "Can I go in goal? I've got asthma, I can't run around much."

"Yep. You're in goal. Now, anyone left footed?"

Esme's hand shot up. "Me."

"Alright, good. You're going to play in front of Jas. On the wing." She picked another kid. "Krishna, you're going to play on the right. Both of you whip that ball into the box."

"Where's the box?" Stella asked.

"It's an imaginary box." Jas smiled at her. "Basically, in front of the goal so we can score."

"Exactly." Sammy-Jo nodded. "Jas, you're defence with Stella, and I'll run the midfield."

"I can't believe we're playing football with proper footballers." Esme giggled.

"At the end of the day, we wanna win," Sammy-Jo continued, ignoring the gushing comment and then look of awe they all had on their faces. "But…it's supposed to be fun, so…" She looked up and saw Nora's team all ready and waiting. "Let's enjoy it, eh?"

They all ran off into their makeshift positions and Sammy-Jo trotted up to the middle where Nora had the ball under her foot.

"You ready to go down?" Nora said.

Sammy-Jo sniffed, jutting her chin. "You can try, Brady."

They both grinned.

"Toss a coin?" Nora asked, indicating kick-off.

"Nah, have at it." Sammy-Jo retreated. "Okay, kids, let's do this."

Nora turned and passed the ball to one of the girls on her own team, who kicked it hard towards Kayla. Nifty footwork moved the ball down the edge of the pretend pitch, and she spun around Krishna when he dived in to tackle her.

"Whoop," Kayla said, grinning as she moved in on Pete and the goal. Jas whipped across and slid in, taking the ball from her feet. "Aw Jas, you meany, I was on for a goal then."

"Next time, Kay." Jas laughed.

The ball rolled towards Sammy-Jo, and she flicked it up and over the head of an oncoming boy who had an idea that he was going to do something.

"Ooo, nice try," she said, turning quickly and passing the ball to Esme, who looked startled, but soon moved and hoofed the ball towards goal.

In what was meant as a cross, she inadvertently put it past the keeper, and they were one up.

"Superstar!!" Sammy-Jo said, running over to her and ruffling her hair.

Esme grinned like Santa had visited twice.

The game was on.

Back and forth, the ball pinged, with all four players setting the kids up to score goals. Ladonya only had to shout "throw in" or "corner kick" until Nora and Sammy-Jo tussled enough to give her an excuse to call a free-kick when Sammy-Jo dramatically fell to the floor and landed on her back.

"Seriously, you're giving her a free-kick for that?" Nora argued playfully. "I've seen better dives at the Olympics."

Sammy-Jo jumped up and brushed herself down. "Don't be a sore loser, Brady, or you'll have to buy the hot chocolate at half-time."

Ladonya looked at her watch. They'd easily been playing for fifteen minutes. "Take the free-kick and then I'll whistle for a break, and Nora can get the hot chocolate."

"Oh that's…call yourself my best friend." Nora poked Ladonya in the ribs.

"Any more of that and you'll be sin-binned." The American grinned.

Sammy-Jo looked around for her players. Only Krishna was shouting for the ball, so she passed it to him. As he ran off, she caught sight of someone else. Three someone elses.

Daisy waved at her from the sidelines. Dolly and Polly both watched on and cheered when Krishna scored. As promised, Ladonya whistled and hit her fingertips into her palm and shouted, "Time-out."

Jogging over to Daisy, Sammy-Jo grinned. "Hey, what are you doing here?"

Twisting in her heels a little, smiling up at Sammy-Jo from under the big woolly hat she wore, Daisy blushed, and Sammy-Jo was thrown for a second. She'd not seen a coy Daisy before.

"Hi," Daisy said, unable to take her eyes from Sammy-Jo. "The uh…they wanted to come to the park so…"

"Can we play?" Polly or Dolly said, yanking on SJ's sleeve.

"Yeah, course you can," Sammy-Jo answered, tearing her eyes away from Daisy to give her attention to the one that had spoken. "One on each team, yeah, and if you're quick get over there and tell Nora, she'll get you a hot chocolate."

The pair didn't wait for Daisy's permission before they were scampering off towards the small hut that sold hot drinks and sandwiches.

"You okay?" Sammy-Jo said once her attention was back on Daisy.

"Yes," Daisy said, still smiling. "It's a nice surprise seeing you here." Her hand reached out and their fingers connected, linking casually before gripping more firmly and holding.

"Yeah?"

Daisy nodded. "I kind of missed you last night."

"Kind of?" Sammy-Jo raised a playful brow.

There it was again, that coyness seeping in. It was attractive; she couldn't deny it. But still, a little confusing given how confident Daisy had been these past few days.

Stepping forward, Daisy chewed her bottom lip before laughing at herself.

"God, how is it that you suddenly make me feel shy?"

"I dunno, how is it?" Sammy-Jo grinned, her other hand landing on Daisy's hip and sliding around her waist to pull her closer. "Did you really miss me?"

Daisy nodded. "Hm-hm. Is it weird that I like having you in my bed so much?"

"Only if it's weird that I like being there."

They were inches apart, almost nose to nose. Something was crackling between them. Something hot and vibrant, ready to ignite.

"Come over later," Sammy-Jo said, her lips ghosting Daisy's.

"Maybe," Daisy offered back before their lips touched and she sucked Sammy-Jo's bottom lip between her own. Letting it go, she said, "If we weren't in front of all these kids, I'd let you drag me into the bushes."

"Don't tell me maybe…come over and let me—"

"Let you what?" Daisy said with a cute tilt of her head. Her coyness was now dissipating with every second they touched each other.

"Let me get to know you better."

Daisy smiled and pulled back just a little. Everyone was walking back towards the pitch, all eyes on them.

She pushed up on her toes and kissed Sammy-Jo.

"Alright."

Chapter Thirty-Nine

"Four Diet Cokes, and a soda and lime, please," Sammy-Jo ordered for them all.

Sadie grabbed a glass from the shelf above the bar, her eyes moving from one to the other. "I'm not even going to ask what you lot have been up to."

Sammy-Jo grinned. "You should join us next time."

The first glass of Coke was placed down on the bar and pushed towards her.

"I think I'll be just fine here, in the warm and not…" Sadie peered over and took in the entire state of Sammy-Jo's clothing. "Covered in mud and soaking wet."

"You don't know what you're missing." Sammy-Jo laughed and passed the drink along.

"So much fun," Kayla said, taking it from SJ. "And we won."

"You did not win, we stopped counting after 36-32." Sammy-Jo frowned.

"But we had 36," Kayla said, trying to wind her up.

Nora's arm came around her shoulder. "Don't poke the bear. She was happy." Nora laughed and pulled Kayla away.

"Nobody won," Sammy-Jo mumbled and turned back to take the next two drinks.

"I dunno, I saw you talking to that woman…looked like you were winning that." Nora waggled her brows. "Is she—"

"Daisy," Sammy-Jo blurted out. "That's Daisy, the one I walked home and…" She took a sip from one of the glasses. "Spent Christmas with."

Nora nodded slowly, knowingly. "You like her."

"Did ya see her?"

"Yeah, but it's not all about how hot someone is, is it?"

Sammy-Jo shrugged. "No, I guess not. She's nice. Funny. Daring…" She couldn't stop the grin that began to spread wider across her face as she talked Daisy up. "And smart, you know, she gets me."

"Sounds good."

"Yeah, I just—"

"Don't lose her," Sadie said, apparently listening in to every word of their conversation. "Don't waste time worrying about the things you can't know, or change. Just grab it."

Sammy-Jo and Nora stared at her.

"Sorry, that wasn't my business, was it?" Sadie smiled and passed the last glass over. "£14.80."

"You sound like you know what you're talking about," Nora said.

Sammy-Jo pressed her card against the machine Sadie held out.

"Just a bit." Sadie smiled. "It worked out in the end, but so many wasted years. If you think you've found someone special, then you've nothing to lose. If it works out, perfect."

"And if it doesn't?" Sammy-Jo asked.

"Then you had some fun and found out. What ifs are a bugger to ignore." Sadie winked and wandered away down the bar to serve someone else.

Nora nudged her. "Come on, let's enjoy the afternoon. You can think about Daisy later."

"And I scored five goals," Polly stated, holding her palm up with all of her fingers extended. She flopped down into the armchair next to Dolly. "And Nora said I was a natural."

"Nora Brady?" her dad exclaimed. "You played with Nora Brady?"

Polly shrugged. "She just said Nora, and Kayla."

"I was on Sammy-Jo's team, with Jas," Dolly jumped in, just as excited.

"Nora Brady, Kayla Smith, and Jas Khan?" their dad continued to repeat, his voice getting slightly higher each time.

"And Ladonya, she was the ref," Polly added, still with no clue why any of this was any more exciting than her five goals.

"I scored a hat-trick too," Dolly piped up.

"Daisy?" Chris called out. "That's awesome girls, I didn't think you liked football."

"We didn't, but we do now," Dolly said.

"Yep?" Daisy asked, appearing in the doorway.

Chris stood up and stared seriously at his eldest. "The girls played football with Nora Brady?"

Daisy laughed. "If that's Nora's surname, then yes."

"Oh my god, what did I do to deserve three kids who don't know a thing about football?"

"Is she someone important?" Daisy asked. "SJ likes her. They hang out a lot."

His eyes bugged. "If you decide to marry Sammy-Jo, I won't object, alright?"

Daisy laughed. "If Bill gets my car fixed, I'll see what I can do about meeting her." She winked and walked away.

"Don't joke with me, Daisy!" he called after her.

Chapter Forty

Sammy-Jo moved from room to room, checking that every possible surface was dusted, carpets hoovered, and any unnecessary items were put away.

She realised quite quickly that she was doing it for two reasons. Firstly, to make a good impression, and secondly, to keep herself busy while she waited.

Allegra had called already and would be hanging out with Kayla and Jas, and if Sammy-Jo was lucky, that would mean staying over and talking about various boys and men they were dating.

Another ten minutes and Daisy would be here. Her socked feet skidded to a halt on the kitchen tiles, and she yanked the freezer door open and pulled out a pizza. There was garlic bread too, but she hesitated. What if she ate that, and Daisy didn't? She'd need to remember to brush her teeth; nobody wanted garlic breath when they were kissing someone.

Her next issue was how to cook it. She was a professional athlete, she didn't eat stuff like this regularly, and if she did she would usually order in, but with it being Christmas, Allegra had persuaded her to buy a ton of crap they wouldn't normally touch.

"It's Christmas, SJ," Allegra had said, while dropping things into the basket Sammy-Jo carried. Most of it Sammy-Jo had taken back out and put back onto the shelf. Nobody needed brandy butter sauce if they expected to be fit and ready to play the minute the Christmas break was over.

She turned the oven on, twisting the temperature dial around to 180 degrees and then she ripped the box open and pulled the cellophane off the pizza before sliding it onto the middle rack and closing the oven door.

"Right," she said to herself as she looked around. There was nothing more to do other than wait and check herself in the mirror one last time.

She was wearing ripped, baggy blue jeans and a white vest covered with a white shirt, rolled at the sleeves. She liked this look a lot. It suited her. Casual but a little sexy. Her hair was down, a curling mane that reached the middle of her back almost, pushed back off her face.

She was about to start fiddling with it when the doorbell rang, and her stomach reacted with that butterfly tumble. "Jesus, sort yourself out, Costa." She laughed as she rubbed her tummy and moved barefooted towards the door.

"Hey," she said confidently when she opened the door and revealed Daisy on the doorstep.

"Hello." Daisy grinned. It was cold out, and she was wrapped accordingly, but it wasn't snowing, or raining, like they had now predicted it might. "Are you letting me in, or are we going out?"

"Out?"

"Well, you're all dressed up and looking…" Daisy took a step back and looked Sammy-Jo up and down. "Kinda hot."

"Kinda?" Sammy-Jo questioned again. "No, we're not going out, and I am not 'kinda hot,' just 'hot' will suffice." Sammy-Jo reached for Daisy and pulled her closer. "And if you're lucky, I'll show you just how hot I am."

"Right here, on the doorstep?" Daisy teased, before her lips puckered and she planted a kiss on Sammy-Jo's lips.

"Mm, maybe," SJ mumbled as the kiss became more passionate and she found herself pushed against the door frame.

Daisy sighed, her eyes still closed as she pulled away and slowly opened them. "You're right, you are hot."

"Told you so." Sammy-Jo winked and pulled her inside, closing the door behind them. "Coat off," she demanded and grabbed the bobble hat from Daisy's head.

"Just the coat?" Daisy continued to tease as she unzipped it slowly.

"For now. I want to be sitting comfortably when you take the rest off." Sammy-Jo grinned and headed back down the hallway and into the kitchen. She checked the oven. The pizza was cooked and on the verge of being charred if it stayed in there much longer. "I cooked a pizza. You hungry?"

"I could eat," Daisy answered, leaning against the door frame watching Sammy-Jo move around the small kitchen looking for a pizza cutter and plates.

Sammy-Jo stopped all movement and stared at her. "Don't worry, you won't starve." It was only now that she realised Daisy had tried to dress more than casually. A black dress that looked more like something she'd wear in the summer fell loosely down her body, stopping just above her ankles. It had thin straps and no bra – at least, not one that had straps. "You uh… You look…stunning."

Daisy scoffed. "Hardly, but I appreciate the complim—"

Moving quickly, Sammy-Jo took hold of her chin and stared down at her. "You're stunning, nothing else. No counter argument, no buts or maybes, just stunning."

"Okay." Daisy smiled and blushed a little at the way Sammy-Jo's eyes bore into her own. "Thank you." Her hand reached up to touch Sammy-Jo's cheek. "I've never…" She studied Sammy-Jo's face more intently. "Nobody's ever looked at me the way you do."

"Then everyone else is walking around blind."

"Not you though."

Sammy-Jo shook her head. "No, not me. You're beautiful, and I don't just mean…I mean, everything, I like everything about you."

Chapter Forty-One

With her knees straddled either side of Sammy-Jo's hips, Daisy sat up and breathed deeply. The impromptu kissing session had gotten steamy. Her palms rested against Sammy-Jo's chest.

"Do you want to take this upstairs?" Sammy-Jo asked.

"Where's your housemate?"

"Allegra?" Sammy-Jo asked, which even to her own ears must have seemed like a dim question. Who else would Daisy be talking about? She answered quickly, "She's at her boyfriend's."

Daisy grinned and reached for one of the straps on her dress. Letting it fall off her shoulder, she pulled her arm free. "So, let's stay here then."

Sammy-Jo watched, enwrapped, as the other arm shook itself free and the dress slid down at the front, revealing Daisy's ample breasts.

"What are you thinking?" Daisy asked.

"'Fab tits' a good enough answer?"

"Maybe," Daisy said, leaning forward until her breasts hovered above Sammy-Jo's eager mouth. "I like it when you suck my nipples."

"When I do? Or anyone?"

Daisy smirked. "Don't get jealous and ruin it."

"I'm not. I'm just asking."

Daisy studied the wounded puppy look on her face.

"You," she said, deciding it wouldn't kill her to give Sammy-Jo a little reassurance; after all, it wasn't a lie.

"Yeah, me too." Sammy-Jo pulled her closer and closed her mouth around the nearest to her, her neck craning up somewhat.

"Just like that." Daisy moaned. She reached for Sammy-Jo's hand and pulled it until she got the gist and slid it between Daisy's legs. "Touch me."

The groan emitted next would have told anyone else in the house that Sammy-Jo had just infiltrated her being, not just physically but in every other way too.

Every movement thrust Sammy-Jo deeper and when Daisy groaned again, it almost smothered the sound of the front door opening and voices moving closer down the hall.

In an instant, Sammy-Jo whipped the blanket from the back of the couch and pulled it over Daisy, yanking her forward against her chest. She didn't have time to remove her fingers from where they nestled, still inside of Daisy, when the living room door pushed open and Allegra's blonde head popped around it to say, "Hey."

Daisy hid her face in the crook of Sammy-Jo's neck and pretended they were just cuddling.

"Alright, what are you doing back?" Sammy-Jo inquired as Allegra came fully into the room.

"You must be Daisy." Allegra grinned.

Slowly, Daisy raised her head, aware that every subtle movement did something to her beneath the blanket.

"Hi. Yep, that's me. You must be Allegra."

Allegra's grin widened when the blanket slipped to reveal a bare shoulder.

"I thought you were out tonight," Sammy-Jo said.

"Clearly." Allegra turned back to the door. "We just stopped in to pick some things up, and then you'll have the place all to yourself and you can…go back to whatever it is you were doing." She stifled the chuckle that threatened to escape.

When she left the room, Sammy-Jo went to move her hand, but Daisy clamped around it.

"No." She gave her own smirk. "Carry on."

"But…Allegra could come in—"

"Yes, sweetheart, she could…" She leaned down to kiss SJ, grinding her hips to make her point. "That's hot, don't you think?"

"Fuck, yeah," Sammy-Jo managed to say before her mouth was engulfed with Daisy's tongue.

Chapter Forty-Two

Saturday 28th December

Sammy-Jo sighed contentedly when she rolled over and instead of a cold empty side of the bed, she was reminded of the warm body sharing it.

She could get used to this.

"Mm, you're all warm and snuggly," Daisy said, pushing herself back into the warmth of the embrace.

"Course I am." Sammy-Jo nuzzled against Daisy's shoulder and kissed the bare skin. "Why don't you stay?"

Daisy chuckled. "Because I need to go home and help Mum get ready for the New Year bash she's throwing."

"New Year bash?"

"Hm, just some neighbours, nothing too big but she prides herself on throwing a great party and I said I'd go shopping with her."

Sammy-Jo tightened her hold. "Okay, but I meant stay…"

The silence was palpable.

Releasing her grip, Sammy-Jo said, "I – that was a bit…"

Daisy twisted around to face her. "Do you know how easy it would be for me to say yes? I like you, enough to want to see where this might lead after I go home."

"I get it. I know that I am counting my chickens before they're hatched. It's just…I like this. You being here, us hanging out, and it might be the most lesbian cliché ever and a whole U-Haul moment, and I know that I am being completely spontaneous and I've no idea if we'd work out or not, but—" She threw the covers back and bounced naked onto her knees. "I want to find out."

Daisy chuckled. “So do I…just not as quickly as you do, Speedy.” She sat up and cupped Sammy-Jo’s chin. “Look, it’s less than a two-hour drive to my place, and I have to move soon anyway, so we’ll cross that bridge when it happens, but right now, I just want to enjoy this, knowing that we’re going to keep seeing each other.” She kissed her. “Can we do that?”

Sammy-Jo nodded. “Yes, course we can. I’m sorry, I just—"

“Shh…I like it SJ, I like that you want this.”

“Yeah?”

“Are you kidding? The hot, athlete with the best hair wants me?” Daisy pushed her over and jumped, straddling Sammy-Jo’s waist as she stared into her lover’s eyes and saw everything she needed right there.

“Hot?”

“Oh yeah.” Daisy inched forward.

“Best hair?”

“Fab hair.” Her lips ghosted over Sammy-Jo’s. “I love it tickling my thighs,” she whispered.

“Like last night?”

“Yeah, definitely like last night…Allegra hadn’t even left.”

“I know…it was exhilarating.”

“Hm-hm, so very…” She kissed her. “…very...” Another kiss. “…hot.”

Chapter Forty-Three

By the time Daisy finally got up, showered and headed back to her parents', it was almost lunchtime, and her mum wasn't impressed.

"You didn't have to come if you didn't want to," Eileen said once Daisy was changed and ready to head out to the store.

"I do want to go; I just got caught up and lost track of the time."

"Hm." Eileen's lips pressed together, and one brow raised dramatically. "And I guess that had nothing to with Sammy-Jo and your Christmas romance, did it?"

"Might have." Daisy grinned. "I'm twenty-seven Mum, I'm allowed to do the sex thing."

"Oh behave. You think I didn't know you've been doing the sex thing since Gwen?" She laughed at Daisy's shocked face. "You weren't exactly quiet about it, Daisy Rose."

"I think we were. It could have been a lot noisier," she said in an attempt to embarrass her mother more than she was feeling embarrassed herself.

"Hm and if you had, me and your dad would have given you something to think about."

"Eww, below the belt, Mother."

Eileen laughed. "Yes, it was definitely below the belt."

"Oh grim, I shall never look at either of you again." Daisy feigned disgust.

"You can add up, can't you? If the twins are seven, then you were nineteen when they were conceived…and just to be clear, we still do the sex thing."

Daisy gasped and opened the door to escape more than anything. "Fine, you win, you win. Just stop talking about you and Dad doing it."

"Right, coat on. Let's get going before there's nothing left to buy. I dunno why it becomes like the apocalypse every Christmas and New Year. You'd think the shops were shut for a month with the way people load up their trolleys."

In the car, Eileen navigated what was left of the snow and turned towards town.

"Bath Street will be busy today," she said, catching Daisy checking her phone out of the corner of her eye. "You know you can spend a few hours not talking to each other."

"I know."

"I thought that was the plan. To take some space and see how you felt."

"I know," Daisy repeated. "It's just…she makes me feel happy."

"Sex will do that," Eileen said wisely. "All those hormones flooding—"

"It's not just that. I like her…I really like her, and we have a lot in common, and enough differences to be independent. She's literally everything I want, and she's willing to try and make it work, so…yeah, I'm excited about it, about her."

"I wasn't being critical, Daisy. I like Sammy-Jo, and I like seeing you happy, and if it also means you'd be visiting more…well, I'm not going to stand in the way."

"She asked me to stay."

"That's a lot of commitment. You'd be giving everything up…not that I don't agree. I think you'd be happier here. But Daisy…" Eileen stopped the car at the traffic light and turned to look at her eldest. "You can only do that if it's what you want to do. Not Sammy-Jo, not me, or your dad."

"I know." Daisy stared out the window and caught sight of someone. Pressing the window down, she called out. "Diana!"

The blonde head whipped around, looking to see who was yelling at her, and then she smiled and waved.

"Daisy! Pub later?"

"Okay," Daisy called back, just as the lights changed and Eileen was forced to pull away. "That was Diana."

"I guessed that when you called her Diana." Eileen chuckled. "She seems nice."

"She is." Daisy thought for a moment. "Is it weird that in the space of a week, I've made a really good friend, met lots of other potential friends and possibly the love I've been looking for, and all on the doorstep of my family?"

"Almost like you're being shown a path."

"That's what I was thinking. But it could just be all shiny and happy because it's Christmas and everyone is in that kind of mood. We're all off work and just having fun. What would it be like once everyone's lives go back to normal?"

"I guess…you're going to have to find out."

Chapter Forty-Four

Diana waited at the table while Shannon queued at the bar with Scarlett. It was still early, and she watched her mother animatedly joining in with a conversation on another table.

The Lesbian Businesswomen's Group, or LBG, she'd set up earlier in the year was gathering for a 'meeting' regarding next year's agenda. Diana was quite sure it was just an excuse to catch up and have drinks on expenses.

But if she were honest, she was proud of what her mother was achieving. Late in life lesbianism and soulmate love with Scarlett, her career taking off since being made redundant from her last job, and now, here she was hanging with the bigwigs of lesbian business.

"Hey," Daisy said, scooting around the bench seat to sit beside her.

"Oh, I didn't see you arrive." Diana chuckled, hugging her new friend.

"I snuck in. What's going on over there?" Daisy pointed at the group.

"It's the LBW," Diana said, smiling before following up with, "Bath Street's lesbian mafia."

"Really?" Daisy giggled. "They don't look too scary."

"Oh, they're pussycats unless someone treads on someone else's toes in business, and then they're like hellcats supporting one another."

"Blimey."

"You've met my mother; she started it. That's Gabby Dean, she owns the women's football team."

"Sammy-Jo's team?"

Diana nodded. "Yep. And the dark-haired one on the left, that's Georgia Samuels."

"She runs the café, Aston's?"

"Owns it, alongside a very small marketing firm she's just created. That's what they're all in cahoots about now. They will support the business in any way they can."

"So, what does your mother own?"

"Technically nothing, though she now has shares in the company she works for…big hotel chain." They both watched as another woman joined them, all smiles and hellos. "That's Natalie, she owns Come Again, the sex store chain? And she's the girlfriend of Sadie, who owns this place."

"Some very important women then."

"They like to think so." Diana laughed. She caught sight of Shannon making drinking signs and pointing to Daisy. "I think Shannon is trying to ask if you want a drink."

Daisy looked over and nodded. "Small white wine?" she mouthed quietly and got the thumbs up from Shannon.

"So, how's things with this Sammy-Jo?" Diana asked. "You hardly said anything in your text other than your dad wants you to marry her because she's his favourite footballer."

Daisy sighed. "Is it too soon to be talking about love?"

"Probably, yes." Diana laughed. "But I am not the one to ask about that because I couldn't see it when it was standing in front of my face." She laughed and smiled over at Shannon again. "My sister, Zara, would tell you that it's never too early if you've found the right one."

"That's cute."

"So, have you found the right one?"

"Maybe…I guess I just feel a little out of sorts because it has been so whirlwind."

"Many a marriage begins that way," Diana said sagely, before adding, "But so did many a divorce."

Daisy laughed.

"Hi Daisy," Scarlett said, placing a small white wine in front of her and a large red in front of Diana.

"Hi Scarlett, how are you?"

"All good, lovely Christmas, you?"

"Fabulous," Daisy answered.

"She's in love," Diana piped up and nudged Daisy.

"Oh, with that one you were looking for?" Shannon asked as she joined the table and placed her own and Scarlett's drinks down.

"Yes, SJ, or Sammy-Jo, she's just…" Daisy drifted off as her eyes were drawn to the opening door. "…right there." She smiled as Sammy-Jo and her friends all bundled through the door and headed to the bar.

"I'll be right back," Daisy said, clambering out from behind the table to head off Sammy-Jo, but Allegra gave SJ the heads up and as she turned around, Daisy flung her arms around her neck. "I didn't know you were coming here?"

"Last-minute thing." Sammy-Jo grinned. "Miss me?"

"Only a little bit," Daisy lied with a smile. "I'm just over there with some friends. Why don't you all join us?"

"I will see what everyone says, but I'll come over anyway and say hi." She stared into Daisy's eyes. "I'd love to meet your friends."

Stepping forward, Daisy said, "You turn me on."

Grabbing her waist and pulling her closer, Sammy-Jo said, "Well, why don't you let me take you home later and get this dress off of you?"

Pushing up on tiptoes, Daisy whispered against her ear, "Why do we have to go home for that?"

Sammy-Jo blushed. "Good point."

"Find me later, lover." Daisy kissed her quickly and then turned on her heel and returned to her friends.

"What did you just say to her? I can feel the heat from here." Diana laughed when Daisy sat down.

"I might have suggested she's getting lucky later."

"I might try that with Claudia," Scarlett said.

"Who are you kidding?" Diana said. "If anyone around here would blush, it wouldn't be Mother, it would be you, and we've all been there when it's happened."

"You don't know the half of it." Scarlett chuckled and sipped her beer.

Chapter Forty-Five

By the time the pub began to get busy, both tables had merged into one. Georgia had gone home, but Gabby, Claudia, and Natalie had been pulled into the ever-growing circle of Daisy's new friends, made easier by the fact that SJ's friend Nora was married to Gabby, and Claudia was with Scarlett, and Natalie was happy to hang around until Sadie finished work.

"I love how much of a community you all have here," Daisy said, looking around.

"We certainly do make the most of it," Claudia answered.

Daisy squeezed up and made room for Sammy-Jo, her palm landing on the athlete's thigh and slipping between them intimately.

"Hey," SJ said, smiling and leaning in to kiss her. "You having a good time?"

"Hey yourself." Daisy laughed. "Yes, it's so much fun."

Diana leaned across. "Daisy, have you met Gabby and Natalie?"

"No." She turned to find two older, attractive women smiling at her. "It's lovely to meet you," Daisy said to them both.

Gabby looked back and forth between them. "*The* Daisy?"

Sammy-Jo nodded. "Yeah."

"Well, looks like we'll be seeing more of you." Gabby grinned at Daisy. "Nora said we should all go for a meal."

"That would be lovely," Daisy said before Sammy-Jo could answer. "I'm here till the new year, but I'll be back." She looked at Sammy-Jo.

"Yeah, we'd like that," Sammy-Jo said. "I want Daisy to meet you all properly, you know."

"She wants me to stay." Daisy chuckled and squeezed SJ's hand.

"You should," Diana chipped in. "You hate your job, you have to move anyway…come to Bath Street!"

"Oh, how simple you make that sound." Daisy laughed. "I like it here, I do, and I'd be closer to my family, but I do need to work, so…until I can't bear it any longer, I have to stay in Kent."

"What is it that you do?" Gabby asked.

"Marketing, for a company that has no real ideas about how to do it, but it's paying my bills so…" She shrugged.

"I'm sure something will come up," Gabby said, turning to Natalie.

"Yes, we'll ask around and see if anyone's hiring."

"Really?" Daisy said. "I mean…it would be kind of awesome."

"It would be more than awesome." Sammy-Jo grinned.

"No promises, but we know quite a lot of people around here." Natalie winked. "And we can't see young lovers pulled apart over a silly thing like a job."

Sammy-Jo pulled Daisy closer. "She's already the best Christmas present. I'd give everything for a happy New Year."

Daisy kissed her cheek. "You're such a charmer."

"Isn't she just? Gabby laughed. "Who are you and what have you done with Sammy-Jo?"

"Lap it up and get used to it. I'm the new and improved Sammy-Jo."

"Amen to that." Gabby laughed.

Chapter Forty-Six

The upbeat music played loudly as Daisy grabbed Sammy-Jo's hand and pulled her onto the makeshift dance floor that had been created for the Christmas period.

"I'm not really a dancer," Sammy-Jo tried to argue, but Daisy was having none of it.

"Put your hands on my waist," Daisy instructed, before turning around and backing up until she fit against Sammy-Jo. Her arm raised up and her hand reached behind until she could slide her palm behind Sammy-Jo's head, tangling in her hair. She craned her neck and pulled Sammy-Jo's mouth closer. "Just move with me."

Her hips swayed and it took a moment before Sammy-Jo relaxed enough and pressed her hips forward, moving side to side with Daisy.

"You're so fucking hot," Sammy-Jo said against her ear. "I want to take you home and take off this dress."

Daisy grabbed Sammy-Jo's hand and pulled it around her waist, holding it against her stomach. "I already told you, we don't need to go home for that."

"You're serious, aren't you?"

Spinning around, Daisy slid her arms around Sammy-Jo's neck. "Put your hands on my arse, and yes, you know I am deadly serious." She locked eyes with Sammy-Jo and grinned when her backside was squeezed and her dress inched up a little. "I'm sure you can get imaginative, SJ."

"I'm not fucking in the toilets. I don't care how clean they look."

Daisy laughed. The dance floor was filling up and other people jostled around them as more and more got braver with a little bit of alcohol in them.

"You could fuck me here," Daisy said, raising up on her toes to speak against Sammy-Jo's ear. Her backside was squeezed once again. "You'd like that, would you?"

"I'm not going to deny that the idea turns me on, but…I can't afford to get caught doing that, not with…I'm back on track with the boss and the team."

Daisy grinned, bit her ear lobe and then reached behind and grabbed Sammy-Jo's hand. "Toilet it is then."

"Daisy!" Sammy-Jo said but didn't do anything to stop herself from being pulled towards the loos and a promise of something exciting.

Bounding through the door, Daisy giggled as she continued to drag Sammy-Jo towards the free cubicle at the end of the row.

Squeezed inside, she lifted her dress up and over her head, handing it to Sammy-Jo.

"Hang it on the back of the door," she whispered, stifling more giggles.

Sammy-Jo took it but stood stock still, just staring at her. She stood in her underwear, music blaring through the walls getting louder every time someone opened the door and came in or went out.

"You're bloody crazy," Sammy-Jo finally said, hooking the dress onto the back of the door. When she turned back, Daisy held out her bra. "Fuck, Daisy…this is…"

"It's everything you fantasise about."

Sammy-Jo pulled her bottom lip between her teeth. "You're who I fantasise about." She took the bra and laughed as she hung it around her neck like a scarf. Moving in, she caught Daisy easily in the confined space and started a kiss that would ignite any dampened fire.

"I want you," Daisy whispered. "To touch me, and get me all hot and bothered, but not…"

"Not what?"

"Not finish…I want to edge."

"You want me to stop just when you're about to—"

Daisy nodded. "It's…" She let out a breath. "It drives me wild."

"Okay."

"And then later, when I can't stand it any longer…all you'll have to do is say something against my ear that makes me shiver and—"

"And?"

"I'll finally enjoy it." She grinned and pulled Sammy-Jo's hand lower.

"How will I know when?"

"I'll tell you, silly. Now…are you going to torture me or not." Daisy grinned and flung her arms around Sammy-Jo's neck, resuming the kiss.

When they left the bathroom ten or fifteen minutes later, it was Allegra who Sammy-Jo spotted first, giving her a look that suggested she knew what they'd been doing. Or was that just Sammy-Jo's paranoia about being caught?

She couldn't lie; the idea was what made it exciting. Daisy made everything exciting, she thought as she watched her dance her way back into the crowd of new friends that were merging.

Was that weird also? That within a week of meeting, they were already creating pathways that both of them could walk down?

Her teammates, half of whom were straight and with their boyfriends, were mingling just as happily as everyone else. She caught Daisy's eye, and they shared a smile. Was it really only a week? It felt longer, so much longer, and if she thought about it, she knew more about Daisy than she had about almost every woman she'd ever slept with and scarily, Daisy knew more about her than she'd ever shared with anyone else.

And it wasn't freaking her out.

That had to be a good thing, didn't it?

She felt a hand on her arm and turned to find Diana grinning at her.

"You know, we're all rooting for you, right?"

"Are you?"

Diana laughed, the alcohol clearly working to loosen her up. "Yes, Daisy really likes you, and I can see why. You like her just as much. It's cute, and we all like Daisy, so…make her stay."

"I'm trying." Sammy-Jo grinned at the idea. "I'm not losing her."

They both looked over at Daisy dancing with the group. But when she hooked a finger in a come hither kind of way, Sammy-Jo tensed. That was the signal.

"If you'll excuse me, I think I'm going to go and dance."

"Of course," Diana said, but Sammy-Jo was already moving towards Daisy, who now faced her while still dancing.

"Hey lover," she said when Sammy-Jo finally reached her. She turned slowly and backed against Sammy-Jo. "Excite me some more."

This time, Sammy-Jo didn't need showing what to do with her hands. She instinctively moved one towards Daisy's stomach, holding her firmly against her, while the other roamed and touched. She pressed her mouth closer to Daisy's ear and let her tongue lick the lobe.

They danced that way for three songs before Daisy turned and faced her, arms stretched up around Sammy-Jo's neck, her backside gripped firmly.

She nestled comfortably into Sammy-Jo's neck and moaned a little as every movement caused her body to react.

And all Sammy-Jo needed to say was, "Show me."

Chapter Forty-Seven

Sunday 29th December

"I'm sorry, I just can't," Sammy-Jo said.

Daisy sprung up from the bed. "It's fine, I just—" She shook her head. "I just assumed you would, and I didn't think to ask." She turned and stared down at Sammy-Jo with those eyes that might just be Sammy-Jo's downfall. "Is there no way you can get out of it?"

"Nope, it's the club's party. It's written in stone and last year…" She looked away and puffed out her cheeks before releasing the breath. "I fucked up big time last year. Huge. Not big, huge. I almost threw my entire career down the toilet, so this year I need to make amends and show everyone how far I've come."

"I get it," Daisy said sadly as she flopped down onto the bed again.

"You can come with me."

"I can't. It's Mum's big night and if I'm not there when I'm here in town, she'd be devastated."

"Yeah, I guess."

Daisy smiled at her. "It's just one night, we can manage, can't we?"

"Yeah, but we don't have to like it." Sammy-Jo giggled and pulled Daisy closer. "And we've got two more nights before then, so…"

"What do you suggest we do?"

"Paris?"

"Paris!" Daisy exclaimed. "Now?"

"Why not? I bet we can get a shuttle over and be back tomorrow."

Daisy thought about it.

"As much as that sounds delightful…I don't have my passport with me."

"Bummer," Sammy-Jo said. "Alright, Bath?"

"What's in Bath?"

Sammy-Jo shrugged. "History, a fancy hotel and lots of sex?"

"And we'd be back by tomorrow?"

Sammy-Jo nodded. "Yep."

Frowning, Daisy asked, "And how would we get there? We can't risk a train, it would be just my luck that we'd be stuck there and then we'd both miss New Year's Eve."

"Hold that thought," Sammy-Jo said. Moving into action, she bent over the edge of her bed and found her jeans. Yanking her phone from the pocket, she checked the battery and then swiped until she pressed the call button.

"Who are you calling?"

"I'm calli— Oh, hey, Nora, it's me…I know you know it's me. It's just what people say… Yes, I know that, anyway I wanted to ask a favour…hm yes, I'll tell you that later…yes, that is correct. So, the favour… Can I borrow your car?...no, I'm not going to do that… Yes." She blew her cheeks out and listened, rolling her eyes at Daisy. "So, is that a yes?...thank you, I owe you one…yes, I know that too… Okay, be round in a bit."

"You're borrowing a car?"

Sammy-Jo nodded, pleased with herself. "Yep, gotta go around and get it though in the next hour cos they're going out."

Daisy jumped up. "So, why are we still laying in bed?"

Daisy gasped as they walked up to the gate where Nora lived with Gabby.

"Bloody hell, this is—"

"I know, Gabby is doing alright for herself, and Nora's Nora Brady, so she's popular with brands."

"Still, it's a statement, isn't it?"

"I guess so, never really thought about it." She pressed the buzzer and waited. Nobody answered, the door just clicked and buzzed, Sammy-Jo pushed it open, and stepped inside to the small courtyard driveway.

In front of them was Gabby's white, brand spanking new Range Rover, the one Sammy-Jo had told the twins about. Next to that was a motorbike covered with a big winter jacket that was tightly secured around it and beside that was a small black Porsche.

Daisy gawped. "Are we…is that?" She pointed to the Porsche.

"It's second-hand, don't get that excited," Sammy-Jo said. "Come on, let's get the keys and then we can get packed and go."

The door was already open, and Sammy-Jo walked in to find Gabby looking at herself in the mirror in the hallway, putting her earrings in.

"Hello you two," she said, looking at them both through the glass. "Nora will be down in a sec, she's just run up to grab my watch."

"You've got an amazing home," Daisy gushed.

"Thank you, it's still a work in progress but we like it." Gabby's smile got wider when she heard the thumping feet of her wife running down the stairs. "Here she is."

Nora passed a gold watch to Gabby and kissed her cheek before she turned to Daisy and said, "Hello." Then she turned to Sammy-Jo and held out a set of keys. "I've added you to my insurance, but please do not make me have to use it."

"I won't. We're just going to drive to Bath, stay the night in a nice hotel and drive back tomorrow, alright?"

"Cool, well there should be enough fuel to get you there," Nora said.

"Thank you so much, Nora, we really appreciate it," Daisy said to her.

"You're welcome, have a nice time."

Sammy-Jo narrowed her eyes at them. "Where are you two going?"

Gabby answered, "It's the Women in Business luncheon."

"Did you do that yesterday?"

"No, that was just my little group. Today is a wider field, it's not limited to LGBT," Gabby explained, and then turning to Daisy she said, "I'll keep my ear out and ask around."

"That would be great, thank you," Daisy gushed some more.

"Right, come on, or we'll never get anything done," Sammy-Jo said. Turning to Nora at the door and holding up the keys she said, "Seriously, thanks for this."

"Will you go?" Nora laughed.

Chapter Forty-Eight

"Mum, Dad," Polly shouted. "Daisy just pulled up in a flash car with Sammy-Jo."

"Stop nosing out the window," Eileen said but watched her husband do exactly that.

"It's a Porsche," he said a little too excitedly.

"It's a car," Eileen offered, bringing some normality to things. But she too got up and went to look. They all watched as Daisy and Sammy-Jo kissed. "You know, I think this might be the reason she finally comes home?"

"I hope so. Never felt right her being so far away."

"I know."

"And she can't take us to the park," Dolly piped up.

They all watched the lovebirds climb from the car and walk towards the gate, then dispersed back to their seats as though they hadn't moved or seen a thing.

"Mum, Dad, I'm just popping in to get some stuff," Daisy called out when the front door opened. The sound of footsteps running up the stairs followed.

"Well, I guess she's staying out again," Eileen said.

"I can't believe our daughter is a WAG," Chris said, putting his paper back down.

"What's a wag?" Polly asked. Dolly looked up for the answer too.

"It means wives and girlfriends, the papers use it when they talk about the partners of footballers," Eileen explained.

"So, Sammy-Jo is Daisy's girlfriend now?" Polly asked.

“Is Daisy gonna be her wife?” Dolly asked.

“They’ve only just met,” Eileen said.

“Imagine though, watching the football from a VIP box.” Chris grinned.

Eileen rolled her eyes. “Honestly, Christopher.”

“What?” he laughed. “A man can dream.”

The sound of footsteps and laughter coming down the stairs made them all turn and look at the lounge door.

It was Daisy whose head appeared.

“Hey, just so you know, we’re going to Bath for the night, but I’ll be back tomorrow to help organise the party.”

“Bath, it’s lovely there,” Chris said. “How are you getting there?”

Eileen shot him a look.

“Oh, Sammy-Jo borrowed Nora’s car.”

“Nora Brady?” Chris said with more enthusiasm. “You’re driving around in Nora’s Porsche.”

“Stalker much, Dad?” Daisy laughed.

“No, I just…” He glanced towards the window. “So, you’ll be back tomorrow, fabulous. Are you coming to the party, SJ?”

Sammy-Jo leaned in and over Daisy’s head to appear around the door. “Oh hey, Mr Foster, Uh, nah, got the club Christmas do.”

“Oh, that’s a shame,” Eileen said. “For us, not you.” She chuckled.

“Yeah, them’s the breaks. But I promise, I’ll have her back safe and sound tomorrow.”

“We trust you. Go and have some fun.”

“Right, now you’re all happy about what I do and who I do it with…” Daisy teased. “I’ll see you tomorrow.”

"Have fun," Dolly said.

"Cheers, Doll. Later, Poll."

"Bye."

Chapter Forty-Nine

Sammy-Jo pulled the car into the entrance of the hotel and roared up the drive, parking right outside of the door.

"Wow, it's beautiful," Daisy said. She'd pestered all the way for the name of the hotel Sammy-Jo had booked for them, but she wouldn't give it up.

"Surprised?" Sammy-Jo smiled.

"Yeah, and no…I mean, it's gorgeous, but I kind of knew you'd pick something like this."

"Happy?"

Daisy leaned across the car. "Very," she said, kissing her softly. "Now I know why you said to pack the dress."

Sammy-Jo laughed. "Well, I kind of like you wearing that. You look hot, but yeah, I knew you'd want to dress up."

"Are we going in?"

"Unless you want to sit in Nora's car and make out." Sammy-Jo chuckled. "She'd kill me if she found out."

Daisy's attention was taken past Sammy-Jo's face and out of the window to a young man in a smart uniform.

"Hm, I'm not one for an actual audience."

Sammy-Jo turned to look behind her.

"Ah, yeah, probably not a good idea." She waved at him, and then switched the engine off. "Come on then."

"Good afternoon, I'm James, and I'd love to park your vehicle for you."

"Okay James, but listen up." Sammy-Jo leaned in towards him while Daisy grabbed their bags. "I've borrowed this car from a very good friend, and if anything happens to it, I'll be needing a funeral director, am I clear?"

"Yes, ma'am, I can assure you that I am very cautious when it comes to moving vehicles. If you let me know your name, I'll add the details to your booking and then all you'll have to do is speak with reception—"

"I got it, James, not my first rodeo." She tossed him the key. "Sammy-Jo Costa."

He smiled at her.

"And James…" She waited for him to turn back to her. "Thank you."

"You're very welcome," he answered and then turned to another uniformed colleague. "Harris will take your bags."

Daisy's eyes bulged when they were shown into the room. It was bigger than her flat, bigger than the entire downstairs of her parents' house.

"Wow, SJ, this is… Can we afford this?"

Sammy-Jo wrapped her arms around Daisy's shoulders from behind and kissed the side of her head.

"This is my treat. I told you I'd get you something for Christmas."

"Aww, you're so romantic," Daisy answered, turning in her arms. "What do I get you?"

"You already gave me the best Christmas gift."

"I did? What did I give you?"

"You. That's all I needed, just you."

"You're so sweet, you know that?" Daisy kissed her slowly.

When Sammy-Jo pulled back, she chuckled. “Don’t tell anyone else. I have a reputation to maintain.”

Daisy laughed. “Oh, I’ll keep your secret, so long as you don’t change with me.”

“Never. I’ve grown a lot this last year. Meeting you has shown me what it is that I want.”

“Me?”

Sammy-Jo nodded. “I’m serious, I know what I want, Daisy.”

“Me too.”

Chapter Fifty

Claudia moved around the room and headed towards the table where Natalie and Gabby were waving at her. Bottles of champagne were opened, and glasses filled.

"Hey," she said as she slid into her seat.

"Nora is going to pick us all up later," Gabby said, pouring a glass for Claudia. "So, we are going to enjoy this afternoon."

"Sounds like a plan."

"I've already warned Sadie that I will not be available for anything that requires thinking about until tomorrow." Natalie raised her glass. "To all the women who love us."

They clinked glasses.

"Where's Georgia? I wanted to talk to her about Daisy," Gabby asked.

"The young blonde woman from last night?" Natalie clarified. "I am so bad with names lately."

"Age darling, it happens to the best of us." Claudia laughed. "I'm not sure where Georgia is though." She looked around to see if she could see her anywhere. "What did you want to ask her, anyway?"

"Well, Daisy is looking to change jobs and she's in marketing, so I thought Georgia might have an idea about any jobs available…or I wondered if her new venture might be looking to recruit."

"Well, that sounds like a good plan. But if it goes the wrong way, I could look into whether we have any opportunities at Come Again," Natalie offered. She waved over a waitress and pointed to the empty champagne bottle, mouthing a silent 'thank you.' "I'd have to speak with HR."

"That would be awesome," Gabby said. "I'd see what we have available at the club, but I'm thinking it best to keep that very separate if she's planning to continue dating Sammy-Jo."

"Isn't she the one who gave you a hell of a time last Christmas?" Claudia asked. She pulled the bowl of Nocellara olives closer and plucked one, popping it into her mouth.

Gabby sighed. "Yes, though we have worked through that, and I've got to say, she's been a model pro ever since. I'm happy for her, and Daisy seems like a great person."

"Hm, Diana is taken with her. Even Scarlett liked her," Claudia added.

"So, we're in agreement. We'll do what we can to find the perfect job for Daisy, so that she and Sammy-Jo can have their happy ever after?" Gabby grinned. "God, I feel like a modern day Cilla Black."

"I mean, we always have vacancies at several hotels, but I don't know about head office. I can ask though," Claudia said. "I am starving. I hope they're serving something more than olives."

"I can see they're already bringing food around, so it won't be long," Natalie said with a little conspiratorial wink. "Oh, here comes Georgia." She waved her over. "She doesn't look so happy. Do you think everything is okay?"

"I'm sure we will find out," Gabby said with a raised brow and a little smirk of mischief.

"Georgia, we saved a seat," Natalie said.

Sitting down, Georgia blew out a breath and reached for a glass, pouring some champagne and swigging it down.

"Everything all right?" Claudia asked.

"Honestly, Robbie has decided that she's old enough to stay out all night and not let anyone know she's safe."

"Oh dear," Claudia said, the only other mother out of the four of them.

“Yeah, not the best. Pippa was going out of her mind. And Robbie strolls in this morning with a bullshit story about sending a text and it’s not her fault it didn’t go through.”

“Sounds fun,” Gabby said, topping up her glass.

“Then she kicked off because she’s grounded.”

“She’s usually such a thoughtful kid. What’s brought all this on?” Natalie asked.

Georgia shrugged. “Not a clue, but Cassie said there’s a couple of new kids started this year and she’s seen Robbie hanging out with them.”

“Gotta love a snitch.” Gabby chuckled.

“It’s the best. I find out more from Cassie than I do from Max or Roberta.”

“Well, she’s home now and you’ve put those parental boundaries in, and she’s a good kid at heart, so hopefully that will be the end of it,” Claudia offered, with a gentle touch of her hand against Georgia’s arm. “And you can always send her back to Scarlett’s art therapy group.”

“Yes I can.” Georgia smiled. “She at least enjoys that.”

“So, now that we know you’re all good, I have a question for you.” Gabby grinned.

“Sounds ominous. Go on.” Georgia laughed.

“We have a new friend who needs a job, in marketing. Are you recruiting?”

“I’m not sure, but I’m happy to meet and have a chat if it would help.”

“It can’t hurt,” Gabby said just as her phone rang. She glanced at it. “Oh, I have to take this…new player coming in.”

“I want the details,” Georgia called after her as she walked away to speak privately. “So, this new friend? Tell me about her.”

Chapter Fifty-One

"What do you want to do first?" Daisy asked. "Go for a walk?"

"Yeah, that might be good. Unless you fancied the spa?" Sammy-Jo stood at the window staring out at the countryside and the city of Bath ahead of that.

"Mm, a massage would be good, can't deny that," Daisy said, sidling up behind her and pressing herself up against her back. "You feel tense," she said, squeezing Sammy-Jo's shoulders.

"I dunno why. This is the most relaxed I've felt in…ever." Sammy-Jo chuckled. She turned around. "How about a stroll around the grounds and then we'll have some lunch?" Her arms wrapped around Daisy's waist and tugged her closer. "Then we'll go get a facial."

"What happened to the massage?"

"Well…I thought I could…give you a long, slow, sensual massage later."

"Oh…is that before or after dinner?" Daisy ran her hand up Sammy-Jo's chest and over her shoulder until it met its pair behind her neck.

"Whatever works for you."

"It all works for me." Daisy laughed. When Sammy-Jo didn't smile, she asked, "What's wrong?"

"Nothing, I—"

"Sammy-Jo Costa, don't you start lying to me."

Now, SJ smiled. "I'm not, I just…is this real?"

"What do you mean?" Daisy frowned.

"I guess I'm waiting for the other shoe to drop, or worse, that I'll sabotage things because I can't quite believe that it's all going to turn out…because it never does."

"Honestly, I don't know. And I think I have the same concerns. It's barely been a week."

"I know, right, and not that I'm complaining about it, because it's been the best week ever." Sammy-Jo grinned before becoming serious again. "But what if…we've had lots of sex, good sex…great sex," she emphasised. "What if that's all it is?"

"Let's sit down," Daisy said, leading Sammy-Jo to the bed. "This is why I've been reticent about moving back, or at least, thinking about it. I like you so much, but I'm a realist and this feels like…you ever had a holiday fling?"

Sammy-Jo shook her head. "No, I've had holiday one-night stands."

"Well…" Daisy grinned. "A fling is more…emotional, it's like you meet this person and then you're stuck in this little bubble where everything is exciting and heightened and all the feelings and emotions explode and you feel like you've met your person, and then boom, just like that, one of you is going home and you never see them again and it's the worst feeling."

"Sounds awful."

"Yeah, but in the moment, it feels like the best thing you've ever done."

"And that's what this feels like?"

Daisy nodded. "A little bit."

"So, how do we find out?" Sammy-Jo asked. "How do we know if this is going to last, because you're going to go home and—"

"Yeah, I know. But this is different because I'll be coming back and you can come and visit me and…it's time isn't it? That's the only way to find out. We can call it a holiday fling and then go our separate ways—"

"I don't want to do that."

"Or we can just give ourselves time to find out."

"Let's do that," Sammy-Jo said emphatically.

Daisy smiled. "Alright, so…let's explore something."

"What?"

"No sex," Daisy said.

"Huh?"

Daisy laughed. "While we're here. Let's not have sex. Let's talk, spend time with each other, do stuff together."

"Like an old married couple?"

"Hm, don't let my mother hear you say that, or she will give you chapter and verse about her and my dad's sex life," Daisy joked. "But yes, let's pretend we're a married couple and do all sorts of couple things, but no—"

"Sexy times. Got it." Sammy-Jo smile., "So, shall we go for a walk?"

"Yes, I'd love that." Daisy went to stand up, but Sammy-Jo grabbed her wrist. "What is it?"

"No sex, but…kissing's allowed, right?"

Leaning down, Daisy pressed her lips against Sammy-Jo's. "Yeah, kissing is definitely allowed."

"Okay, I can do that."

"Can you?" Daisy teased.

Sammy-Jo nodded. "If it means proving that we're more than sex, then yeah, I can do that."

Chapter Fifty-Two

"So, we've walked the gardens," Daisy counted on her fingers, "enjoyed some lunch, and a massage…what do you want to do next?"

Sammy-Jo worked her neck from side to side while she considered it. She felt quite relaxed and chilled right now.

"Nothing," she answered. "Let's just go down to the bar, get a drink and chill."

Daisy smiled at her. "And talk to each other?"

"Yep, like an old married couple would do."

"What if…instead of going down to the bar…we ordered room service and stretched out, stuck a film on and cuddled," Daisy said, offering an alternative.

Sammy-Jo shrugged. "Can do. Don't you want to talk?"

"Yeah, I just…" Daisy sighed. "I don't want to put a table between us. We should be able to lay on a bed and snuggle, and not have sex."

"Oh, it's a test," Sammy-Jo said, understanding now.

"Not a test as such, just…" Now Daisy shrugged. "I dunno. It's hard; I really want you to ravish me." She laughed.

"Well, I'm not gonna. I don't break that easily, Dr Foster, no matter how cute you look pouting like that."

"Damn, has my pouting worn off already?" Daisy chuckled.

"Only for the next…" Sammy-Jo checked her watch. "Seventeen hours."

"God, that long." Daisy laughed. "Okay, fine, let's go to the bar. Are you still allowed to drink?"

"It's not forbidden. But I don't want to overdo it. Once we hit New Year's Day, that will be it for alcohol. I'll be back in training, and you'll have to find other things to do to occupy your time." Sammy-Jo grabbed her wallet and shoved it into her pocket.

"Good, because I am buying us champagne."

"Can you afford that?"

Daisy poked her. "Never you mind, but one thing you should know about me is that I don't do or say anything that I don't want to. So, if I want to buy champagne, I will."

"Fair enough. I just wanted to be clear that...I don't expect you to."

"Good, and just to be clear, I didn't expect you to pay for all of this." Daisy waved her hand around at the room.

"It's your Christmas present."

Daisy grabbed a hold of her collars and pulled Sammy-Jo lower to kiss her. "I already had it…I got you."

"Nice save."

Sammy-Jo refilled their champagne flutes and then nibbled on an olive.

"I could get used to this," she said, looking around the room. The Christmas decorations and tree were still up, and the fireplace they sat beside roared. It was warm, and cosy, and romantic.

"Me too," Daisy replied, snuggling against Sammy-Jo's side. "It's magical."

"It is. We could make it a regular event. Come back here every Christmas."

Daisy grinned. "I'd need a big pay rise."

Sammy-Jo shrugged. "I'd just need to score a few more goals and then my bonus kicks in."

"You get paid more if you score?" Daisy asked, reaching for an olive.

"Oh yeah, I'm an attacking midfielder. My job is to link the rest of midfield and the attack. I get a bonus for every assist and another bonus for every goal. This is the first season I might actually do alright though."

"Why's that?"

"We just have a better squad. Nora Brady signing was a blessing. With that came The Sledge." Daisy looked perplexed. "Sorry, I mean Kunkel, Dorit Kunkel, German international. She only signed for one season, but Gabby managed to get her to stay for two more, so with them signing we were able to swing it with Beth Nailor. So, more goals. And obviously, I'm playing and not benched for being a twat."

"I see. I guess I should probably come along and watch you play."

Sammy-Jo shrugged again. "Well yeah, but you don't have to. I wouldn't expect you—"

Daisy pressed a finger against her lips. "I want to."

"Oh, well in that case, yes. And you should wear my shirt."

"To the game?" Daisy asked coyly.

"Where else would— Oh, well, yeah, I mean…yeah that would be hot, actually," Sammy-Jo said, imagining the scenario.

"I suggest you find me one then." Daisy grinned. "For when we get home and are allowed to have sex again."

Chapter Fifty-Three

Back in the room, Sammy-Jo stripped off, not bothered about her nakedness. She strolled into the bathroom and flicked the switch for the shower.

Daisy laughed when she followed in order to brush her teeth. "What are you wearing?"

Sammy-Jo frowned. "It's a shower cap, they're free, and if I get my hair wet, I'll be spending all night drying it. Otherwise, it will frizz, and I'm not leaving the room if that happens."

"Babe, your mane is never going to stay under that. Come here and let me tie it up."

Sammy-Jo huffed like a five-year-old not being allowed to stick its finger in an electrical socket, but she did as she was told and stood dramatically shivering while Daisy pulled the plastic hat off her head. It ripped.

"See, useless." Daisy showed her. Picking up her brush, she began to pull Sammy-Jo's hair up and into a big pineapple-style ponytail, and then with deft fingers, she wound it around itself before grabbing another band and holding it in place. "There. That should hold long enough for you to get a shower."

Looking at herself in the mirror, Sammy-Jo pulled a face. "Bit girly, but—"

"What are you talking about? All the hot tomboy lesbians are rocking a bun."

"Well, not this one… I like it swishing so I can whack people with it when I tackle them."

Daisy winced. "Is that allowed?"

Sammy-Jo shrugged. "Not been booked for it, so yeah, I guess it must be. It's a risk I'm willing to take." She grinned. "You joining me?"

"No, that would be…" She stepped back and enjoyed the view. "Very dangerous. I'll jump in after; leave it running for me."

Leaving the bathroom, Daisy ventured over to the window, near the desk, where a small coffee and tea caddy sat beside a kettle. She flicked it on and prepared to make them both a hot chocolate with the sachets, when she noticed something outside of the window.

It was snowing again.

"Oh no," she muttered just as the kettle boiled.

"What's up?" Sammy-Jo said, already out of the shower. A towel was wrapped tightly around her.

"You were quick."

"Wasn't much to do on my own. Quick swish and boom, here I am." She made a pose and then laughed before crossing the room. "What did you say… Oh, no," she said herself when she saw out of the window what Daisy had seen.

"It's snowing hard."

"Yeah, it'll be gone tomorrow, you watch. We'll get some sleep, and then by the time we go down for breakfast, it will be raining and all washed away. You watch."

"But what if it's not? What if it's like it was before Christmas? We can't just walk home."

"Do you want to leave now?"

Daisy spun and stared up at her. "What? No, we can't…can we?"

"We can do what we want, Daisy. Is that what you want?"

Daisy looked around at the beautiful room, the huge bed and the decadent quilt and pillows. "We could get stuck here."

Sammy-Jo nodded. "Yeah, it's a risk."

Daisy screwed up her mouth as she contemplated it. "If this was about sex, I'd be all up for taking a risk, but my mum is so excited about the party. If we didn't get back and I missed helping her with it…"

Putting her arm around her, Sammy-Jo said, "I'll call down to reception and have the car brought round."

"I feel so bad," Daisy said, tears welling in her eyes. "You went to all this trouble, and it's cost a fortune and…"

"Shit," Sammy-Jo said. "We can't leave."

Daisy stopped crying and frowned. "What?"

"We drank a bottle of champagne; neither of us is under the limit. And that's not a risk I am willing to take."

"No, of course not." Daisy threw her hands up. "So, we make the most of it then, and what will be will be, but I'm going to call my mum now and let her know."

"Yeah, I'm starting to learn that things happen for a reason and sometimes you just have to go with it. Unless that reason makes me an arsehole, then I'm supposed to say no." She grinned, and Daisy couldn't not smile at that.

"You're not an arsehole, at least, not to me." Daisy hugged her.

"I'm glad you think so. I'll call Nora and let her know we might be keeping her car another day…or two. And you'd better turn the shower off."

Chapter Fifty-Four

Nora answered on the third ring. "What have you done to my car?"

"Cheers mate, that's just charming, isn't it?" Sammy-Jo said. She pulled her legs up and sat on the bed, still wrapped in her towel, watching Daisy speak to her mum. "The car is fine, but…"

"Go on," Nora said hesitantly.

"It's started snowing here again, lots of snow. We were going to leave and head home, but we can't."

"Why not? It would be the sensible thing to do."

"Yeah, and had we known it was going to turn horrible again, we wouldn't have drunk the bottle of champagne earlier."

"Fuck. Well, yeah, then you can't drive."

"Exactly," Sammy-Jo said, noticing Daisy's shoulders sag. "So, we're going to see what the weather is like in the morning and then decide on whether it's safe to travel. I just wanted to warn you in case we get stuck here for another day…or two."

She heard Gabby in the background saying something excitedly and Nora said, "Yes okay I'll tell her."

"Tell me what?"

"Firstly, do whatever you need to do to get home in one piece. I can work something out here, Gabby can drive me anywhere if I need to go," Nora said, ever the placid, logical one. "And…Satty Basra is joining from PSG."

"What?" Sammy-Jo exclaimed so loudly that Daisy swung around and asked, "Are you alright?" She nodded. "Satty Basra, the Satty Basra, from the hero of London City to PSG, and now Bath Street Harriers?"

"The very one. Gabby spoke to her people this afternoon. Apparently things aren't great with her ex playing there, so she wants a move to the WSL and as close to London as possible. Chelsea and Arsenal are already overrun in that position, but we aren't, not with Astrid's cruciate injury."

"Fuck, that's…we might end up staying in the top six if she's on form."

"I know, right? Anyway, gotta go. Let me know when you plan to return."

"Will do."

She closed the phone off and listened in as Daisy continued talking to her mum.

"Yeah, it is…" Daisy said, smiling over at Sammy-Jo. "Yep, I know."

Sammy-Jo stood up and dropped her towel, causing Daisy to blush and stammer.

"I-I uh, yeah, that's exactly it." She mouthed, "Put that on."

Wriggling her hips, Sammy-Jo laughed and began dancing around the room until Daisy giggled.

"Yeah, sorry, I'm listening," she said into the phone as her mum continued talking. "Yep, we will. If it's clear in the morning, we will head back."

Sammy-Jo found a t-shirt and pulled it on, laughing to herself while Daisy closed up the call with her mum.

"You are a sod, you know that?" Daisy said, chasing her around the room until they both ended up on the bed with Daisy straddling Sammy-Jo's thighs.

"Uh…what are you doing?"

"Pinning you to the bed until you learn to behave yourself."

"That's never going to happen." Sammy-Jo laughed and with a heave of her hips and an upward thrust, she managed to twist and turn and throw Daisy onto her back, reversing their situation. "Oh, look at that," she gloated.

Daisy smiled smugly. "Of course, you'd think you won, but the reality is… I have you just where I want you."

"Really?"

"Hm-hm." Daisy nodded and slid her palms up and under Sammy-Jo's shirt.

"Uh-uh…" Sammy-Jo grabbed her hands. "No sex, remember."

"Who said anything about sex…"

"Daisy," Sammy-Jo warned.

"What, SJ?" she said, her fingertips just managing to move under Sammy-Jo's grip.

"You are mean if you start this."

Daisy breathed deeply and stilled her fingers. "You're right, but the parameters of our stay have changed."

"No, they haven't. We were staying till tomorrow, that hasn't changed. And we're going home tomorrow…but if we can't go home…then tomorrow we can renegotiate the terms of our stay."

"Fuck, that was sexy. You're right, I'm sorry." Daisy smiled, and when Sammy-Jo released her and fell to the side, she said, "Can you bring that Sammy-Jo out again?"

"You like bossy SJ?"

"Don't you?" Daisy asked, sitting up.

"I guess…though she gets me in trouble a lot." She smiled sadly. "And I'm really trying not to get in trouble anymore."

"Well, there is trouble and then there is fun. Knowing the difference is what matters. I can help you learn."

"Maybe it's not me that's trouble." Sammy-Jo smiled, narrowing her eyes. "Shall we order snacks and watch a film?"

"Yes, I'm going to jump in the shower."

Chapter Fifty-Five

Daisy chuckled as she stood there in nothing but a towel watching Sammy-Jo. The bun had gone, as she knew it would have.

"What?" Sammy-Jo said, frowning at her. Her hand was midway between her mouth and the bowl of crisps in her lap.

"Nothing, you look comfy."

The crisp entered and was chomped noisily as Sammy-Jo answered, "I am. Hurry up and get in here."

Now it was Daisy who frowned.

"What?" Sammy-Jo said again.

"I didn't pack pyjamas. I kind of assumed I wouldn't be needing them."

"Oh."

"Unlike you, who seems to have been much more organised."

Sammy-Jo shrugged. "To be fair, I kind of cheated."

Daisy's eyes narrowed. "How?"

"So, I have a case packed for away games: spare underwear, sleeping stuff, everything I need for a night away. I wash it and re-pack it so it's always ready to go."

"I see. Well, that is kind of smart."

Sammy-Jo beamed. "I know, I just grabbed it and threw in a couple of extra—" Her eyes lit up and she moved the bowl of chips before jumping up and jogging across the room to her case.

She hadn't unpacked.

"Here, you can wear this." She turned, holding up a t-shirt with 'badass' written across it in a graffiti style with only a little creasing.

"Thank you," Daisy said, taking it from her. "It's very…you." She grinned and slipped it on over the top of the towel that was still wrapped around her.

"It's a bit big, but you girls wear nightshirts like that, don't you?" Sammy-Jo said, nodding to herself at how good it looked on Daisy.

"Us girls?"

"Yeah, you know what I mean."

"Do I?" Daisy laughed. "What are you then?"

"Well, I'm a girl obviously, but I'm not a girly girl, that's all I meant. Like, I'm a vest and shorts girl." She used her hands to indicate her own attire. "I don't wear dresses, even nighttime ones."

"Uh-uh…got it." Daisy smiled. "So, I'm the girly girl."

"Yeah." Sammy-Jo shrugged and jumped back onto the bed, knocking the crisps over. "Shit," she said, shuffling them back into the bowl. "You wear heels, and make-up and dresses, and you look stunning and gorgeous and…yeah, you're girly."

"You're not stunning and gorgeous?"

Sammy-Jo stopped what she was doing and thought for a moment. "I don't—" She pressed her lips together, her brow furrowing. "I used to think I was…"

Daisy climbed onto the bed. "You are."

Pulling a funny face, Sammy-Jo laughed it off. "Nah."

"You are," Daisy reiterated. "Despite the attempts to try and appear invisible, it's impossible. The world sees you." Daisy's eyes twinkled. "And all of this hair."

Subconsciously or not, Sammy-Jo reached up and ran her hands through it. "My hair is stunning, I'll give you that."

"Your hair is stunning, but it's also where you hide."

"I don't hide," Sammy-Jo said defensively.

Daisy placed a soothing hand on her and the tension disappeared instantly.

"I am badass," Sammy-Jo said, pointing to the t-shirt Daisy wore. "Like literally the toughest player on the pitch."

"Hm-hm." Daisy nodded. "But…we're in a hotel room, in a bed and nowhere near a football pitch."

"Does that matter?"

Staring at her, Daisy, scoffed. "Yeah, it matters. You don't have to be tough with me."

"I do, that's my job."

"Your job? Do I look like I need protecting?" Daisy laughed. "My point is, no matter if you're masc or a tomboy or not girly, all of those women using those labels can still be pretty, beautiful, stunning and gorgeous, and you are all of that. And the thing that I find a real turn on, is that I know who you are to everyone else…but with me, you let out a little vulnerability and that's sexy, and I'm just saying that if you wanted to do more of that, I would like it."

"Yeah?" Sammy-Jo said shyly.

"Yeah," Daisy mocked playfully. "I like all the dashing hero stuff and the protective nature that you have. That's also sexy, but when it's supported by a foundation of stable security and someone who's able to emotionally connect and be vulnerable when they need to…that's stratospheric sexy."

"So, what you're saying is you like it when we talk, and when I don't pretend everything is alright, and when I can ask for my needs to be met?"

"Yes."

"Have you been talking to my therapist?" Sammy-Jo laughed.

"No, should I?"

"Probably."

Daisy flopped down into the space beside Sammy-Jo and snuggled. “It’s kind of hot that you see one. I mean, that says a lot about you and how willing you are to fix things.”

“Yeah, well I didn’t really have much choice in the matter at first. Gabby said I either went or found another club.”

“She seems so easy-going.”

“Ha, yeah right.” Sammy-Jo moved her arm and pulled Daisy closer. “You don’t get where Gabby has gotten without being tough, but…she’s fair and open and…I guess I could be a bit more like her.”

“Role model, I like it.”

“But we won’t tell her.”

“Nope, our secret.”

Chapter Fifty-Six

Monday 30th December.

Waking up with Daisy curled around her was heaven for Sammy-Jo. It really was like all her Christmases had come at once, but the nagging fear that it would all go wrong poked hard at the back of her mind.

People like Daisy didn't work out for people like Sammy-Jo. People like Daisy would soon see through her and realise she was nothing but trouble and that at some point she would do something to fuck it all up and then Daisy would be gone.

And the Sammy-Jo of old would believe that nonsense and create an issue to sabotage, or just avoid dating the likes of Daisy and find herself another toxic idiot like Krista.

But not this version of Sammy-Jo.

This was just her traumas being triggered. And if they were triggered, it was because Daisy was exactly who she should be allowing to love her.

Love? Did she just say love?

Easing herself out from Daisy's arms, she slid off of the bed and padded barefoot to the window. Reaching for the curtain, she stopped. Did she want it to be snowing still? So, they would be locked away here for another night? She grinned; it might be nice, unless Daisy planned to continue the no sex rule.

Laughing to herself, she eased the curtain back just enough to look out without the daylight pouring in and waking Daisy.

Snow covered the hills and fields and the lawn. But it wasn't snowing. Several millimetres must have come down in the night, but it had stopped, so that was a good sign, wasn't it?

She let the curtain fall back, and then turned to see last night's dinner plates on the floor and Daisy staring at her.

"Well?" Daisy said. Because what else did she need to say? They both understood what she was asking.

Sammy-Jo shrugged. "Not sure. There's snow on the ground, but it's not snowing. So, if that holds then maybe later the roads will have cleared a bit and we can take a chance."

She went back to the window and opened the curtains fully now Daisy was awake.

"Want to go down for breakfast?"

Daisy stretched and yawned. "Yeah, I guess so."

"Maybe someone who works here will have a better idea of what it's like out there. And if it's bad, then I'll speak to the manager about another night here." She chewed her fingernail and looked at the floor.

"What's that look for?" Daisy grinned.

"What look?"

"You look pensive, is everything alright?"

Sammy-Jo stopped chewing and smiled like a kid that had been caught doing something they shouldn't.

"Well, I was thinking that if we did have to stay another night…are we gonna extend the no sex rule?"

"Oh," Daisy chuckled and got out of bed, "I mean, I hadn't thought about it."

"It's fine if you do want to…I can go without—"

"Shush," Daisy said, putting her finger to Sammy-Jo's lips. "Whether we stay here, or go home, I'm not sure I want another night with restrictions. It was nice, and I think we both passed the test. We can entertain each other and communicate without being sexually intimate."

"Yeah."

"But I do kind of want to enjoy this honeymoon period for as long as it lasts."

Sammy-Jo's mouth gaped open. "As long as it lasts?" She grabbed Daisy around the waist and hauled her up off her feet and onto the bed, giggling and grasping. Hovering over her, Sammy-Jo's hair fell and framed them both in a secluded face to face space. "It's never going to stop."

"Course it will." Daisy continued to giggle. "You'll be playing again, and exhausted from all that running around, and I'll have to get up at six in the morning again to go to work, and we'll be driving back and forth…"

"Move in with me."

Daisy sighed and pushed Sammy-Jo up. "You make it all sound so easy."

"Because it is," Sammy-Jo said, rolling onto her side but still looking at Daisy. "Allegra won't care. She's at John's all the time anyway. And I have room, I don't have much and what I do have isn't sentimental. We can clear it out and move your stuff in and—"

Daisy put her hand against Sammy-Jo's chest. "I'll think about it, alright, but even if we did do something as crazy as that, it will still take time. I'd still have to find another job, and give a month's notice and organise—"

This time Sammy-Jo placed her finger to Daisy's lips and grinned. "You'll think about it was all you needed to say."

Daisy attempted to bite the finger that lingered against her lips. "I'm beginning to see how you get into so much trouble."

Beaming, Sammy-Jo jumped up. "I know, but this could be good trouble." She grabbed a towel. "Wanna share the shower?"

"With no sex?" Daisy said with a straight face.

The smile on Sammy-Jo's face dropped.

"I'm just kidding. But…I'm putting your hair up in a bun again…it's sexy."

"Whatever," Sammy-Jo snarked before grinning and turning on her heel. Lightning speed had her in the bathroom and turning on the water before Daisy had moved.

When she finally appeared in the doorway, Sammy-Jo's jaw dropped.

"Naked Daisy is kind of one of my new favourite things," she said.

"Hm, naked and wet." Daisy smiled mischievously, before reaching for a brush.

Sammy-Jo sagged dramatically but gave in with no fight when Daisy proceeded to navigate her mane and style it back into the man bun.

She watched it all through the mirror. The way Daisy focused and bit her lower lip as she concentrated. Her fingers moved in a way Sammy-Jo didn't understand, because hair for her was not about style. Daisy had been right; it was protection. Her sanctuary to hide behind.

"There. Now you can ravish me." Daisy giggled. The room had filled with steam, and she thrust her hand under the water to check the temperature. Deeming it perfect, she backed her way in and stood under the water, letting it cascade over her.

Sammy-Jo frowned. "You're getting your hair wet."

"Mine won't take three hours to dry." Sammy-Jo went to speak. "Ah," Daisy said, holding a finger up. "And I'm not letting you go outside with it wet and tied up."

"You're very bossy today."

Daisy laughed. "So put me in my place."

"Jesus," Sammy-Jo muttered and moved in. "I've never met anyone like you," she said honestly, drizzling soap into her hand and lathering it up.

"Like me?"

"Yeah, just…things you say…they hit me right—"

"Right?" Daisy stepped closer and with her right hand, reached down and between Sammy-Jo's thighs, cupping her. "There?"

"Hm-hm," Sammy-Jo answered, her own hands, soapy and wet, now slathered soap up and down Daisy's back. "Right there," she said before Daisy tilted her head up and they met in a kiss.

Daisy's fingers moved slowly.

Sammy-Jo's tongue matched it right up until the moment that Daisy slid inside of her. The speed was still slow and deliberate, but it was too much for Sammy-Jo to focus and she pulled back from the kiss. They'd not done this before. It was always Sammy-Jo that used that move. She'd been a strictly outside kind of girl when it came to sex.

"Okay?" Daisy asked gently, clearly understanding that this was new.

"Yeah, I just…" She'd tensed up, she knew that, and she was grateful that Daisy noticed at least.

"At your speed, alright?"

"I don't want you to stop…but gently, alright?" Her hand moved to grip Daisy's wrist. She wasn't sure why yet, whether to take control and pull her away the minute it all became too much, or to steer her. She opened her eyes and found Daisy smiling at her and she felt suddenly safe.

"You feel so good," Daisy said and smiled again when she clearly hit the spot because despite the slow speed and the gentle movements, Sammy-Jo's hips thrust involuntarily, and she made a little gasp sound. "Like that?"

Sammy-Jo nodded. "Yeah, that's uh…okay, don't stop, okay?"

"I won't." Daisy kissed her throat.

Chapter Fifty-Seven

The drive that led away from the hotel and out onto the country lane was clear of snow. Staff had salted it the night before and again that morning, but the lane was different. Less traffic meant only two lines of clear tarmac, where other cars cut through the snow, could be navigated.

"Maybe we should just stay another night," Daisy said, looking straight ahead while Sammy-Jo concentrated.

It was barely midday and weather reports were predicting more snow later that night, but for the rest of the afternoon, it was meant to be clear.

"We'll get to the main road and see what it's like. If it looks like a mess, we can turn around and come back."

"Okay," Daisy said. She reached out and flicked the stereo on. Christmas music was still playing despite Christmas being over. "I've never driven in the snow. I mean, not when it's had a chance to lay."

"It's not fun," Sammy-Jo admitted.

Daisy smiled to herself thinking back to when they first met and the way the snow had come down. In hindsight, it was probably a good thing that her car had broken down. She hadn't had to drive in it, and she'd met the woman in the car with her, who was feeling more and more like a permanent fixture.

Had it really only been ten days? Ten amplified days; her mother was right about that. They'd spent a lot of time together in those ten days, but still it wasn't any more than a few weeks of dating equivalent, was it?

She checked her phone and noticed a text from Diana.

"Are you busy tonight?" she asked Sammy-Jo.

Sammy-Jo glanced at her quickly. "No, I don't think so."

"Diana messaged. Everyone is heading to Blanca's later. Do you fancy it?"

"Let me think. Another night hanging out with you. Dancing with you. Maybe staying over with you…hell yes, I fancy it." She laughed until the car swerved a little on an ice patch. "Shit."

Daisy reached out, her palm landing on Sammy-Jo's thigh. "That was—"

"Scary," Sammy-Jo said for them both.

They were only travelling a little over 20 mph. It felt like an eternity. The tree overhang was a saving grace with the way even the bare branches had shielded the road from a real layer of snow.

Daisy messaged back that they'd see them there.

"I don't think it's much further now till we get to the main road."

Sammy-Jo didn't answer, but she nodded, intensely focused on not crashing Nora's car.

Her phone beeped a reply.

Diana: How are things going? X

Daisy: Pretty good. We're just driving back from a romantic night away. I know it's crazy, but…she might actually be the one. X

Diana: Sometimes crazy is what we need. Honestly, if you'd met me before I met Shannon, you wouldn't recognise me. The right person is the right person. Time doesn't matter. X

Daisy: I guess so, I just don't want to be one of those cliché lesbians who U-Haul after two dates. X

Diana: Well, you'll know what is best for you. Just make sure it's your decision and nobody else's. If you want to do something crazy, do it. We only live once, Zara keeps telling me, and I hate to agree with her, but on this… I probably do. Drive safe and see you tonight. X

"Ooo I can see the road," Sammy-Jo said excitedly. Daisy looked up from her phone and watched as the end of the lane came into view and they both held their breath as the main road became visible.

"It's clear." Daisy clapped. The tarmac was shiny and wet, but the snow was gone. The road had clearly been salted by the council overnight. "So, as long as we stick to main roads and motorways, we should get home in a few hours?"

"I think so." Sammy-Jo grinned as she waited to turn into the road. "I'll take it easy though. Black ice could still be a problem."

Daisy checked her watch. It was just gone midday. "We should be home by four. Enough time to put our feet up for a bit, have something to eat and then get changed and ready to hit the dancefloor."

"Sounds like a plan to me," Sammy-Jo said, edging the car forward and into the gap created in the traffic.

A song came on that Daisy liked, and she turned it up, started singing and then eased back into her seat. She could relax now, and just enjoy the drive.

Chapter Fifty-Eight

The three-hour journey took nearer five by the time Sammy-Jo dropped Daisy off at her parents and then headed over to give the car back to Nora.

"Had a good time?" Nora asked, taking the keys from her and giving the car a cursory glance for damage.

"The car's fine," Sammy-Jo said, feeling a little irked. "And yeah, great time actually."

"Great. You coming in?"

"Uh." Sammy-Jo checked her watch. "Yeah, a quick coffee would be nice. I'm exhausted."

"Oh yeah." Nora laughed and winked and led them up the steps towards the huge door that would lead into the house.

"No, not cos of that," Sammy-Jo said, following Nora. "It's tiring driving back in snow when you're not in your own car and concentrating hard to make sure you don't crash it." She closed the door and continued talking. "It took a lot longer too, and there were a couple of accidents we had to manoeuvre past."

"Well, I'm grateful for the extra care you took with Portia."

Sammy-Jo rolled her eyes at the car's name.

"I'm grateful for you lending me it."

"Her, not it. Portia is a girl," Nora said.

"It's a car - an inanimate object," Sammy-Jo argued.

"What is?" Gabby was sitting at the island in the kitchen when they entered the room. She smiled at Sammy-Jo.

"Portia!" Nora said indignantly. "Honestly, she has no idea."

"Of course, darling," Gabby said rubbing Nora's bicep. But she winked at Sammy-Jo. "Coffee?"

"Please," Sammy-Jo said, taking a stool.

"How are things going with Daisy?" Gabby asked, as she began to fiddle and fill the contraption that would eventually produce decent coffee-shop-grade coffee.

"Really good, I think."

Nora's phone rang, and she made her excuses and left the kitchen.

"You think?" Gabby asked, turning to look at Sammy-Jo. "You looked pretty cosy last time we saw you both."

"I guess I'm positive but also prepared for it not working out."

"Why wouldn't it work out?"

Sammy-Jo shrugged. "No relationship is guaranteed, is it?"

"No, but generally most people don't get into them with the idea that it won't work out," Gabby answered, pressing a large button with a flourish and leaving the coffee maker to gurgle and produce nectar.

"I know. When I'm with her, I feel totally into it and that it will all be fine, and then the minute we're apart my brain starts finding reasons to prepare for doom."

Gabby took the stool opposite. "Are you worrying that if she leaves town, that will be it?"

Sammy-Jo nodded. "I mean, I know it's not the end of the world, but she's a 9 to 5 week and I'm busy at the weekends…so when do we see each other?" She held her hands out and blew out her cheeks. "It will fizzle out, won't it."

"Maybe…but maybe you'll communicate with each other and come up with a solution. If you really want it to work, SJ, then it will."

"I just want for once to be happy, and she's not like anyone I've ever dated before. She's so much better—" She noticed the smirk on Gabby's face, forgetting that they had dated all those years ago. "For me, she's better for me than anyone I've tried to… I've never tried to make anything work with anyone else before," she admitted. "It was always just fun, or I knew it wouldn't last, or I dunno…but this, with her, it feels so different. And it terrifies me, but at the same time it excites me beyond belief."

"I think what we have here is a severe case of Sammy-Jo's finally fallen in love."

"Is that what it is?"

Gabby laughed. "Oh, a bad case, absolutely."

"Does it ever stop being scary?"

"Yeah, it does. But probably something you might want to talk about with your therapist. Are you still seeing her?"

She nodded. "Yeah, once a month now though. I will talk to her. I feel a bit all over the place, but in a happy way and I just want to be sure that—"

"Daisy's a good person. Everyone can see that, and everyone can see how well you go together, so speak with your therapist if you need to but don't doubt yourself. This isn't a Krista rerun."

"Yeah, I know. I'm being an idiot about it."

"It's understandable. I think the thing to remember is to enjoy each day. Stop worrying about what might or might not happen. Trust yourself."

The machine beeped and Gabby got up to pour two cups of steaming coffee. "Grab the milk," she instructed, and Sammy-Jo got up and went to the fridge. "Oh, and I've put the word out for Daisy with the LBG today. Any jobs going, and she'll be the first to know."

"Really?" Sammy-Jo's eyes lit up. "That's awesome."

"For someone who has only just been introduced to people, she's already gained some friends. That says a lot about someone in my book."

"Yeah." Sammy-Jo grinned. "Yeah, it does."

Chapter Fifty-Nine

Allegra pranced around the living room singing into the TV remote in her pyjamas and dressing gown. Her wet hair was wrapped in a towel, and her face was covered in something green.

"Attractive," Sammy-Jo said, standing in the doorway laughing to herself.

"Fucking hell, SJ." Allegra gasped, hand to her chest in shock. "When did you get back?"

"Just now." Sammy-Jo shrugged and entered the room, flopping down onto the couch. "I take it John isn't here?"

"Of course he isn't, do you think I'd be wearing this if he was?" She pointed to her pyjamas, not her face.

"Yeah, that would be terrible."

Allegra sat down beside Sammy-Jo and pulled her feet up. "So, how's things with you?"

"Yeah, good. I'm really…I asked Daisy to move in with us."

Allegra's eyes widened. "Wow, okay…and she said?"

"She's thinking about it."

Allegra nodded. "I mean, it's your house, so of course. Is this you asking me to move out?"

"What? No. Why would you think that?" Sammy-Jo straightened up. "I—" She sagged again. "I should have spoken to you first, shouldn't I?"

Allegra made a face, "I mean, maybe. I don't know. I'm just your lodger so, I guess you don't need to ask me for permission, but we would all have to live together, so maybe a conversation would have been nice."

"Yeah, sorry. It wasn't something I really thought much about before I asked her."

"You don't think it's a bit quick? You barely know her."

"Yeah, you're right, it is, but I dunno, it feels right and yeah, it's scary as fuck if I'm honest, but I can't ignore how I feel."

"I'm not saying you should. Just…I worry about you, you know, after Twat Face."

"Do ya?"

Allegra kicked her. "You're like the big sister I never had, and although that makes you annoying as fuck, it means I care about you, and I want what's best for you."

Sammy-Jo felt her eyes mist up.

"Shut up, stop being nice to me."

Leaning forward to take a closer look, Allegra grinned. "Oh my God, are you tearing up?"

"No." Sammy-Jo laughed and wiped her eyes.

"You bloody are!" Allegra laughed. "I like it…'bout time the softer side of you showed up."

"I'm still a fucking machine," Sammy-Jo chuckled.

"On the pitch, you can be what you like…off it…maybe this Daisy is good for you after all."

"I know she is." Sammy-Jo bashed her own knees. "Anyway, can't sit around blithering on with you. I'm going out." She jumped up. "You wanna come?"

"Is it a date?"

"Like I'd bring you on a blooming date." She held out her hand and pulled Allegra to her feet. "It's a pre-New Year drink at Blanca's. You can meet Daisy properly."

"Oh, well now you're talking," Allegra said, pushing SJ towards the stairs. "You need a shower. I'm not being seen out with you looking like this."

"What's wrong with this?"

"Plaid. Just because the lesbians like it, doesn't mean you have to wear it."

"I like it," Sammy-Jo complained with every step she took, Allegra slapping her backside to make her move faster. "But fine, I was going to get changed anyway."

"Good. Put those skinny black jeans on, the cropped vest and the white shirt over the top. And Sammy-Jo?"

"What?" she said at the top of the stairs.

"Decent underwear, yeah?"

Chapter Sixty

"Two more nights to let our hair down and then we're back on it for the next part of the season, so stop being a Debbie Downer and enjoy yourself," Sammy-Jo overheard Jas telling Kayla outside the bar when she and Allegra arrived.

"What's the matter?" Sammy-Jo asked. It was cold, and warm air billowed like a white cloud. "Is she still moping?"

"I'm not moping. I'm allowed to be disappointed," Kayla said defiantly.

Allegra pushed Sammy-Jo out of the way and put her arm around Kayla's shoulders. "Yes, you are." She glared at the other two. "But you have to remember, we can only change the things we can control, and you can't do anything about this other than get back on that pitch and show them why they made a mistake."

"I know, and that's what I intend to do. Only everyone else thinks because I don't want to drink, it means I'm boring."

"I didn't say you were boring." Jas stepped up. "And you don't have to drink. I'm just saying you've got to put it to bed and enjoy yourself."

"Can we go inside and do this? It's bloody freezing," Sammy-Jo complained while scoping out the area for any sign of Daisy. She didn't see her, not that she was really expecting to; they were early.

Yanking the door open, she led the little group inside and up to the bar.

"Have we got seats already?" she asked Jas.

"Yeah, the rest of the gang are in the corner." Jas pointed towards a loud group, with Handsy clearly on form.

Glancing around, Sammy-Jo noticed other faces she recognised from Gabby's little circle and Daisy's new friends.

"She'll be here soon." Allegra nudged her. "You missing her already? God, you have got it bad."

"Shut up, and don't embarrass me."

"Like I would." Allegra laughed. "I mean, you do such a good job of it yourself."

Sammy-Jo laughed too.

"You've really changed, you know that, right?" Allegra said as they shuffled forward, closer to the bar but still behind several other people.

"I hope so, but I'm glad people have noticed."

"They do. And appreciate it. You're much more fun now we can take the piss out of you."

"You're such a shit."

"I know, and you love it." Allegra grabbed her cheeks and pulled her forward, planting a big kiss on her lips.

"Ew, gerroff," Sammy-Jo said just as she caught sight of something blonde heading towards her.

"What the hell?" Daisy said, poking her hard in the shoulder.

"Hey, don't poke her like that," Allegra stepped in.

"Oh, no…nope, no, no," Sammy-Jo said, grabbing each of them and putting herself in the middle. "Big misunderstanding. Do not make it into something it's not." She looked to Allegra and then Daisy. "This is my idiot flatmate, Allegra, you met her very briefly the night we—" She stopped talking. "Before… you met her before. Anyway, she's just being a dick."

Allegra shook Sammy-Jo's grip of her wrist off.

"You are a little firecracker, aren't you?" Allegra smiled at Daisy. "I'm sorry, I get a little protective over her." She held out her hand. "Nice to meet you properly, before we're all drunk."

"Oh god, I feel like such an idiot." Daisy took Allegra's hand and shook it before she turned back to Sammy-Jo. "I'm sorry, that was such a dick move. I just had a flash of Nadia, and my head went to the wrong place."

"Get me a pint, will ya?" Sammy-Jo said to Allegra, before she pulled Daisy into a hug. "Let's go outside for a minute."

"Sure," Daisy said before following Sammy-Jo.

The door opened before Sammy-Jo reached it, and in walked Nora with Gabby in tow. "Alright? Nora frowned. "You not stopping?"

"Yeah, just getting some air."

"Hi." Daisy waved over Sammy-Jo's shoulder.

"Oh, I see." Gabby winked and pulled Nora away. "Leave them be."

"I was just asking…Oh—" Was all Sammy-Jo heard from Nora before they'd stepped out into the cold and found a quiet spot overlooking the river.

"I'm really sorry. God, Allegra must think I'm a right…"

"I don't care what Allegra thinks," Sammy-Jo said. "Well, I do, but whatever it is it won't change my opinion on anything."

"Good. Because I am so—"

"Thing is Daisy, I can't do that again," Sammy-Jo interrupted. "I can't be with someone who doesn't trust me, or worse, that I can't trust."

"That's not fair, Sammy-Jo. I literally walked in to find you kissing someone."

"Yeah, and you jumped straight to the idea that I was doing the dirty."

Daisy scoffed. "And if the shoe was on the other foot, you'd be okay with that, would you?"

Sammy-Jo shrugged. "I dunno, but it wasn't the other shoe. And after everything Krista—"

“Don’t you dare put this on the same page as your psychopath ex. That’s not fair.” Daisy stamped her foot. “God, you know what, forget it. Have a good night.”

“Daisy!” Sammy-Jo called after her. “Where are you going?”

“Home. And don’t follow me!” she shouted back.

Sammy-Jo kicked the floor in frustration and watched, hands on hips, as Daisy stormed off towards the bridge.

“Everything alright?” Allegra asked sheepishly. “I didn’t think—”

“No, you didn’t, and now I’ve lost the best thing that ever happened to me.” She threw her hands up. “Thanks a bunch, Leggy.”

“Great,” Allegra said to herself, watching Sammy-Jo storm into the pub in one direction, and turning to see Daisy already on the other side of the embankment, head down, hands thrust into her pockets.

Chapter Sixty-One

New Year's Eve

Allegra chewed on a nail as she stared out of the living room window at two kids kicking a ball through the slush. Sammy-Jo was still in bed, where she assumed she might stay for a few more hours, given the state of her the night before - for which Allegra felt guilty.

"How was I to know Daisy's ex had cheated, or even know she would walk into the pub right that second?" she said to John. He sat on the sofa listening. "And now, Sammy-Jo hates me—"

"She doesn't hate you," he said. "She's just Sammy-Jo; this is her default setting when things go wrong in her life."

Allegra turned to face him and smiled. "You're not wrong there. But even so, she was doing so well with all the therapy and stuff and along came Daisy and gave Sammy-Jo an opportunity, and I've gone and ruined it."

"You didn't ruin anything. You said yourself, they barely know each other. Maybe this is what they needed…a little pin to burst the bubble." He got up and walked over to her, wrapping his arms around her. "This is how they will know if it's right or not."

"I guess so. I just hate seeing her like that."

"No, it wasn't pretty, and I'm glad you called me to help. I'm not sure you'd have managed on your own. She's quite belligerent when she doesn't want to do something." He grinned.

"I'm just glad we got her out before anyone else noticed, or she made a complete tit of herself. No way am I letting her do a rerun of last Christmas."

"Ah, the dreadful ex and her plot to bring down Brady. All very *Eastenders*." John kissed the top of her head. "She's lucky to have a friend like you."

Creaky floorboards above alerted them to the fact that Sammy-Jo was up, and they both listened for further sounds of movement. A *thud, thud, thud*, repeated and then the living room door opened, and Sammy-Jo stood in the doorway grimacing, hair like a rat's nest. It was a good job that she rarely wore make-up because no doubt it would be smeared all over her face.

The silence was palpable, a standoff where nobody seemed to know what to say. At any other time, one of them would make a joke, or Allegra would say something like, "Look at the state of her." But it didn't feel appropriate. Not if she was going to salvage their friendship.

So, she was surprised when Sammy-Jo mumbled, "Sorry." She ran her hand through her mane and muttered an expletive when her fingers got caught. "Last night, I went too far and had too much to drink and probably took everything out on you. So, I'm sorry if I said or did anything—"

"You didn't," Allegra said quickly. "I mean you were a total arsehole but…nothing that I'd hold against you."

Sammy-Jo looked away. "Okay, well, I'm just getting some water and then I'm going back to bed."

"Alright. Shall I wake you up later? We can get ready tog—"

"Nah, I'm not going. I'll just be miserable, and we don't need me fucking it all up two years running," she said. "But thanks though." She turned to go back into the hall and into the kitchen.

"SJ?" Allegra called out. "Why don't you…just call her? I'm sure you can work it out."

"She doesn't trust me, Legs."

"So, what that's it? You're breaking up?"

Sammy-Jo shrugged. "I don't think we were ever together, were we? It's a fling, that's all."

"Yesterday, you wanted her to move in," Allegra said, inching closer.

"Yeah," Sammy-Jo said sadly, her eyes misting up. "I'm going back to bed."

Chapter Sixty-Two

Eileen watched her eldest shuffle into the kitchen. She sipped her tea as Daisy opened the bread bin and pulled two slices from the bag, popping them into the toaster.

"Do you want to talk about it now?"

Daisy glanced over her shoulder at her mother before grunting, "Nope."

"Alright, well, you'd better shake yourself out of that mood then, young lady, because nobody is walking around on tippy toes to avoid your wrath."

"I don't have—" Daisy pressed her lips together and breathed through her nose until the anger passed. And then she burst into tears.

"Oh, sweetheart, whatever is wrong?" Eileen said, putting her cup down and pulling the chair next to her out. "Come and sit down."

Daisy didn't argue. She left the toast and dropped into the seat, instantly hugged.

"She dumped me."

"Who? SJ? Whatever for?" Eileen asked, kissing Daisy's head. She rubbed comforting circles on her back, just like she'd done when she was little and someone had upset her.

Rubbing her eyes dry, Daisy sat up. "I walked into the pub and there was some woman kissing her."

"You what?" Eileen felt her own anger burn.

"No, it wasn't like that, but I thought it was, and I got mad and accused her or…" She shook her head. "I don't remember what I said, but then the woman started to get arsey and Sammy-Jo stepped in between us and explained it was just her flatmate, Allegra, and of course, the minute she said it, I remembered from before when—"

"Take a breath, sweetheart."

Daisy sighed. "We went outside, and I apologised for getting the wrong end of the stick. After Nadia and all the cheating with her, I just… I panicked I guess…"

"That's understandable; surely Sammy-Jo could work that out."

"Clearly not, because she said she couldn't do this again. She couldn't be with someone who didn't trust her, and after everything Krista had done…and then I got mad, because how dare she compare me to that, to her, this woman who tried to kill her friend?"

"Well, no. Nobody would want that."

"Right?" Daisy rubbed her face out of frustration. "So, I left, I came home and well, that's it." She sniffed. "Diana texted and said Sammy-Jo got really drunk, and Allegra had to call her boyfriend to help take her home."

The toaster popped.

"Sounds to me like both of you got triggered and reacted badly. Have you called her this morning?"

"No, why would I?"

Eileen smiled. "Because you like her, and yesterday you were all for making it work, and now you've had your first argument. This is all fixable, if you want it to be."

"I'm not the one who ended it. I'll be damned if I'm going to chase around after her."

"I'm not saying you should chase after her. I'm saying, have a really long think about things before you bang a final nail in. Relationships take hard work and commitment to fix them. We can all take space, and we can all blow up now and then, but if it's real between you, then you'll have to work it out."

Daisy huffed. "I know, but can't I just be a selfish brat for a few hours? I'm angry still, and I don't want to take that into a conversation. That's if she'll even talk to me."

"She will."

"How can you be so sure?"

"Alright, put it this way. If she won't, then you know this will never work and you can go home tomorrow and back to your life and forget all about her."

"And if she does?"

"Then maybe she is the one you hope she is." She patted Daisy's knee. "Now, eat your toast, and then we have a buffet to make."

Chapter Sixty-Three

Sammy-Jo kicked off the covers and dragged herself out of bed and back down the stairs. She'd heard the door shut and knew Allegra had left to go to the party.

In a pair of comfy sweatpants and a jumper, she switched the TV on and then her games console. This was all she needed, she'd decided. A quiet night in front of the TV with the Xbox and a cup of tea.

Wandering into the kitchen, she found a note from Allegra.

Left you some dinner in the microwave.

If you change your mind, you know where we are.

Leggy.

P.S. stop being an idiot and change your mind.

She smiled as she read it. It was gone eight p.m. already. She could just go upstairs and get changed and turn up, but then a flash of the previous year popped into her head.

"Come on, fuck it, let's just go," Krista urged. "What are they going to say? It's your club."

"Nothing. I'm the captain; I can bring who I like. I can do what I want."

"So, let's go…or – no… doesn't matter," Krista had said, smiling sadly.

"What?"

"It's just…I wondered if maybe you…" Her eyes misted over. "Maybe you're ashamed of me?"

"No, course not." She moved quickly and pulled Krista close. "You really want to go?" A firm nodding answered. "I mean, we're already drunk. We'll have to get a cab."

"Just drive, it will be fine."

"Are you mad?" SJ slurred. "Get a cab." She swigged once more from the vodka bottle. "Or stay in."

"No, come on. You're Sammy-Jo Costa, remember? This is your team, and they're taking it all away from you. You need to show them. You trust me, right?"

"Yeah, bloody Nora Brady ruining everything."

Sammy-Jo cringed at what had followed.

To this day, she swore Krista had put something in her drink when she wasn't looking. She'd never been that off her face in her life. Even last night's drunkenness had been nothing like the way she was that night with Krista.

She'd trusted her.

At the time, there was something of a camaraderie about her. The way she'd soothe Sammy-Jo's ego and encourage the bitterness to build. All of her worries and concerns around football, and Nora, and Gabby were being heard.

For a long while, Sammy-Jo had hated herself, hated the way she'd been so easily manipulated, but Gabby had been right; therapy had been what she'd needed and now, a whole year later, she finally felt in control of her life.

She thumped the cushion.

Why couldn't she just meet someone and be happy like everyone else managed to do?

She liked Daisy, and for the first time in that year, she'd let someone get under her skin.

The TV flickered and she picked up the remote to turn it off.

"Stop being ridiculous," she told herself. "You're not going to sit here moping; that's old SJ."

The twins ran around the room like whirlwinds, dancing to the playlist they'd helped their dad create over the last few weeks. That was the planning that had gone into this one night.

People chatted and laughed and shimmied their hips in every corner of the room, hallway, and kitchen.

"I didn't know you had so many friends," Daisy said, squeezing into the space beside her mum at the kitchen table that was holding all of the food for the buffet.

"Oh, thought it was only you who made friends quickly." Her mum laughed and nudged her. "Where do you think you get it from?"

Daisy smiled as best as she could considering she felt so miserable still. "True, and just so you know, I could have been at various other parties. You're lucky I chose yours."

"So lucky." Eileen laughed and picked up a triangle of sandwich. "Are you okay?"

"Yeah, I guess so. I kind of hoped she'd have called or texted, but…" She shrugged.

"You could call her? Invite her over?"

"Nah, she's got her work thing. The women's team have their Christmas party at New Year, so, it's a big deal and last year was…" She scrunched her mouth. "It was an event Sammy-Jo regrets, so…she needs that."

"Fair enough." Eileen passed her a plate. "Get something to eat."

"Yes, Mum." Daisy laughed. Her attention went to someone entering the room. Bill.

"Hey Daisy, I should have the car done for you in the morning."

"Really? That would be awesome, thanks Bill."

"Yeah, it's a simple enough job. The part came in this morning, and I picked it up earlier. You'll be glad to have it back I imagine."

Daisy smiled. "Yeah, I need to get home so I can…" She glanced at her mum for her reaction. "Organise moving…here."

Eileen was about to pop a pickled onion into her mouth and stopped midair. “Here?”

“If the offer is still open. I figured there are worse places to be, and whether I have a job or not, I’ll get one, and I like it here. I can see why you moved.”

“That’s—”

“Daisy’s moving home?” Dolly said from out of nowhere.

“She is?” Polly said, her head popping out from under the table.

“How did you get there? You were both dancing a moment ago.” Daisy laughed at them.

“We’re sneaky,” Polly admitted. “Is it true though?”

“Yeah, I think so. I need to go and sort out my flat and pack my things, hand my notice in and stuff—”

“This is awesome!” Dolly shouted, before running off to tell their dad.

Eileen hugged Daisy close. “Go and find Sammy-Jo. Tell her, fix it before it’s too late.”

Daisy shook her head. “I can’t. It’s at the training ground and I can’t just walk in.”

Bill put his hand up. “Actually…” Daisy stared at him and waited. “There’s a hole in the fence where some of the kids go and sneak in.”

“Is that legal? I’d be trespassing,” Daisy said, looking a little unsure until she looked at Eileen’s face. “Okay, fine, but if I’m arrested, you’re bailing me out.”

Chapter Sixty-Four

Stomping down the road, Sammy-Jo wished she'd added an extra layer, and bought better gloves. The wind chill was murderous. However, the adrenaline pushed her onwards and when she finally got there, she stood outside and re-thought her decision.

Music blared out and she could see lots of people moving about inside. The Christmas tree was lit up still and twinkling in the background, but the steamed-up windows made it difficult to pinpoint anyone familiar.

What if Daisy didn't want to see her?

Then you'll know and can move on, she told herself but still hesitated. It was just a stupid misunderstanding. If they couldn't work this out, then there wasn't any point anyway, was there?

She walked up to the door and raised a hand to grab the knocker, but her gloves were too bulky.

"For fuck's sake," she mumbled and shoved the fingertips of one glove into her mouth to pull her hand free. This time, she grabbed the knocker and knocked on the door with it three times.

Nobody answered.

She moved across to the window and tried to look in, get someone's attention, but it was too steamed up and the music was loud. Despite that, she knocked on the window.

Nothing.

"Damn it."

Rubbing her hands together, she went back to the door and tried again. This time, it opened.

"Oh, hey. I'm looking for Daisy," she said to the man holding the door with one hand and a can of lager with the other.

"Daisy?"

"Yes, Daisy, she lives here," Sammy-Jo said, trying to look past him.

"Nah, I think she went out. Try the pub." Someone shouted at him to stop letting the cold in and he closed the door before Sammy-Jo could ask which pub.

"Charming!" Sammy-Jo said, turning on her heel. "The pub?"

The idea that Daisy had left her mum's party when she'd made such a big deal about it didn't sit right, but what else did she have to go on?

She pulled her glove back on and got moving.

"Bill, what if we get caught?" Daisy whispered. The pair of them, and her dad, were hunkered down in some bushes at the far end of the complex.

"We won't."

"You might," her dad said, chuckling. "But we won't. And anyway, that's the fun of it."

"Not helping." Daisy punched him playfully.

"The worst that will happen is you'll get chucked out, but the likelihood is, you'll be able to ask for Sammy-Jo and hopefully, she'll get wind you're there and come to your rescue and you'll find each other," Bill said.

"Who knew you were such a romantic, Bill." Daisy laughed.

Bill blushed and pulled her arm. "Come on, we have to find the gap."

They all shuffled along, bent over and mumbling to themselves about branches hitting and scratching them, catching on clothes and dumping large piles of snow on top of them.

"Seriously, if she won't speak to me after this, then…"

"Here it is," Bill said, reaching for the fence.

"You sure you wanna do this?" her dad said, taking hold of one side of the wire fence while Bill pulled the other to create a hole as big as it could get.

Daisy nodded. "Yeah, what have I got to lose?"

"Ya freedom." Bill laughed.

Rolling her eyes, Daisy stepped through the gap. Her coat caught on a loose wire. She moved back and shrugged her coat off, throwing it through.

"Okay, wish me luck."

"Good luck," they both said in unison.

Ahead of her was a pitch, at least she assumed it was. It was a wide expanse of space with a completely untouched carpet of white snow still covering it. Netless goalposts stood to one side. Looming in the distance was a white building, all dark but for a few windows near the bottom.

The entire area was lit up by bright lights around the building that bounced off of the snow and would light her up like a beacon in her red jacket.

Probably should have considered that, she thought.

"Stick to the sides," Bill said in a loud enough whisper. She glanced back and saw the pair of them watching her. They both held their thumbs up.

"Right," she told herself. "Let's do this."

With just a hint of nerves tumbling around in her tummy, she started to move quickly, hunched over, keeping to the hedges that lined the fence. She had a couple of hundred yards to go until she reached the cover of a smaller structure where she could rest and take stock of her surroundings.

Ahead, she could see the car park through the gap. Several cars were parked up and more arriving. She ducked down out of the line of headlights that swung around and would have lit her up had she stepped out.

"It's like being James Bond." She giggled. The thrill of it all was starting to make it fun.

She poked her head around the edge of the building and saw that the coast was clear for her to dart across the open space towards the main building.

"So, far, so good."

The sound of two people talking made her stop in her tracks. Back pressed up against the wall, she looked like a target for a firing squad.

"Is she okay though?" one voice asked.

"Yeah, you know how it is. Just wants a bit of quiet time."

"I guess. We should check on her tomorrow though, right?"

"I'm sure she'd like that," the second voice assured. "We better get back inside. They'll have the search party out otherwise."

Daisy counted to twenty, and then slid around the corner. There was nobody else around, so she shrugged off her coat once more and pushed it into the corner before taking a breath and stepping into the foyer through the main doors.

A huge 'Welcome to Bath Street' sign was lit up across the reception area. Catching a glimpse of herself, she smiled and tried to look confident. She was dressed for a party, all she had to do was follow the music and—

"Can I help you?" a voice from behind said. "You look a little lost."

Daisy held her breath before turning around and smiling at the unfamiliar face.

"Hi, yes, I was looking for the loos, Sammy-Jo said they were this way but…" She held her hands out and played innocent.

"Sammy-Jo said?" The woman was about Daisy's age. She had a slight accent, Scandinavian maybe.

"Yes, I'm Daisy, her plus one."

The woman nodded, but still looked at her curiously. "We didn't think SJ was coming. She told Allegra she was staying at home."

Daisy felt the panic rush through her. Not quite so thrilling to be breaking in here if Sammy-Jo was absent. And why was she not here?

"Oh I—"

"Everything alright?" asked another voice, one that sounded vaguely familiar. Daisy winced as she spun around and found herself face to face with Sammy-Jo's flatmate. "Daisy?"

"Allegra, hi." Daisy waved half-heartedly as she recognised one of the voices from outside a moment ago.

Allegra looked at the other woman. "It's okay Astrid, I've got it."

They both watched as the tall blonde walked away without a backwards glance.

"So…" Allegra said, closing the space between them. "You're here with SJ?"

Daisy pushed her tongue into her cheek before saying, "You know that I'm not, but I'd like to speak to her, if that's possible."

"Unfortunately, she's not here."

Now the conversation outside made sense, Daisy thought. "Where is she?"

"At home, as far as I am aware," Allegra answered. "Why do you want to see her?"

"Does it matter?" Daisy said. She felt a little defensive standing here, caught and embarrassed.

Allegra moved around her and blocked any thoughts of a quick escape. "I think so. She's very…she liked you a lot, and now she's licking her wounds and that concerns me."

"I just want to talk to her, that's all." Daisy relaxed a little. "It's all just a silly misunderstanding and I want to fix it."

Allegra nodded. "I get it, I do. But you have to understand just how hurt she is."

"I know and I—"

"Not by you," Allegra said quickly. "You have no clue what the impact was when Krista did what she did. The impact it had on Sammy-Jo. She's not over that. She thinks she is, but really, this…" She waved her hand a Daisy. "This isn't an argument at all really; it's about trust."

"I know and I do trust her," Daisy said.

"But she doesn't trust herself," Allegra pointed out. "She doesn't trust herself to pick a girl who will just love her." Allegra smiled. "She puts on this big brave mask, the inflated ego comes into play, and nothing bothers SJ Costa. But the reality is, she's terrified that she will let you in and you'll just leave the moment it gets difficult with her, because it will. She still has shit to fix."

"I didn't realise." Daisy shrank down, shoulders sagging.

"Well, you wouldn't. You've only known her what? A week?"

"A bit longer, but I get your point." Daisy chewed her lip. "But I want to talk to her still. It's the right thing to do, isn't it?"

Allegra smiled. "She's at home." She stepped aside so that Daisy could pass. "Oh, and Daisy?"

"Yes?"

"Do not hurt her. Fix it, or leave, but don't do it unkindly, or unfairly. She doesn't deserve any more shit."

"I have no intention of hurting her."

"Good, because if you end up moving in, I'd prefer it if we were friends." Allegra smiled. "I'll order you a cab. Wait here."

Chapter Sixty-Five

It was quicker to go to Blanca's first and see if Daisy was there before heading over to Art.

Arriving at the bar, she was hot underneath the layers and the moment she set foot inside, she began peeling them off.

Blanca's was packed, as she expected it would be. Glancing around, she noticed a few familiar faces, but nobody that she thought Daisy would be out with.

Checking her watch, she noticed that it was just after 9 p.m. Relatively early in the New Year's Eve party celebrating.

She made a decision. Have a pint here and wait to see if Daisy turned up. If she wasn't here by ten, she'd go over to Art and find her there.

Simple.

Except for the part where she had to push her way to the bar and wave a tenner in her hand until someone noticed her and poured her a pint.

"Is Sadie working?" she asked the girl behind the bar. She'd probably have noticed if Daisy had come in.

"No," she said, shaking her head. "She's gone to a party with Natalie."

"Oh, okay, never mind then." She handed over her money and took the drink, sipping it while she waited for her change.

She noticed a girl staring at her from across the room, the slow smile creeping onto her face as she looked Sammy-Jo up and down, and then the confident bravado as she pushed off from the wall and made her way over.

"Alright?" she asked.

"Great, thanks," Sammy-Jo answered, aware this was about to become a little awkward. "I'm seeing someone." She blurted before the girl could say anything more.

"Cool." She held her hands up and backed away a couple of steps. "Shame though, you're hot."

"Uh, thanks." Sammy-Jo felt the blood rush to her cheeks. "Have a good night."

"I will. Come find me if she doesn't show up." She winked and then turned away, heading back to her spot against the wall.

Sammy-Jo slid her hand into her pocket for her phone, deciding it was probably easier to just message Daisy and avoid any other potential misunderstandings between them.

"Shit."

Her pocket was empty. She had a minute of panic, patting down all of her pockets, and then she had a vision of her phone on the cabinet charging in the living room.

"For fuck's sake," she mumbled and downed the rest of her drink. "You're an idiot."

Daisy gave the cab driver Sammy-Jo's address and sat back in her seat, slowly warming up. Now the adrenaline had subsided, she'd realised how cold it was and silently prayed there wouldn't be any more snow.

With her car fixed, she had every intention of getting back to her flat tomorrow so she could go to work on the second and tell Stella she was quitting, and then she could start packing up her flat and organising storage.

She smiled to herself.

Everyone had been right; moving here would be the best thing she could do. She'd have her parents for support, and she'd see more of the twins and get to be a proper big sister. She'd find a job eventually, and if things went the way she hoped, she'd have Sammy-Jo to enjoy it all with. If it didn't, well, she still had her budding new friendships all over town. Living here would be great for someone like Daisy.

The car took turning after turning, over the bridge out of Bath Street and into Amberfield, and then they were passing her mum and dad's house.

"Anywhere along here will do," she said, leaning forward and pointing to the part of the street where Sammy-Jo lived.

The car pulled over and she held out her card to tap on the payment machine.

"Have a good night," the driver said.

"Thank you."

The door closed with a heavy slam behind her, and she looked along the quiet road. Nobody was around. Hardly surprising, she thought. It was party season, or pub night, or cosy on the sofa indoors night, not out on the street in the freezing cold.

The cab drove away, and she walked the few feet to Sammy-Jo's gate and pushed it open, rehearsing in her head what she planned to say when Sammy-Jo opened the door.

She did a *tap-tappity-tap* on the window and waited.

And waited.

It was dark inside, but that didn't mean anything. The lounge was towards the back of the house. With the door closed, you wouldn't see any light or hear a TV.

She rapped her knuckles again.

Still nothing.

Bending down, she pushed the letterbox open and called out. "SJ?"

Silence. No movement. She knocked again.

"SJ, please don't ignore me. I just want to talk."

Nothing.

“This is ridiculous,” Daisy mumbled to herself. If Allegra was telling the truth, then Sammy-Jo was at home, but it sure didn’t seem like she was.

She pulled her phone from her pocket and rang Sammy-Jo. The tinny sound of it ringing came from inside.

Daisy bent down again and peered through the letter box. The ringing was a little louder.

“Sammy-Jo Costa, I can hear your phone ringing, I know you’re in there. Will you please answer the door?”

Chapter Sixty-Six

At ten exactly, Sammy-Jo gave up on the idea that Daisy was coming to Blanca's. More people had arrived, but none of them had been Daisy or any of the new friends she was hanging out with lately.

Sammy-Jo heaved her coat back on and stepped out and back into the cold night air, never more grateful for the woolly hat she pulled onto her head.

It was probably a good 15-minute walk to get to Art if she was taking a fast pace, which she was. She could have jogged it, but the idea of sweating under these layers didn't sit right, and she wasn't wearing the right clothes and shoes, so a fast walk would have to do.

Of course, she thought, there was no rule that said Daisy would only be in a gay bar. She could have gone to any of the pubs in the area, although it still didn't make any sense.

Daisy had been absolute in her need to attend her mum's big party. Why would she leave to go to the pub? And who with? That was the question Sammy-Jo was trying not to focus on too much.

It was an old thought pattern, one she was trying not to get stuck in again. Daisy had done nothing to suggest she would be the kind of girl who jumped from one fire to another.

They'd only argued last night; there was no way Daisy was on a date with anyone else, Sammy-Jo was sure of that. But her brain still tried to tell her otherwise.

"Ruminating over things we can't control, or we have no proof of, will only create a fantasy response, whether that's positive or negative, Sammy-Jo."

She could hear her therapist's voice clearly in her mind.

Dodging a group of people all a little worse for wear but happy and loud, Sammy-Jo grinned as she stepped into the road, and almost got hit by a car.

"Shit," she said, quickly stepping back. "Focus on getting there in one piece and not getting killed." She laughed at herself but felt the adrenaline rush the near miss had caused.

Finally, she rounded the corner and there was Art. People were spewing out onto the road outside with plastic cups and cigarettes in hand.

She squeezed through the throng and the door opened as someone was coming out. She slipped inside and took a good look around.

Art was smaller than Blanca's in square feet, which made it feel even more packed as she tried to see over the tops of heads if Daisy was there, or at least any of her friends.

Pushing through the crowd, she was pretty sure she wasn't upstairs, which meant attempting to get down the narrow staircase that already had several people on their way up.

Waiting patiently wasn't one of Sammy-Jo's strong points in a normal situation, but trying to locate Daisy just aggravated it more and in the end, she gave up being polite and when the next space opened, she moved quickly down the stairs and forced those at the bottom to back up and let her through.

She spotted a blonde in the corner, and breathed a sigh of relief. She was pretty sure it was Diana.

"Diana?" she called out, but the music was too loud, and the woman continued to dance, unaware that anyone was shouting at her. "Diana?" Sammy-Jo said again as she inched towards her.

It was only when she was a mere three feet away that someone pointed to Sammy-Jo and Diana spun around.

"Hey, Sammy-Jo, right?" Diana said, leaning in closer and raising her voice. "Happy New Year." She looked behind SJ, and then she said something that made Sammy-Jo's heart sink. "Is Daisy with you?"

"No," Sammy-Jo said, shaking her head. "I was hoping I'd find her here."

"Oh, no, she told me she was going to be at her parents'."

"Yeah, I went there, and someone said she'd left and gone to the pub."

Diana looked perplexed. "That's weird. Maybe she went to Blanca's?"

Sammy-Jo shook her head again, worry beginning to creep in. "No, she's not there."

Diana pulled her phone free and sent Daisy a text.

Diana: Where are you?

Chapter Sixty-Seven

Daisy's phone pinged and she swiped the screen, instantly expecting it to be Sammy-Jo.

It wasn't, it was just Diana. She could read the message without opening it fully and pushed the phone back into her pocket. Diana could wait until later. She knew Daisy wasn't coming out tonight.

She gave it one last try and banged on Sammy-Jo's door as loudly as she could.

"Oi." A man's voice came from the left of her. "Will you stop banging and shouting? She's not in."

Daisy turned to find an older man with greying hair and matching trousers with a red jumper on. His cheeks were crimson, and he was glaring at her from next door. The grumpy neighbour.

"Sorry," Daisy said. "I'm just trying to get hold of Sammy-Jo."

"Well, she's not in, is she?" he said, looking at her as though she were dim. "She went out, about two hours ago."

Daisy wondered how he knew that, but then she noticed the gap in the curtains of his living room.

"Oh, right, well then, I guess I'll go. I'm sorry for bothering you."

His response was a grunt, and then he walked inside and shut his front door, leaving Daisy with more questions than she had answers for.

Maybe she's gone to the party after all, and you've missed each other, she thought to herself. *But then Allegra would have told her that I'd come looking for her and she'd have called me. Unless she really doesn't want to speak to me, and we really are over.*

She turned onto the street and began the short walk back to her parents', eyes scanning every potential person walking in her direction, but none of them looked like they'd be Sammy-Jo.

It wasn't long before she was walking up the path and putting her key into the door. The sound of music and laughter did little to lift her spirits, but she plastered a smile on her face anyway.

"Hey, Daisy," her mum said a little loudly, clearly a lot more drunk. Daisy giggled to herself; it was good to see her parents let their hair down. "Did you find her?" Eileen asked.

"No, she didn't go to the party," Daisy said forlornly and reached for an egg mayonnaise filled vol-au-vont. She nibbled the edge.

"Oh, that's—"

"Allegra said she'd stayed at home and called me a taxi and I went there, but she wasn't at home either. So…" She shrugged. "I guess she found something to entertain her."

"Aw, sweetie, I am sorry." Eileen hugged her. "But you know what? You're here, with family, and that's what matters. And in…" She squinted to see her watch. "Thirty-five minutes, it's a new year and everything re-sets. It's a go-again moment, and that's what you're going to do."

Daisy smiled. "Yeah, I know. Pick myself up, dust myself down…"

"Re-adjust that princess crown," Eileen finished off the saying she'd said throughout Daisy's childhood whenever anything had gone wrong.

"I will. I just…I'm gutted. I could kick myself for reacting the way that I did."

"We all have things we wish we'd done differently. Tomorrow, you're going to go home and kick-start the next chapter, and I'm going to get your dad organising that spare room a little better. Maybe a lick of paint."

"Sounds good, as long as it isn't pink."

"No pink. I'll make sure." Eileen grinned. "Oh, I can't wait to have you home again."

Diana had dragged her group through the motions of several Steps songs that had been spliced together by the DJ.

In all honesty, Sammy-Jo had to admit they were a fun bunch, and she could see why and how Daisy had befriended them all so easily.

Thinking of Daisy made her feel sad again. Where was she? And why hadn't she answered Diana's text?

It was a quarter to midnight.

Grabbing her coat, she made her way across to Diana.

"I'm going to get going. Happy New Year."

"Oh, you should stay," Diana slurred a little. The cocktails were definitely flowing. "At least stay till the bong goes?"

Sammy-Jo laughed at that. "I just think if I head off now, I might get a cab. Save me walking home."

"I can get you a lift when Mum and Scarlett pick us up. They've gone to a party with Natalie and Sadie," she explained.

Sammy-Jo was vaguely aware of these people, but she didn't want to be a burden to them, especially on the busiest night of the year.

"Seriously, I'll be fine. But thanks. Enjoy the rest of the night." She backed away before Diana could stop her, and this time when she came to the stairs, she didn't give anyone at the top an opportunity to come down before she was bounding up them, pushing her way through the bar and spilling out onto the street.

Feeling the urge to cry, she kept moving, going as fast as she could and fighting the overwhelming feelings that were building up. She couldn't cry, not on New Year's Eve; it was bad luck.

And her luck was bad enough right now.

Chapter Sixty-Eight

New Year's Day

In the end, Daisy had enjoyed the party. She'd made the decision that there was nothing much else she could do right now, that Sammy-Jo would contact her when she was ready, and she was okay with that.

She'd consumed several glasses of rum and Coke, and it was almost four in the morning when she finally fell into bed just a little worse for wear.

Waking up, her head pounded just enough that she knew paracetamols would be required and several coffees. She was thankful that the twins hadn't woken her any earlier.

"Oh, you're up." Eileen grinned. "Was just going to send the girls up to terrorise you. Bill has finished the car, and ya breakfast will be ready in five minutes."

Daisy looked at the clock; it was almost midday. "Blimey, I didn't intend to sleep this late."

"You didn't intend to drink that much either," her dad said, entering the kitchen with two empty mugs. "Bill said to tell you that you'll need a couple of new tyres pretty soon."

"Ugh, it's one thing after another. I might just sell her when I get back here. I can walk into town or get a bus."

"You could do that." Eileen smiled. "I still can't believe you're going to be moving home." She passed Daisy a mug of coffee.

"Don't get too excited. Once I'm on my feet again, I'll be finding my own place. But yeah…I'm looking forward to some home-cooked dinners again." She took a sip of her coffee and winced at the heat, blowing it a few more times.

"Gladly. Now, what time are you off?"

"I'll have breakfast." She yawned. "And then I'll grab a shower and set off. I might as well leave my things here. No point taking them home just to bring them back again."

"That's a good idea," Eileen answered and caught the slice of toast that popped up a little too quickly. She placed it and the three other slices onto a plate and placed them on the table, following it up with a bowl of beans and some grated cheese. "Best cure for a hangover."

The house was silent. Allegra was at John's, and Sammy-Jo had no reason to get up, so she flicked the TV on and watched the usual New Year's Day rubbish.

She dozed on and off until her stomach grumbled, and she knew she needed food. The kebab she'd got on the way home had been huge, and half of it was still in the fridge. All she had to do was warm it up in the oven while she made a cup of tea and grabbed a shower.

When she got downstairs, she reminded herself that she was a professional athlete and maybe, just maybe, eggs would be a better option.

It was midday. An omelette would work, she thought and moved around the kitchen finding her ingredients. She had everything frying up nicely in the pan when she remembered her phone and went to check it for messages.

She didn't get any further than one missed call.

The previous night, from Daisy.

"Fuck," she said, feeling the sensations of panic, fear and excitement, all rapidly move through her. She quickly pressed the call button and listened.

"I'm sorry, your call cannot be taken right now."

"Damn it." She disconnected and turned the hob off, running up the stairs and into the bathroom, her phone and the messages from Allegra forgotten.

She switched the shower on and stripped off while the water warmed up and then she was about to jump in when she remembered her hair. No way was she getting that wet.

With barely a soaking, she was washed and out again in less than a minute, towel drying as she crossed the hallway and started pulling on clean clothes, and then she was out the door.

Before she'd reached the end of the path, her neighbour, Mr Willis, shouted his usual greeting.

"Oi, tell your mates to keep it down."

"Happy New Year to you too, Mr Willis," she said, pulling the gate open. As she closed it, she looked up at him. "What mates?"

"Last night, banging on your door and shouting through the letterbox, bloody racket. I told her to keep it down."

"Who, what did she look like?"

"I dunno, a girl. Blonde hair."

"Daisy!" She grinned and set off without a backward glance at Mr Willis.

Chapter Sixty-Nine

"Daisy!" Sammy-Jo shouted as her fist banged on the door loud enough to wake half the street from their hangovers.

The door opened and Dolly, or it could have been Polly, looked up at her with wide eyes.

"Hey, is Daisy here?"

"Nope," the kid said with a shake of her head.

"Sammy-Jo, is that you?" Eileen asked. Coming to the door, she shooed the kids away. "Daisy isn't here."

"What? Where…I mean…she's—" Sammy-Jo twisted one way and then the other, her hand on her head, trying to understand. "But last night…she came to my place."

"I know, and you wouldn't let her in."

"No, no." Sammy-Jo shook her head. "No, I wasn't home. I came here."

Eileen frowned. "Come inside. I'll make a cup of tea while we talk."

"I need to—"

"Sammy-Jo, come inside."

Her shoulders sagged, and she huffed, but did as she was told and stepped into the warmth.

"You can take your coat off."

Once again, she did as she was instructed and shrugged off her coat, before following Eileen into the kitchen.

"Sit yourself down and tell me what you think has happened."

"We had an argument—"

"I know that bit," Eileen said without any judgement. She just continued to make the tea.

"So, last night I was supposed to go to my club's Christmas party, but I wasn't in the mood, and I stayed at home. And then I kind of thought, 'this is silly, I like Daisy,' and so…I got dressed and I came here to talk to her."

"You came here?"

"Yes." SJ nodded. "It took ages for someone to open the door and then when they did, I asked for Daisy, but they said she'd gone out. I asked where and they just shrugged and said the pub."

"The pub?" Eileen's face scrunched up. "Why would they say that?"

Sammy-Jo shrugged. "I don't know, but I figured okay, I'll go and find her."

"Why didn't you just call her?"

"I left my phone at home," Sammy-Jo admitted sheepishly. "So, I went to Blanca's, but she wasn't there. I waited an hour, and she didn't come, so I left and walked into town to Art. She wasn't there, but her friends were, and Diana sent a message, but Daisy never answered. In the end I just went home. Then just now I finally looked at my phone and saw she'd tried to call me, and Mr Willis said someone was banging on my door, so…"

Eileen chuckled. "Honestly, it's like a comedy sketch show." She passed Sammy-Jo a mug of tea. "Daisy went to find you."

"She did?"

"Yep." Eileen took a seat at the table. "She went to the party, but you weren't there, so she went to your place because your flatmate said you were there, only you weren't there because you were out looking for her."

"Oh god, I need to speak to her but her phone's off."

"If she's driving, then she has it switched off, plus it was dead this morning and she's charging it on the way—"

"So, she's gone?"

"She's gone, yes. Bill fixed the car this morning and so—"

"I need to speak to her. Not on the phone, I need to say what I have to say in person."

Eileen sighed, got up and opened a drawer. She found a notebook and a pen and scribbled something down.

"Finish your tea, and then—" She passed the note. "That's her address."

Sammy-Jo went to stand up.

"I said, finish your tea first. You need to calm down and have a plan. How are you going to get there?"

"I'll—" She sat down and slumped in the chair. "Nora, I'll ask Nora if I can borrow her car again."

"Okay, and you'll need some clothes packed, because no doubt you'll be staying the night, and Daisy has work in the morning so—"

"Yes, okay, I can… You're right."

"I usually am. You'll get used to that." Eileen smiled at her, and for the first time in the last 48 hours, Sammy-Jo felt herself relax.

Chapter Seventy

"You might as well buy it at this rate," Nora said, handing over the keys. "When are you coming back?"

"I'll be two days tops. Sunday at the latest."

"Sunday? It's Thursday." Nora's vocal pitch raised.

"Oh, don't be such a grump," Gabby said, walking up behind her wife. "You're a huge cog in this romance; don't spoil it." She kissed Nora's cheek.

"I guess, when you put it like that," Nora answered. "But remember that when I take your car, and you have to get a taxi."

"Darling, I don't do taxis. You know that I'll hire a driver, a handsome butch one to—"

"No, fine, I'll drive you," Nora gave in with a grin.

"I wanna be playful like you two," Sammy-Jo said.

Gabby's brow raised. "Who said I'm playing?" She smirked playfully. "Drive carefully, SJ."

"I will." Sammy-Jo backed away from the door. "And I'll bring her back in one piece."

Nora grinned. "I know you will, have fun."

"Oh Sammy-Jo, I almost forgot. When you manage to convince her to come back, let her know there's a job waiting if she wants it."

"A job? That's awesome, where?"

"Natalie spoke with her marketing department, and apparently the opportunity to hire someone was snapped at, so…"

"I'll tell her. Thank you both."

Sammy-Jo threw her bag onto the passenger seat and then typed Daisy's address into the sat nav on her phone and clipped it into the phone holder on the dashboard.

One hour and thirty-five minutes. That was the predicted travel time. But it was New Year's Day, and a lot less traffic on the road than usual. If she was lucky, she'd shave a few minutes off of that.

She revved the engine and waited for the electronic gates to fully open, and then she pulled forward and onto the road.

Daisy parked her car and finally relaxed. The motorways were pretty clear, but smaller roads still had a lot of slushy snow and ice. It was amazing the difference between two parts of the country.

She pulled her key free, turning the engine off in the process, grabbed her bag and phone to climb out of the car and promptly slipped the moment her foot hit the pavement.

"Whoa," she said, managing to avoid sliding straight out of the car. "Home sweet home." She sighed and took more care.

It was a matter of minutes to walk up around to the door, run up the stairs and put her key into the lock. The flat was freezing.

She'd been gone for pretty much two weeks and the heating had been set to the minimum time length just to keep it ticking along while she was gone. The first thing she did was whack it on high.

Dumping her bag down, she opened it and pulled out the three plastic food boxes of leftovers her mum had packed for her.

"You won't want to go shopping tonight, will you?" she'd said to Daisy as she'd squeezed them into her bag.

Grabbing a plate, she opened the first box and took out several triangles of sandwiches, biting into one instantly when her tummy rumbled.

By the time she'd finished filling her plate, and eaten the food in front of the TV, she'd forgotten all about her phone and the promised call to say she was home.

She fell asleep.

Chapter Seventy One

It was dark by the time Sammy-Jo edged the Porsche into the street where Daisy lived. She felt the butterflies fluttering inside of herself and for a brief second wondered if she would be welcomed.

But common sense quickly prevailed, and she nosed along the road with one eye on the numbers of the houses. She had no idea what Daisy's flat looked like, and there were several small blocks intermingled between old Victorian-style conversions.

84C would at least be on the right-hand side of the street. Passing 12, she pushed the accelerator a little more and moved along, skipping several houses. This time when she slowed, she saw 68.

Now, her heart beat faster. Daisy was within reach.

The last house was 82, and then there was a small purpose-built block of what looked to be no more than six apartments. There was a small turn in, and she nosed the car into the small car park for residents and their visitors.

Her heart leapt when she saw Daisy's car. She parked in the empty space next to it and then switched the engine off.

This was it. Make or break.

She was hopeful; a positive outcome seemed more likely given the effort Daisy had gone to the previous night. Allegra's messages had given her all the details on that, and she'd giggled at the idea of Daisy sneaking into the party.

It was a good sign, wasn't it? It was why she'd packed an overnight bag.

But still, there was always the nagging doubt, the fear lurking that in the time it had taken for Daisy to drive away, she'd have changed her mind.

"Stop it," she told her reflection in the rear mirror. "Stop ruining it before you've even spoken to her."

She climbed out of the car and pulled her coat back on. It might only be a short distance to the warmth of Daisy's flat, but it was freezing enough that even those few steps would be shivery.

Glancing at her bag, she couldn't decide whether to take it and look presumptuous or leave it.

Once again, she told herself to stop it. "Overthinking doesn't help."

She grabbed the bag, locked the car and walked towards the building. One step became two, became fifteen and then she was there, at the door.

Grateful there wasn't an intercom, she yanked the big door open and stepped inside.

There were six flats in total, spread out over three floors, with no lift. A-B were on the ground floor. Daisy's flat would be on the first floor. Two flights of stairs.

Grinning and filled with a sudden sense of excitement, Sammy-Jo launched herself up the steps. Taking two at a time, it was mere seconds till she reached the top.

Flat C was on the left.

Standing at the door, Sammy-Jo composed herself before she raised a hand and lifted the knocker, letting it bang twice, not too loudly, but loud enough.

And she waited.

After half a minute, she tried again, a little louder this time. Readjusting her bag over her shoulder, she glanced around. The tiny landing was tidy and clean. Daisy's neighbour had a pot plant hanging.

Still nothing.

Bending down, she opened the letterbox and was hit with a waft of warm air. Peering in, all she could see was the darkened hallway.

All the lights were off.

Rummaging in her pocket for her phone, she hit Daisy's number and listened.

"The number you have called is unavailable."

"Bloody hell, why haven't you switched your phone on?" she muttered to herself. Her shoulders sagged as she pressed the button for another number.

"Everything alright?" Allegra said into her ear.

"No, I've got here and she's not in."

"Oh, well, maybe she's popped to the shops. She must have emptied her fridge before she left for that length of time."

Sammy-Jo straightened up. That made sense. "Okay, so…I should just wait, right?"

"Well, it's a long way to go to just turn around at the first hurdle, isn't it?"

"I guess, yeah. Okay, I'll just—" There was a sound behind her. A chain moving. "Gotta go, I think she's—" She disconnected the call just as the door opened and a sleepy-looking Daisy peered out from the darkness.

"SJ?"

"Hey."

Chapter Seventy-Two

Daisy opened the door wider and beckoned her in.

"Sorry, I fell asleep on the sofa. I woke up when I thought I heard a noise and then I heard someone talking and— How long have you been out there?"

"Not long. Few minutes. I did knock, was probably that that woke you up. Sorry."

"No, it's fine. I— What are you doing here?" she asked, hopeful. If Sammy-Jo had come all this way, it had to be a good thing, right?

"I just…" Sammy-Jo dropped her bag to the floor. "I didn't want things to end that way."

"Oh." Daisy felt her gut punched and the smile slid away. This was just a more polite goodbye.

"What I mean is…" Sammy-Jo patted her forehead and looked sheepishly away before she finally settled her gaze back on Daisy's face. "What I meant to say was… I don't want things to end."

"Really?" Daisy asked, feeling a lot better than she did ten seconds ago. "Because I don't want that either…things to end, I don't want to end things." She shook her head and laughed. Why couldn't she speak properly?

"I really like you, Daisy, and I know it's fast, and I know everyone will think I'm just falling back into my old patterns and stuff but I'm not. This is, this feels…between us, its all— I can't explain it."

"Different?"

Sammy-Jo smiled at her and said, "Yeah, and I don't care what anyone else thinks. I want to be with you, and work things out instead of blowing it all up or choosing someone who isn't good for me." She took Daisy's hand. "And I didn't want to start this new year without you knowing that."

Daisy's heart melted in that moment, that one sweet, vulnerable moment.

"You came all this way?" Daisy whispered.

"Risk and reward, right?" Sammy-Jo answered, stepping closer. "I don't want to lose you, especially over some silly misunderstanding that triggered us. We can work through those, can't we?"

"I think so, yes," Daisy answered, letting her palm slide up Sammy-Jo's chest and rest over her shoulder. Her lips grazed Sammy-Jo's cheek.

"I can't promise that there won't be a lot of moments when I'm triggered by something stupid, but—"

Daisy placed her finger over Sammy-Jo's lips. "It wasn't stupid. Our reactions were, but feeling like you did wasn't stupid. We've both been hurt in the past, and we need to work on that."

"Alright."

"But…I realised when I was driving back here, that all I could think about was you. And how awful it would be to move and not speak to you again," Daisy admitted.

"Well, now you don't have to – wait, what?"

"I'll explain in a minute. Are you going to take your coat off?"

Sammy-Jo looked down at herself and laughed. "Are you inviting me in to stay?"

Daisy reached for the zip and tugged it lower. "Well, I can hardly not, seeing as you came all this way." When the coat was undone, Sammy-Jo shrugged it off but stopped when she noticed Daisy frown. "How did you even find me?"

"Got your address from your mum."

"Ah, that makes sense."

"It seems like we kept missing each other yesterday. She told me you went to the party, and then Allegra filled me in, and I went to your parents', but some bloke said you'd gone out and he thought it was to the pub, so I went to Blanca's, and then Art. I saw Diana. She messaged you, but you didn't answer."

"Oh damn." Daisy jumped suddenly and ran from the room to the kitchen where her phone was. She switched it back on as she returned to the lounge. "It ran out overnight and I charged it on the drive back. I was meant to call Mum and let her know I arrived home safely."

"You'd better call her; she'll be worried."

Daisy smiled. "Yes, and then…" She checked the time. "I need to go and buy some milk and breakfast. We can pick up a pizza and then…"

"Then?"

Tilting her head a little, Daisy licked her lip, ending in a soft bite before she said, "I'm going to need you to cash in on that reward part of the equation."

Sammy-Jo gulped, a lazy smile spreading across her face. "I can do that."

"Good. You brought enough clothes for the weekend, right? Not that you'll be wearing them much."

Squinting at her, Sammy-Jo said, "I thought you had to go to work tomorrow?"

Daisy laughed at the subtle change of subject. "I am popping into the office to deliver a letter, but no. I told Mum that, so I had an escape route if it all got a bit much. I was planning to stay, and then we fell out, so…"

"So, we've got until Sunday night," Sammy-Jo said, working it all out in her head. "I need to have the car back by Sunday, but I didn't specify a time." She grinned. "What letter do you need to deliver? Can't we do it now?"

"I haven't written it yet," Daisy admitted. "Plus, I kind of want to see Stella's face when she reads it."

Sammy-Jo frowned.

"Mum didn't tell you?" Daisy said, taken aback. She'd assumed her mum had blabbed everything.

"No, are you gonna tell me what's happening?"

Daisy breathed deeply before spurting out, "I'm handing my notice in. I'm moving to Amberfield."

"Really?" Sammy-Jo's face lit up. "You're really going to do it?"

Daisy nodded, grinning at her. "I am. I spoke with Mum and Dad. I'm going to move in with them for a bit and see what's what, you know, get a job, see how things with us go."

Sammy-Jo looked up at the ceiling and seemed to mumble something.

"What are you doing?" Daisy chuckled.

"Thanking the goddess. When I picked up the car, I spoke to Gabby. She said to tell you, there's a job going in the marketing department at Natalie's firm?"

"Gabby's friend Natalie, who owns Come Again?"

Sammy-Jo shrugged. "I guess so."

Daisy launched at Sammy-Jo, jumping up and wrapping her arms around her, legs following as she found her mouth with her own and kissed her hard.

Staggering back under the welcome assault, Sammy-Jo managed to find the sofa with the back of her thighs before she fell over the arm of it, Daisy landing straddled across her.

"Even without a job, I'm still moving," Daisy clarified.

"But with the job, it makes it more likely you'll stay!"

Chapter Seventy-Three

Daisy barely had the key out of the lock and the door open when Sammy-Jo barged past, dropped the shopping bags and then turned around to focus on her prey.

Giggling, Daisy backed up against the now closed door.

"Sammy-Jo, can I not even get in—"

"Nope," Sammy-Jo said, pressing forward until there was nowhere for Daisy to run, not that she wanted to.

She'd spent the entire hour they'd taken to drive to the shop, get all the things she needed and then drive home again, teasing Sammy-Jo with everything she wanted to do with her.

"Now, you must pay," Sammy-Jo said, bending enough to grasp the back of Daisy's legs and scoop her up until she was wrapped around her and being carried.

Their mouths met, ravenous for one another. Sammy-Jo stumbled as she twisted, pushing Daisy against the wall with a gentle thump.

Her tongue slid effortlessly, warm and wet, around Daisy's mouth, breathing through her nose until Daisy took control of the kissing and the one nostril that wasn't blocked from the cold became squished against Daisy's nose.

"Bedroom." Sammy-Jo gasped for breath. "Bedroom, kitchen, floor. I don't care. Pick one."

Daisy giggled again. "Door on your left."

Sammy-Jo readjusted Daisy's weight in her arms and then turned enough to walk towards the open doorway. The lights were off, but she could just make out the shape of something big in the room.

"That better be the bed," she said before tossing Daisy down on top of it and then landing on top of her.

Pulling at clothing they both fought to remove, Sammy-Jo won out when she managed to yank Daisy's jeans down, only getting stuck when she remembered the boots.

"Fuck's sake," she muttered and tried to pull them free without undoing the laces. Daisy sat up on her elbows and watched gleefully as Sammy-Jo pulled at them, swearing and muttering to herself until finally, she tossed one and then the other to the floor.

"If you weren't quite so impatient." Daisy laughed.

"If you weren't quite such a tease…" Sammy-Jo's lips curled into a smile. She added the jeans and socks with the boots. "Now, what did you say about how long I can do this for?"

"I said nothing." Daisy squealed when her underwear followed.

"Oh, you said something." Sammy-Jo balanced on her knees. "Take that off," she said, pointing to Daisy's jumper.

Pushing herself up into a sitting position, Daisy smiled. "Make me."

"You did not just say that." Sammy-Jo's jaw dropped comically. There was no protest though when she lifted the hem and pulled the woollen sweater over Daisy's head and dropped it onto the bed beside them. "You know, you can't keep it up."

"I can…" Daisy squealed again when Sammy-Jo tickled her. "I can…you can't—"

"Oh, I can." Sammy-Jo laughed. She flung an arm around Daisy's waist, twisted and somehow managed to end up sitting with Daisy in her lap.

"How did you do that?"

"I have several talents you have yet to enjoy," Sammy-Jo boasted. "I spend most of my time in a gym or running around a football pitch. Picking you up and tossing you around isn't hard."

"Stop turning me on." Daisy grinned and slid her arm around Sammy-Jo's neck. "I kind of like being tossed around."

"Excellent," Sammy-Jo said, though her focus was on divesting Daisy of the t-shirt and bra. When those last vestiges of clothing were gone and Daisy was naked and warm against her body, Sammy-Jo cupped her cheek. The urgent need seemingly dissipated as something else filled the void.

Their eyes locked, and Sammy-Jo's fingers moved deftly as though tracing every part of Daisy's face.

"What are you doing?" Daisy asked.

"No idea," Sammy-Jo said, somewhat mesmerised. "Can I just—"

"As long as you're touching me, I don't care what you do," Daisy gushed. "I like your hands on me. I like the way you're looking at me."

"How am I looking at you?"

Daisy gulped, licking her lips a little nervously before she said, "Like you love me."

"Maybe I do."

"Oh, that's—"

"Too much?" Sammy-Jo panicked and pulled her hand away, but Daisy grabbed it and put it back.

"No, I was going to say, that's kind of how I feel too."

"Oh, well that's alright then." Sammy-Jo smiled and felt a new sense of confidence wash over her. "So, am I fucking you senseless or making love to you now?"

"Hm, I think it can be both." Daisy leaned forward and kissed her. "Or maybe start off with one and finish with the other." The kiss deepened. "But there's a small problem."

"Uh, what?"

"I'm the only one naked."

Sammy-Jo laughed. "Yes, because you're the one who needs to be." She moved with lightning speed again, this time tossing Daisy onto her bed again and pouncing like a panther between her open thighs. She reached up, pulled the band out of her hair and let it fall around her face.

"My woman's lion's mane," Daisy said, pushing her fingers into it and wrapping the hair tightly around them, forcing Sammy-Jo forward. "Make me roar, baby."

Sammy-Jo's mouth suctioned around her, and she let out more of a squeak than a roar, and Sammy-Jo smiled against her, receiving a poke as reward.

"Are you laughing at my roar?"

Sammy-Jo looked up at her, like an alligator. "No, never," she said, her tongue lashing Daisy's clit before she could respond. This time it wasn't a squeal but a loud sigh as her back arched and her hips thrust upward.

"Don't stop," she pleaded, mewling and writhing with every stroke of Sammy-Jo's strong, talented tongue. She tried to focus on the pattern, but it was no use. Sammy-Jo would switch it up every time her hips got into any rhythm. "God, what you do to me," Daisy whispered. "I can't—"

She couldn't get another word out as Sammy-Jo wrapped her arms around her thighs, and just when she least expected it, the licking became sucking, and it was all Daisy could do not to bounce off the bed with the way her body reacted. Thrusting herself into the movement, both hands now entwined in Sammy-Jo's hair in an effort to hold her in place and never let her stop doing what she was doing.

"Sam – Jo," she managed to utter before the roar escaped.

Chapter Seventy-Four

Thursday 2nd January

"I'm not getting out of bed," Sammy-Jo said, refusing to open her eyes despite Daisy opening the curtains and letting the streetlamp light fill the room. "It's not even daylight."

Daisy laughed at her. "You don't have to get up, but I need to go to work."

Rolling over, her arm coming up to cover her eyes, she squinted enough to make out Daisy. She was wearing a fitted black pantsuit, cut and shaped perfectly to her body.

Sitting up fast, Sammy-Jo's eyes opened wide.

"Is that what you wear to work?"

Daisy glanced down at herself. "Yes, is it okay?" She seemed to study her jacket as though there might be a stain on it.

"Oh, yeah it's…what time will you be back?"

Daisy frowned. "I'm not sure, but I won't be long. Why?" she asked slowly, narrowing her eyes at the now very awake girlfriend in her bed.

"Because… I might need to…" Sammy-Jo bit her bottom lip. "Fuck babe, it's hot."

Laughing, Daisy climbed onto the bed, straddling Sammy-Jo and trapping her under the duvet. "You think so?"

"Hm-hm." Sammy-Jo nodded.

"What did you think I'd wear to the office?"

"Hadn't thought about it, but I guess…I dunno. I wish I'd thought of this though."

"Maybe we should have a dress up day." She climbed off of Sammy-Jo and fixed her jacket. "Like I'd come home and find you still in your kit…"

"Match day kit?"

"Is that the skimpy shorts?" Daisy asked as she slid an earring into her left ear.

"I mean, I wouldn't call them skimpy but—" Sammy-Jo noticed the stare. "They are definitely short, and…and I have several pairs…home or away?"

Daisy looked perplexed. "I have no idea what that even means."

Sammy-Jo grinned. "So much to learn. Home kit, we wear at our ground; away kit we wear when we play at other team's grounds."

"And the difference?"

"One's dark blue; the other is currently white."

"Currently?"

Sammy-Jo threw the duvet off and sat on the edge of the bed. "Yes, sometimes they change the away kit to sell more shirts."

"I see, well, I'm not fussed what colour they are as long as…" Daisy moved closer and pushed her way in between Sammy-Jo's open knees. "They're tight, and I can ogle your backside while you do the housework."

"Housework?"

"Yeah, I'm developing a little fantasy." Daisy grinned. "Right, I'll tell you more when I've thought about it, but I need to get going. I'll call you later, okay?" She leaned down and kissed her. "Spare key is on the table."

She walked away, and Sammy-Jo's eyes followed Daisy's backside as she went. "Okay, I get the backside thing."

Glancing over her shoulder, Daisy blew a kiss. "I knew you would. Get up; I need you dressed and ready when I get back."

Chapter Seventy-Five

Her office building was virtually empty with most firms allowing staff the rest of this week off, but not Daytona Marketing. They were highly driven and incredibly uncaring about the welfare of their staff. It was all about the company, the clients and most importantly, the profits.

Daisy sighed when she held her pass up and waited for the beep and click that would signal her arrival inside the office.

Most of the staff had used their annual leave, and the open plan desk area was almost empty apart from Pearl working away on her computer with her headphones in as usual. Daisy smiled. She'd miss people like Pearl, but this job, not a chance.

She could see Stella through the window of her office. Head down, reading. She wasn't a bad person per se, she was just a terrible manager, and she was a complete suck up to the higher-ups and didn't listen to anyone else's opinions.

Knocking on the door, Daisy smiled casually at her through the window. Caught by surprise, Stella sat bolt upright and beckoned her in.

"Daisy, I wasn't expecting you in today," she said, not standing to greet her or offering a handshake, a Happy New Year. That was Stella.

"Happy New Year," Daisy said anyway. "Did you have a nice Christmas?"

The pleasantries seemed to throw Stella off. "I – yes, it was nice enough."

"Good. I did too. So good actually that I've some bad news."

"Oh, what's that?"

"I've decided to move closer to my family and so I'm leaving."

Stella looked shocked by the news. "Okay, so, you'll need to put your notice in writing and—"

"No, I'm leaving now, as in, I won't be back on Monday," Daisy said emphatically. It felt good. Stella's mouth twitched at the corner.

"But…you can't, I need you…we have the Markham project and you're…you're the best I have."

Daisy was aware of that statement already, but it was nice to finally hear it acknowledged.

"The thing is, I've been offered a job. I'm heading to the interview as soon as I leave here." Which explained why she was dressed for work. "I fully expect to get it. My CV speaks for itself, but even if I didn't, I'm not coming in on Monday. I'll be busy moving my things."

"I could get you a pay rise," Stella blurted. "A substantial one."

Closing her eyes and shaking her head, Daisy considered how often she'd asked for that in the past and been rejected.

"It's not about the money, Stella. I want to be nearer my family, a fresh start with my new partner and honestly, I hate working here. It's the most exhausting and tiresome place. My creativity is starved working for Daytona, so there's nothing you could say, or offer, that would make me change my mind about this."

She stood up and held her hand out to shake. It took Stella a moment to catch up and she finally followed Daisy's actions.

"I'm sorry you feel that way. I've always considered you a valuable member of the team."

Daisy sighed. "Maybe let the team know that occasionally. You'd be amazed at how much it would be appreciated to feel appreciated."

She left the office and went over to her desk. Pearl wasn't at her desk and the office felt eerily silent.

There wasn't much that was personal on her desk or in the drawers. Some pens and a packet of Soothers from when she'd had a cold before Christmas. She took out a pen and sat quietly writing notes to her co-workers. Placing each one into a separate envelope and sealing them, she dropped them into the internal mail tray.

Standing, she took one last look around. She was about to leave when she remembered one last thing. Reaching around her neck, she took off the lanyard with her pass and placed it on the desk. Now, she was free.

With Daisy gone, Sammy-Jo didn't see any point in lying about in bed. The heating had kicked in and a hot shower had warmed her up. Now, wearing her hoodie and matching sweatpants, she felt half human again as she munched on a seeded bagel with cream cheese and smoked salmon.

Her phone buzzed on the worktop. Glancing at the screen, she saw that it was Allegra.

"Yep," she said through a half-chewed mouthful.

"Are you stuffing your face?" Allegra asked.

"Yep," Sammy-Jo repeated.

Allegra chuckled. "I was just phoning to see how things are going, but seeing as you're eating and still there, I'm guessing well?"

Sammy-Jo swallowed the mouthful and washed it down with a gulp of tea. "Actually, it's pretty fantastic. I'm coming back today."

"How is that fantastic?"

"Because Daisy is coming with me. She's just gone to work to tell them to stick it."

"Oh my god, you actually convinced her to move in with you? You're both as mad as each other."

Rolling her eyes, Sammy-Jo took herself over to the couch and sat down. "No, she'd already decided that she was moving back. She was going to hand her notice in and move at the end of the month, but…" She paused for dramatic effect. "I spoke to Gabby yesterday and she said there was a job going at her friend Natalie's office, if Daisy wanted it. So…" Another pause only resulted in Allegra yawning dramatically. "So, last night, Gabby spoke to Natalie, who organised for Daisy to come in today to meet with someone called Harry and talk it over."

"So, she hasn't actually got the job yet?"

"Well, no, but she will, she's smart and—point is, regardless, she is moving into her parents'. She'll get the job sorted, and me and her can date and keep getting to know each other and when the time's right, she can move in."

"Wow, well this sounds all very grown up… Clearly, Daisy's idea." She chuckled.

"Fuck and off." Sammy-Jo smiled. "I'm happy, Daisy is happy, and that's all that matters."

"You're right," Allegra said. "And I'm happy for you both. I guess I should get John to put some clothes on if you're going to be back later."

"Oh grim. You better not have been doing it on my sofa."

Allegra roared with laughter. "You'll never know, and that's the fun of it for me. Have a safe trip. Speak to you later."

"Git," Sammy-Jo said before the line went dead.

She grinned when she heard the sound of the key in the door and jumped up, ready for whatever came next.

Chapter Seventy-Six

It had been an easy drive back. Daisy had led in her car with Sammy-Jo following behind. They'd parted ways as they entered into Bath Street, Sammy-Jo taking the car back to Nora and Daisy heading to the Come Again offices.

The building was plush, nothing like the one she'd left that morning. This was all glass and shiny surfaces as she walked through the revolving doors and was greeted by a security guard who took her name and pointed her in the direction of the lifts.

By the time she got to the right floor and found the big double doors that informed her she was in the right place, it was two minutes to three.

At least she wasn't late, she thought.

She pressed the intercom and was buzzed in and met by a woman.

"Hi, I'm Harry. You must be Daisy." The woman smiled warmly.

"Yes, nice to meet you, and thank you so much for making time for me today, I really appreciate it."

She led Daisy down the corridor and into an office that was as bare as you could get. No photos, no posters on the wall. Just a computer screen and keyboard on the desk, a printer on a unit behind it, and brochures and magazines piled neatly next to it.

"Take a seat. Did you want a coffee? Tea?"

"Oh, no I'm fine. Thank you," Daisy said, taking the seat opposite.

"So, tell me about you, Daisy," Harry said with a soft Scottish lilt, sitting back and looking as relaxed as anyone could. She was a confident woman, that much Daisy could tell, but not intimidating.

"Well, I've been quite a studious academic throughout my education." She handed over a copy of her CV. "GCSEs, A-levels and then a degree in business management at Canterbury University. Whereupon I went straight into full-time employment with Daytona—"

Harry smiled and nodded. "That all sounds great, but I really want to know about you, Daisy. Are you the kind of fit we're looking for? Education is important, of course, but I need to know if you're a lion or a mouse."

"I see, of course, well in that case I very much roar. I'm not afraid to speak my mind, with an appropriate tone of course." She laughed a little nervously. "But I felt quite stifled at Daytona. They have a way of doing things that I didn't feel capitalised on the creativity within the room. It was very much a copy and paste style of marketing, whereas I am hoping to find something a little more dynamic. Something I can really get my teeth into and get creative."

Harry grinned. "And to be clear, you're aware of what you might be getting your teeth into here at Come Again?"

As much as Daisy tried not to blush, she wasn't sure she'd pulled it off. "Yes. Absolutely, and one of my favourite brands." She leaned forward. "I'm not afraid to push the limits and boundaries of what society might deem acceptable or not… I live my own life that way. I should point out that I am gay, but as a woman, I am fully behind the concept that we should all feel free to enjoy our sexuality."

Harry laughed. "Half the team are gay; you'll fit right in." She slid a piece of paper across the desk for Daisy to read through. "That's a list of the terms and conditions. Pay scale, bonuses, et cetera. If you're happy with it, then I see no reason why we wouldn't want you onboard being dynamic."

"Really?" Daisy said, quickly glancing over the very generous renumeration package. "In that case, I'd accept. When do I start?"

"We could do a walk around, meet and greet on Monday?"

Daisy nodded. "I can make that work."

"Great. Well, if you get here for ten, I'll meet you downstairs and we can get you all set up with an entry card and HR details. Welcome to the company."

Chapter Seventy-Seven

When Daisy got outside, she smiled at what she found. Sammy-Jo had changed into a nice pair of jeans and a shirt, her hair pulled back off her face and held there by the woollen hat. She was still bundled up underneath a big, quilted jacket.

"Did you go all the way home and then walk back here?"

Sammy-Jo pushed off from the wall and leaned in to kiss her cheek. "No, I drove home, got changed and then dropped the car off and got Nora to drive me here." She grinned with all the confidence of a woman on a mission. "I wanted to be here."

"You're very sweet," Daisy answered and took her hand. "Shall we get something to eat?"

She was about to walk in the direction of her car when she felt her arm tugged. Turning, the look on Sammy-Jo's face made her giggle.

Just to be clear about the face, SJ said, "Really?"

"What?" Daisy said, playing dumb.

"You know what," Sammy-Jo answered, pulling her back until she was pressed up against her and looking up into those big, expectant eyes. "Did you get the job?"

Daisy smiled. "Of course I did."

It was at this point that she was lifted into the air and spun around as though, she imagined, she'd just scored a winning goal at Wembley.

"Now, we can go out and celebrate." Sammy-Jo laughed when she finally put her down. "Any restaurant. You pick."

Daisy ran a finger over her bottom lip as she considered that. "Well, as I'm new to town and you've been here aeons, maybe I should let you guide me on that?"

"Hm, well the best restaurant is Joie, but we won't get in there without booking in advance so… Ooo I know, there's a bougie little place on the high street. I think it's Thai."

Linking arms as they began to walk, Daisy said, "If I'm with you, then it's perfect."

Daisy parked the car on the street, just along from her parents' home. Yanking the handbrake, she turned to Sammy-Jo. "That was delicious. Thank you for treating me."

"You deserve being treated."

"Do you want to just stay in the car, and we can make out?" Daisy smirked.

Sammy-Jo pretended to think about it. "I mean, it's a plan. But…I'm pretty sure Polly or Dolly just spied us from the window." She looked up and along the houses to Daisy's parents' house and the large bay window with the crooked netting.

"Ah, caught before I even got my hand in your pants."

"Nothing stopping you from trying later," Sammy-Jo quipped as she opened the door and stepped out onto the street. With the door closed, she leaned against the car and looked over the roof at Daisy. "In fact, I'm going to insist."

"Ooo, promises." Daisy laughed before she was assaulted by two overeager seven-year-olds running into her. "Hey you two."

"Daisy, you're back already," Dolly said.

"Yeah, I guess so…did you miss me?"

"Not really, you only just left," Polly answered very seriously.

Sammy-Jo laughed until Dolly said, "Are you and Sammy-Jo getting married?"

"Uh no, where did you get that idea from?" Daisy said, pulling a face at Sammy-Jo's look of horror.

They all walked together until they reached the gate, and the twins rushed through. "Cos that's what people in love do," Polly said, and then they were gone, into the house shouting that Daisy was home.

"What's all this?" Eileen said, coming out of the kitchen and into the hall just as Daisy walked back through the door. "Daisy?"

"Hi, Mum."

"Is everything alright?" She glanced over Daisy's shoulder to Sammy-Jo. "You found her then?"

"Yeah, brought her back with me." SJ smiled.

"I can see, what's going on?"

"I've got a job," Daisy said, beaming at her mum.

Elieen frowned. "I know you've got a job."

"No." Daisy laughed. "I've got a new job, here…well, in Bath Street. I jacked in Daytona this morning, had an interview this afternoon and I start on Monday."

"Monday?" Eileen exclaimed. "But we're not ready, your dad and Bill have been stripping the walls. The bed's in bits in the shed…"

"That's okay. I need to go back home tonight. Sammy-Jo is going to help me pack my things and get the flat ready to hand back to the agent. I won't be back until Sunday and then—"

"She can stay with me until her room is ready. I'll take care of her," Sammy-Jo said, leaning over her shoulder. "I mean, if that's what you want." She turned to Daisy.

"I think that would work." Daisy continued to grin. It was becoming contagious as Eileen and Sammy-Jo both copied. "As long as I'm not in your way."

"I've already told you, you can just move in and stay there."

"I know, it's just—"

"Too soon, I get it, but for a few days it's cool, right?" Sammy-Jo asked.

"Yes, it's very cool." Daisy kissed Sammy-Jo's cheek, then she turned to her mother. "We're going to head off. I just wanted to let you know the change of plans."

"Okay, well, drive safe and we'll see you…"

Daisy shrugged. "Not sure, depends on the time we get done and—" She felt Sammy-Jo nudge her in the back. "I will call you. We need to do more packing."

"And I will make sure she does," Sammy-Jo said as she was dragged out of the room and down the hall towards the front door.

Eileen watched them leave the kitchen and didn't hear Chris come in through the back door.

"What's going on? I thought I saw Daisy through the window."

"You did," Eileen said, turning to him with a smile. "She's moving."

"I know, that's why I look like this," he said, pointing to his dusty t-shirt and paint-splattered jeans. "Bill's gone to town to pick up some bits."

"Well, you'd best get a move on. She's moving back now."

Chris frowned. "What do you mean now?"

"She's jacked her job in, had an interview and got another one in Bath Street. She starts on Monday. So, she's going to stay with Sammy-Jo until her room is liveable."

"Bloody hell, is it not all a bit too fast?" Chris asked, rubbing his hand over his short hair. "I mean, I like Sammy-Jo and all, but they've known each other a couple of weeks, and now our Daisy is changing her whole life."

"You might be right, and it will either work out or it won't, but she's here, and I for one am glad of that, and if we have to deal with heartbreak down the line, then we will."

"I suppose so."

"But I have a feeling that those two might actually be well-matched. I'm happy for them, for whatever this is and for however long it lasts. She's happy."

Chris smiled, showing off the same dimples Daisy had. "Yes, that's true…and me and Bill might get a nose in that VIP box at the stadium."

Eileen laughed and whipped him with her tea towel. "You won't be going anywhere till that room's done."

"That's if she comes home. She might like staying at Sammy-Jo's."

"Then we will have a decent spare room until the girls decide they want their own space."

Chris huffed. "Fair enough."

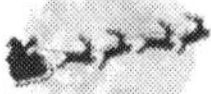

Outside, Daisy stopped at the gate and looked around. Sammy-Jo bumped into her.

"What's up?"

Daisy smiled. "Nothing. I'm just thinking…this is home now."

"Yeah, it is."

"On a scale of one to ten, how crazy would it actually be if I moved in with you?"

Sammy-Jo grinned. "Probably an eight, but I like those kind of odds."

"Risk and reward?" Daisy laughed.

"Exactly. I know I'm a risk—"

Daisy placed a finger against her lips. "You're the reward, idiot. Jacking my job in and moving at all is the risk…and it's a risk I am willing to take."

"Let's take it day by day. We've got the rest of the weekend, and then we've got to get all your stuff packed and moved, so maybe you stay with me for the next week, and if we like it…we keep doing it?"

"That easy, huh?"

Sammy-Jo closed the space between them. Their eyes met and softened as they both considered a life together. "All I want is you."

Epilogue

"Following the Christmas break, the second part of the season has kicked off with Bath Street Harriers continuing to impress. Goals from the usual suspects of Brady and Nailor were supplemented by the addition of new signing, Satty Basra, who joined just a couple of weeks ago and had barely trained with the team.

"Basra comes into a squad already ambitious and way beyond where anyone foresaw they would be in this league. Her exciting bicycle kick goal after an audacious Rabona cross from Costa on 73 minutes had the crowd singing her name already.

"But it was Sammy-Jo Costa who bagged Player of the Match for this reporter. Her nonstop energy to run and run, spraying some sublime passes at times, as well as the already mentioned Rabona, and just a near perfect display from the midfielder, meant her team were unstoppable today. And on this form, Gabby Dean has got to be jumping for joy with the way her team have come together."

Daisy waited with her dad and Bill in the director's box where they'd watched the match.

The men were both ecstatically talking about the game with each other and Gabby, but Daisy had to admit, she didn't really have a clue. She just enjoyed watching Sammy-Jo run around in shorts and got excited about anything she did.

It was a start in her journey to become a footballer's WAG. She laughed to herself at that idea.

The last of the fans had left and the grounds staff were watering the pitch and doing whatever they did to the turf when the match was over. Daisy watched them, oblivious to the fact that Sammy-Jo was creeping up behind her.

"Boo," she said, slipping her arms around Daisy's waist and nuzzling in against her neck. "Miss me?"

Daisy laughed. "I saw you the entire time."

"I know. I saw you too. Why d'ya think I was so good today?" Sammy-Jo boasted. "If I don't get Player of the Match, it's a travesty." She laughed again.

"Does that mean we get to celebrate?" Daisy asked, turning in her arms. "Because, you know there are a lot of risk and rewards we could get up to in here."

Sammy-Jo pulled Daisy closer and glanced around furtively before she grinned. "Changing rooms?"

Daisy nodded but then looked out towards the stands. "What about down there? Or…" She leaned closer and whispered in Sammy-Jo's ear. "On the pitch."

"Fuck. I mean, yes…but…" Sammy-Jo moved them away from any potential ear wigging. "There are cameras, so I'll have to do some investigating and find blind spots."

"God, that sounds so…" Daisy's breath hitched. "Is it really bad that I want to do it right now? I don't think you understand how much I enjoy watching you run around in that kit."

"You like football?"

Daisy raised a brow. "I said, I like watching you run around…in that kit."

"Got it." Sammy-Jo grabbed her hand and began to tug her in the direction of the door. "I've got a spare one at home."

They barely made it through the front door before Sammy-Jo was kissing Daisy and lifting her, pressing her back against the wall as she dealt with closing and locking the door.

Allegra wasn't supposed to be home tonight, but Sammy-Jo was taking no chances on a last-minute interruption.

"You really want me to put my kit on?" Sammy-Jo said, breathing heavily as Daisy began unbuttoning her shirt. "Because I'd really like you to get *your* kit off." She grinned.

"You know, never let anyone tell you you're not a comedian." Daisy smiled, pulling the shirt loose from Sammy-Jo's muscular shoulders.

"I am very funny. It's a gift, a bit like the one where I turn you into a puddle of molten jelly."

"Is that what you do?"

Sammy-Jo nodded. "100 percent. I am extremely dextrous." She waggled her fingers and poked out her tongue.

"God, what I am going to let you do to me in a minute is just…get that kit on," Daisy ordered and slapped her backside playfully when Sammy-Jo turned to run up the stairs.

When she reached the top, she leaned over the banister. "You know you've got five minutes to get naked."

"You better be faster than five minutes, Sammy-Jo Costa, especially if you want me to award you Player of the Match later."

"Ooo." Sammy-Jo's eyes lit up. "I'll be right down." Her head disappeared, but then like whiplash it was back again. "Shall I wear the—"

"No, stop blabbering and get stripping." Daisy laughed at her.

It was all so easy, and no wonder she still hadn't moved into her mum and dad's place. Maybe this was home now. With Sammy-Jo, and Allegra, who Daisy was getting on with quite well, all things considered.

She walked into the lounge, mindlessly removing her clothing as she glanced around at all of her things that were gradually being unpacked and given space in Sammy-Jo's home.

By the time she'd kicked off her boots and yanked her jeans off, she could hear the stampede as Sammy-Jo flew down the stairs, and then the clip-clop sound of her football boots on the wooden flooring.

“Too much?” she asked, entering the room and glancing down at the studded shoes. Then she looked up and noticed that Daisy was in fact naked, as requested.

“You look hot,” Daisy said, closing the space between them. Her fingers reached for the material as she grabbed a handful and pulled Sammy-Jo into a searing kiss.

“Well, I am the Player of the Match,” Sammy-Jo boasted, urging Daisy backwards. “And that means I get a prize.”

“Hm you were, but now I need a different kind of performance from you.” Daisy giggled.

Ghosting her lips against Daisy’s, Sammy-Jo said, “I wonder what you’ll get for Christmas this year?”

Almost allowing the kiss, Daisy answered, “A tree, with lights, lots of lights.”

“I’ll put it on my list to Santa, but I already got everything I need right here.”

“Everything?”

Sammy-Jo nodded, her hands roaming and fingers teasing. “You and me, that’s all I need.”

“Right now, I really need you to…” Daisy stopped talking. Her head fell back as she gasped. “Just like that…”

The End

If you enjoyed this book, or any other of Claire's books, then please consider leaving a review, https://mybook.to/TACCHS

or why not sign up to Claire's monthly eMag and Newsletters for all the up-to-date information on new releases and what Claire is up to?

Subscribe here:

Website:

http://www.itsclastevofficial.co.uk

If you want to connect more with Claire, you can follow her on social media.

Facebook:
https://www.facebook.com/groups/ClaireHightonStevenson

Twitter:

https://twitter.com/ClaStevOfficial

Instagram:

https://www.instagram.com/itsclastevofficial/

TikTok:

@ItsClaStevOfficial

Made in the USA
Columbia, SC
30 November 2024